T0162751

A Wing and A Prayer

The First Book of Gabriel

Ernest Oglesby

iUniverse, Inc.
Bloomington

A Wing and A Prayer
The First Book of Gabriel

iUniverse books may be ordered through booksellers or by contacting:

iUniverse
1663 Liberty Drive
Bloomington, IN 47403
www.iuniverse.com
1-800-Authors (1-800-288-4677)

ISBN: 978-1-4502-4376-6 (sc)
ISBN: 978-1-4502-4378-0 (ebook)
ISBN: 978-1-4502-4377-3 (dj)

Library of Congress Control Number: 2011901153

Printed in the United States of America

iUniverse rev. date: 2/17/2011

Dedication

This book is dedicated to Jane, without whose encouragement and support (and frequent use of the whip), it might never have been finished but remained on one of those shelves where we all leave the things we never get around to finishing.

The first concept was written in my formative years and lay languishing in the dark recesses of my mind for almost thirty years, until I finally decided to get it out, dust it off, and see where the story would lead me. I hope you'll enjoy reading about the journey as much as I enjoyed making it.

The Second Book of Gabriel (Belladonna) awaits.

Roman Britain AD 40

Chapter One

From a distance, they looked like large birds, playfully swooping and soaring together in the skies, disappearing one minute behind the clouds before reappearing and darting here and there in the heavens as though playing a game of tag.

Close up, it was apparent that these were not birds, but humans, albeit with wings. The Celts knew them as Elohim and feared them, their strange screeching tongue and their unnatural physiognomy. They kept to the mountains and high places, except when they foraged for food, sometimes brave enough to steal from the Celt villages.

Such beings were not natural to these shores, but the memory of their arrival was beyond generations, and only the passed-on history of the Druids revealed their full history. They flocked to these shores in advance of the Roman armies, as if fleeing before them.

The Druids instilled such hatred in the Celts for these creatures, and since the early days of their coming, some few of them had been captured and sacrificed to grim gods of the wood. During those sacrifices and ingestion of their spilt blood as part of the old rites, the Druids had quickly learnt of the regenerative powers of that blood and valued it highly. Revered by the rest of the Celtic tribes, Druids held sway and were venerated for their knowledge and leadership.

The Elohim were relatively few in number and grew more cautious of the numerous Celts, yet as the Celts watched and studied, some of these winged creatures grew careless and overconfident.

Lucifer soared, enjoying the wind through his hair, as natural in this environment as any real bird. He swooped, laughing as he raced the frightened smaller-sized birds faster than the fastest hawk; his friend Gabriel was laughing alongside him as they soared through the valleys. The wind in his feathers—was there a better feeling to be had anywhere on this planet?

The snow was light, and yet it obscured their view of the landscape, all white and covered beneath them. Treetops bowed with the weight of the snow. Strangely, the two angels hardly felt the cold when they were flying like this, muscles powering their wings as they strove to outdo each other.

Gabriel taunted him as he plummeted like a stone past him, using gravity to assist his dive, and Lucifer did the same, whooping and screeching after him, eager not to be outdone on their daily exercise. The woods, the dark woods, suddenly so close, as they sought to pull out of their incredibly steep dives to just brush the treetops, out of bravado, as they did most days, unaware their habits had been noted by the Celts.

All of a sudden, the snow-covered treetops shook, and the air was filled with hot rain, and Lucifer fell from the sky screaming, one wing pierced by one of the sharp javelins thrown by the humans hiding in the uppermost of the treetops.

Gabriel swooped lower to aid him, when the stones, hurled with accuracy by the many slingshots, began to fill the air around him, zinging around him and stinging, like bees swarming. Crying out as he was hit again and again, Gabriel fell, his wings clipping the branches as the whooping savages celebrated their catch, the weighted nets cast eagerly and skillfully to trap the two angels and heavy clubs quickly used to beat them unconscious.

Lucifer was afraid. The smoke from the fires assailed his nostrils, and the Celts busied themselves at the direction of the white-robed Druids, preparing the clearing for the ceremony to come.

He lay there groaning, wrapped in the nets with Gabriel, who was still unconscious. He nudged him discreetly. “Gabriel, wake up.” They were both going to die, he was sure. The ground beneath them was wet and coppery with their blood, which still leaked from their wounds. Gabriel woke and tried to stand, gasping with the effort, but the nets and Lucifer's weight kept him on his knees. Scarcely an hour ago, the two of them had been soaring through the heavens as only the Elohim could, performing the sort of maneuvers that every other feathered creature on this planet could only envy. They were as one with the winds, which gave them lift, and flight was as second nature to them as breathing.

Careless, they had descended close to the forest, swooping close to the trees in their abandoned play, when the humans closed their trap. It had been long months since the last of their number had fallen prey to the humans. The majority of the aerie had dispersed, seeking relative safety by avoiding the lowlands.

The wounds were not fatal but would need time to heal, time the humans were not going to give them. Gabriel gritted his teeth as he strained to tear open the nets with his sharp nails, feathers and blood making his hands sticky. "Help me. We must break free of these nets." Lucifer fought not to scream as he tried to pull at the thick nets.

Around them, the woods were filled with the humans, mostly naked bodies covered in that grotesque blue mud. A few wore rough leggings. The Druids were the only ones among them to wear robes, pristine white long beards, wild and unkempt, crowns of holly in their long hair, their eyes wild with the potent drugs they knew and guarded closely unto themselves.

The drums beat loudly, sending a wild rhythm up into the night. The watch fires lit the wood, the tall hazels thick, guarding the sky. The Druids had learnt well from past mistakes, the stone altar open to the sky only in the small clearing and overshadowed by the mighty sacred oak. The Druids drew their strength from the wood, the dark cruel wood.

Lucifer looked around the clearing. Close to the large overhanging oak was a Faery ring comprised of small uneven stones, polished by the elements, seeming so natural and yet equally so sinister, avoided by all except the Druid as though the Celts were afraid to step within. Then his eyes were drawn to the roughly hewn stone of the altar, the dark stains that were still visible there. Men had died here, angels too, he knew. "It's no use," he groaned.

"Shut up, Lucifer. Just shut up and help me. Help me, damn you!" Gabriel swore, pulling at the crude nets with the last vestiges of his strength. Lucifer started to help once more, but the humans soon noticed their efforts and, with loud cries, descended upon them, wielding heavy wooden clubs and raining down blow after blow until both of them slumped almost unconscious to the ground.

When they finally regained consciousness once more, they noticed the Celts standing in close attendance to forestall any further attempts to free themselves from the nets. A tall figure in white robes and holly crown came to address them.

"Bring them food," he addressed some of the other Celts. "Mead too. I would not have them weak from their wounds."

"Why show such concern?" Gabriel asked. "Why have you captured us, if not to put us to death?"

"Your death is of little consequence to me, birdman. I would keep you alive to take from you the secret of your long life. Once done, I leave your final fate to others. Make the most of your time. Tomorrow night, the moon is full, and the altar awaits," He flourished his hand, gesturing towards the cold grey slab of stone in the centre of the clearing.

The Celts were true to their word, bringing them food and mead. Some of their strength was restored, but the nets still weighed them down, and their guards remained in close attendance. Lucifer and Gabriel eventually managed to sleep, despite the cold chill of the evening air. More snow was coming to these lands and not too far away.

Chapter Two

The next day, preparations continued for the evening's planned ceremony. Watch fires around the clearing were tended to, and a perimeter guard of sorts was posted. A light flurry of snow began around midday as the two captured angels were brought more food, which they accepted gratefully. "Eat and be strong, Lucifer," advised Gabriel as he passed the food onto his companion.

The immediate area around the stone altar was open to the skies, and yet the Celts avoided it. Gabriel was quick to notice the shadows, which occasionally flitted across the ground and heard once or twice the keening cries of their fellow angels in the heavens as they sought for their missing comrades. Lucifer tried to call out once in response, but one of the Celts cruelly bludgeoned him to the ground before the cry could leave his lips. The two angels were then bound and gagged to forestall any further attempts at freedom and left to lie in their nets till evening.

At the Druids' command, the nets were removed. The two angels were finally dragged to where the cold stone altar awaited. Death had not been promised, yet what further end could that grim grey stone promise? Struggling once more, they found their bonds too constricting, and the two angels could do nothing as many men pulled on the ropes that bound them to force them facedown across the chiseled stone. The chanting began—cruel, guttural—as the Celts worked themselves into a bloodlust.

Ifys, the High Druid came forward, pulling the sickle-shaped knife from his sash. The sharp metal glinted in the firelight. Lucifer watched, helpless, as the knife was used on Gabriel, his friend's screams almost louder than the obscene chanting. Blood ran red as cartilage and feathers were cut, removed, the coarsely cut channel in the stone funneling the blood flow to where a clay urn waited to be filled.

Relishing the pain he was causing, the Druid cut deep, enjoying the screams as Gabriel lost consciousness once more. Other Druids held up the amputated wings to display to the crowd as they roared their approval. Then the Druid cast the amputated wings next to the Faery ring. Then it was Lucifer's turn to scream.

The two butchered angels lay unconscious across the stone altar, their wounds deep. The High Druid ordered that tar be spread on their wounds, and he used a burning torch himself to light it. The burning flesh awakened both Gabriel and Lucifer, screaming as they found themselves still alive and suffering more agony. Their cries echoed up into the night.

At a signal from the High Druid, soil was thrown over the burning tar, smothering the flames, and they lay face down, panting and sweating, gasping for breath and an escape from such torment. Acolytes were quick to remove the blood-filled urns, careful not to spill a drop as they vanished into the woods. Ifys came up to the altar, stroking Lucifer's golden hair lightly. "We will not make the same mistake with you two," he said cruelly. "Without your wings, you will be easily tamed. Rebuild your strength and your blood, for we will have more of it," he promised.

As Gabriel lay there, trying to ignore the pain of the emasculation and the burning tar, Ifys turned away from the stone altar and raised one of the dismembered wings over to the Faery ring. "Lord Malevar, accept my offering, and aid us against our Roman foes!" the Druid spoke aloud to his followers. Then he began chanting in an unknown tongue, forming sounds Gabriel had not known a human throat could utter. The Druid made invocation to unknown deities, allowing the droplets of blood to spatter the small stones that formed the circumference of the ring itself, and a hushed awe fell upon the whooping Celts as the air itself slowly began to distort.

Gabriel thought he was swooning, imagining things, as his vision blurred. It was as though he was peering through water. He could see but not clearly. The air above the Faery ring of stones looked more liquid than actual air, and the falling snow seemed to disappear when it came to touch it. A voice both grim and yet distant now spoke, cowering the painted Celts, and even the High Druid himself bowed as the voice rang out. "Your offering pleases me. But it is not enough." The words came as though from a mouth unused to speaking such a tongue.

"The wings I give unto you now. You will have the angels themselves by the next full moon. Surely you would not begrudge us some of their blood for ourselves? You know its properties to my kind." The High Druid made his excuses, only too aware of who it was with whom he was speaking.

"My kind has aided yours for centuries. If you wish that aid to continue, then hold true to your word, Druid. You know of my interest in these creatures. The next full moon. No later. Now, give unto me the wings," the voice commanded. Ifys thrust the first severed wing forward, the air obscuring it as though he were immersing it in a stream. Then it just seemed to disappear altogether as the rest of the Celts gasped in awe. The other severed wings followed, all of them disappearing before Gabriel's hazed eyes. He was as awestruck as any of the Celts. This was true magic indeed … The ethereal voice rang out once more. "Be true to your word, Druid. At the next full moon, the angels must cross over."

"As you will, Lord Malevar. I will keep my word," the Druid was quick to reassure the unknown entity.

"Be sure you do. The Dark Elves are not known for their compassion," he warned. The Druid bowed his head in supplication, and the swirling air began to return to normal. The gateway to wherever else had closed. The night was no longer charged with eldritch energy.

Gabriel swallowed hard and turned to where Lucifer lay bound with him on the altar, but his friend was unconscious again and had not witnessed any of this. Hope of some sorts then … They were not to be killed out of hand but given over to what?

He had heard the legends of the "little people" who were supposed to haunt this land since before the coming of mankind, though he had never witnessed anything like that which he had seen this night. Were they aiding the Celts against the Roman persecution?

Automatically, his hands flexed against his bonds, but the ropes held him too tightly, and he was still weakened from his ordeal. In time, his sharpened hard nails would cut through such bonds, but he was not going to get that time. The Druid then nodded to one of the humans, who smiled eagerly as he tore the loincloths from the two wingless angels, leaving them naked. The Druids stepped back to allow the rest of the evening's anticipated entertainment to continue. Gabriel felt the hands running over his buttocks, harsh, cruel laughter behind him. He looked across to where Lucifer was being similarly tormented, one human pulling his head up by his golden locks and spitting in his face.

Then, all at once, above the noise of the drums came a deafening screeching and a tremendous rush of air, which made the trees themselves shiver in their roots. Flames flickered and some torches were blown out. Lucifer looked up. Like a giant eagle come to earth, Michael was there!

Wings flaring wide, causing flurries of snow as he forced the surrounding humans back away from them, Michael, beloved Michael, first among the Elohim, mighty spear held before him as he swooped down into the clearing, bellowing out his hate for these cursed humans, skewered the High Druid fully through, pinning him to the sacred oak which overshadowed the altar before he could react.

It happened in seconds only, the rest of the humans so stunned they just stood frozen as Michael turned his wrath upon them. Mighty wings, some thirty feet from tip to tip, beat the humans back as he grabbed one of the buckets of molten tar and used one of the torches to set it afire before showering them with it.

Screams rang out amid the panic as more flesh burned, and Michael roared as he pulled free his mighty spear and lashed out at the terrified rabble, scattering them like chaff as they sought to flee his wrath. Tears filled his eyes as he saw what had been done to Lucifer and Michael, and his blows literally cut men in two as he wielded the huge spear. Half conscious, Gabriel and Lucifer saw more angels descending as Michael held the humans at bay, their bonds released, and helping hands carried them aloft into the night sky.

Chapter Three

Stolen wine was used to refresh Gabriel and Lucifer as they sought to recover from their wounds, as a conclave of sorts was held amongst the Elohim. Michael, his eyes wet with tears, was leading the debate.

"The time has come to move on. We have lost too many of our brethren to these humans. We must go north, to the wild lands, and hope the Picts are not as numerous."

"And if they breed like the rest of these humans, then where do we go?" asked Uriel.

"Farther north, across the western ocean? We cannot live in peace with these creatures. Some of us have learnt to speak their tongue in part, but we are looked upon as monsters. They fear what is different to themselves. Everywhere these creatures breed, they eventually treat us with fear and hunt us down. We are too few to fight them. We have no womenfolk of our own, and our unions with human women are fraught with danger. We must forever move on, in hope of finding a homeland of our own," Raphael pointed out.

"What of Gabriel and Lucifer? We came too late. Without wings, they are lost to us. Where we go, they cannot follow," Nathaniel stated the obvious.

Michael nodded his head slowly and sorrowfully. "Their rash games have cost them our kinship. They are lost to a life amongst the people who hunted them. This may sound harsh, yet you all know what Lucifer means to me. Would that we could do differently, but you know I speak the truth." He bowed his head in sorrow.

"Aye, we cannot carry them with us. They must make their own way in this world," Uriel spoke for the rest of them. The sad but necessary decision had been made and agreed by all.

The next day, when Gabriel and Lucifer had regained sufficient of their strength, they were brought stolen clothing from one of the villages and flown by some of the Elohim towards the east coast, away from the known Celtic enclaves.

The two had known what their fate had to be and had thought on it long and hard throughout the night. Gabriel watched a tearful good-bye between Michael and Lucifer, and then Michael's glare fell upon him, with all the unspoken curses it could muster in a single glance. Gabriel felt badly enough about the way things had turned out. He blamed himself. Michael blamed him also.

The beating of wings, amid a light flurry of snow, signaled the departure of their brethren. Gabriel and Lucifer took up their burden and began to walk, actually walk, eastwards.

Chapter Four

AD 60

The men laughed and cavorted at the stream's bank as they performed their morning ablutions. Most were bare-chested. Two of them were not, which used to be the subject of much jesting until the jesters learnt the two were quick to show their anger at such remarks. Humour was still something they had to learn.

One of the two men shaved with the aid of a sharp-edged dagger, peering into the water to see the stranger looking back at him. He hardly recognised his own face these days. The eyes, in particular, had a certain coldness about them. The face was lined with the experience of both life and many battles. Yet, it was a *human* face which smiled wistfully back at him out of the water.

Did he fit in here among these men of the Ninth Legion? He was accepted, but he still wasn't sure it had been the right thing to do, allowing themselves to be conscripted into the invading Roman Army. He looked across to Gabriel, who likewise squatted down by the water's edge, applying the edge of a dagger to his face. He too seemed a different person these days. Hiding among the Romans had been his idea and had seemed worthy at the time, but now, four years later, after waging bloody war amongst the Celts, he wasn't so sure.

The Romans had taught them the use of weapons, and war had made them skilled in their use. Gabriel revelled in the fierce bloodletting, seeking revenge against the Celts for their butchery those many years before.

They could not have remained hidden amongst the Celts, for their physiognomy would eventually be noted, and they dare not remove their tunics lest the humans see the scars still livid on their backs. The Romans had accepted their tales of torture at the hands of the Celts, who they had said robbed them of all their wares, crafting a carefully made up tale of merchants arriving by sea from the lands of Gaul, set upon first by pirates and then by the inhabitants of this land.

Lucifer had no love of the Celts and had been quick to revel in the bloody revenge Gabriel insisted in taking, but he was wearying of the endless war. Rome had taught the two of them a lot, but they were teaching the Celts much more. How to hate, organize, and fight. The Celts were quick to learn these things, and the campaigns were getting harder.

Rome was trying to conquer this land by treaty and by force. Where one failed, the other would quickly follow. Yesterday, at a meeting with the elders of the Icenii, their Queen spoke to their commander, revealing the edict of her recently deceased husband, who had bequeathed half his lands to Rome. Half had not been good enough, and the Queen and her daughters had been seized as hostage against the rest of her tribe. The kingdom of the Icenii had been claimed on behalf of Rome.

The Queen had been a proud woman, long blonde hair braided and falling down her back, held together by a crafted golden torque. White linen robes clung proudly to her body as she stood to give her speech to the Roman commander.

Quick to react to the Roman treachery, she had lashed out with a dagger, and only the leather breastplate of their commander's uniform saved him from death. Then she was set upon by other Romans and brought to her knees before him.

A proud woman, defiant to the end as she was dragged away, unconscious. Her two daughters were taken too as the rest of the Council of Elders looked on horrified. Lucifer had heard their screams through the night as they were given to the men of the legion to be used as whores. He had lain awake, trying to ignore the screams, looking occasionally over to Gabriel, who gave the appearance of being able to sleep despite the pitiful sounds echoing into the night.

As they were finishing up at the water's edge, Gabriel walked alongside his friend. "I can see your discomfort in this. Perhaps you're right. Rome has taught us enough. It could be time to move on. This land is too big for Rome to conquer fully with the few legions it has sent here. The Celts are a fierce race but disorganised. If they should ever rise up together, they would sweep the Romans back into the sea," he admitted.

"Where to then? These people have no love of us, and we can be easily seen for what we are," Lucifer explained.

"Perhaps not so, for the Romans have taught us well enough. The legions house many different races from across this world. We can now pass as human, and deserters are not uncommon. We could follow the rest of our kind north into the Pictish Wilderness," Gabriel suggested. "I have heard of no Druids among the Picts, and it is they I fear far more than the Celts themselves."

"It might be best," Lucifer admitted. "Even Rome will not venture that far north. Their campaign against the Druids drives them ever to the west and the mountains we once called home."

Later that day, Gabriel and Lucifer formed part of the ring of soldiers protecting the perimeter of the fort whilst the Elders of the Icenii were allowed in to plead on behalf of their Queen. Their pleas fell on deliberately deaf ears as the commander of this garrison force was under explicit instructions to annex the kingdom of the Icenii come what may.

As an example to the Elders, he had their Queen dragged out into the main square, where a hastily constructed wooden structure had been erected. Boudicca no longer looked her normally regal self. Her hair now hung wildly, for the gold torque had been stolen. A once beautiful face was marked where she had been beaten, and her clean linen gown was now dirty and dishevelled.

Lucifer and others on the wall occasionally glanced back inside the compound to see what was happening, even as they stood guard on the perimeter wall.

The commandant ordered her stripped, and to the gasps of the Elders, Boudicca had her linen gown torn from her body by eager soldiers. Naked, she stood there defiantly, glaring at the commandant as though trying to strike him down with the evil eye. Many of the soldiers openly lusted after her, for her body showed no signs of bearing two adult daughters. At a nod from their commander, soldiers attached ropes to the fetter on her wrists and slung them up and over the tall wooden framework. She cried out once as they hauled on the ropes, pulling her up and off her feet to hang in midair, naked limbs threshing uselessly.

Some of the men tied off the ropes to leave her hanging there. A couple of others amused themselves with the butts of their spears, prodding the woman between her buttocks and between her legs, pushing her back and forth as they humiliated her. But she refused to cry out.

The Elders looked on grimly as the commandant ordered her flogged, and a soldier stepped forward with a long cat-o'-nine- tails made of knotted leather. Gabriel and Lucifer heard the crack of leather on flesh all the way up on the outer wall, though they heard no screams from the helpless woman.

Boudicca threshed in midair, trying to escape the bite of the leather flail, but it was no use. The flogging went on for long minutes until the soldier giving the flogging called, "Enough! She is no longer conscious."

"Let her hang there as an example to all of the power of Rome," ordered the commandant, and the Elders were then removed from the fort, having seen their Queen humbled in such a manner.

Eventually, Lucifer and Gabriel were relieved of duty on the perimeter wall and went to take their midday meal. Boudicca still hung limply from the wooden structure, the blood now drying on her back and buttocks. A few crows had gathered, attracted by the scent of blood.

"This is not a way to make war," Lucifer protested to his friend.

"It is the way Rome makes war," Gabriel chastened him. "Fear not, I think tonight we show Rome what lessons she has taught us." He grinned coldly.

Chapter Five

It was still a few hours before dawn when the two men stole silently across the compound, stowing their few possessions and provisions into their commandant's new chariot, and harnessing two of the horses. Fine horses these Celts had, and the finest had been "requisitioned" for the commandant's use.

Their avenue of escape now determined, the two men returned to the compound square, where the naked Queen still hung by the wrists. Her white skin was pale and visibly striped with dried blood in the moonlight.

One man stood guard over her. A few others on the outer wall concentrated on the forests beyond, and they were tired as the long night was coming to an end.

Lucifer took the man from behind, one hand covering his mouth, the other plunging the dagger into the base of his neck. Gabriel caught the spear as it fell, and the two of them lowered his body gently to the ground.

Quickly now, Gabriel cut the ropes holding the woman aloft, and Lucifer caught her as she fell, wrapping her in his woolen cloak. Boudicca came awake, weary and throat dry from her ordeal, as Lucifer held a leather flask of water for her to drink.

"We are not here as your enemies," he cautioned her to silence.

"My daughters ...," she croaked wearily.

"Soon enough. First, drink," said Gabriel, ever wary and looking about as he stripped the dead soldier. He quickly tied more rope around the dead man's wrists and then threw the ropes over the top of the structure. Finally, he hauled the dead body aloft, tying the ropes in place. From a distance, it would appear as though Boudicca still hung there.

Lucifer carried her to the waiting chariot, where he bade her to lie down out of sight. Then he and Gabriel made their way across the compound to where the two women had been imprisoned. Again, only one guard stood watch outside the small hut where they were kept. Last night's rape had been an example and a reward for the men. It had not been designed to be a regular occurrence, as it would lead to too much lack of discipline in the men.

Gabriel struck swiftly. The guard had no chance. He saw Gabriel approaching, recognised him, and was about to greet him when Gabriel's hand flew up and the cold length of steel flew the short distance from his hand to the guard's throat, a trick Lucifer had not yet mastered. The dagger was quickly retrieved as Gabriel dragged the body out of sight, and Lucifer went inside to where the two women huddled together in sleep.

Wary of Roman treachery, the two of them allowed themselves to be led outside. Then, seeing that there were only two men there, they began to believe Lucifer's words that they were to seek freedom with their mother.

Wrapped in blankets, for there was no time to seek other clothing for them, the two women ran silently to where the chariot awaited. A tearful, if silent, reunion with their mother followed, and whilst Lucifer attended to them, Gabriel went to take care of the last remaining obstacle to their plan.

The gate to the fort was a traditional Roman portcullis, modified only with regard to the available building materials available to them, and was constructed of small saplings. Not sturdy enough to survive a long assault but sufficient for a fort of this size. Its opening was controlled by ropes, pulleys, and counterweights set atop the outer wall.

Gabriel climbed one of the access ladders boldly, in full sight, for he was known amongst the men as a respected warrior who had proved himself since joining the legion. He nodded to a few of the men as he made his way casually along the wall, speaking to a few of his acquaintances as he moved towards his goal.

He looked across to where the chariot stood, the horses moving nervously now as they could sense Lucifer's unease as he held the reins, awaiting Gabriel's signal. There was one man atop the main gate, Marcus Levillus, who was known to Gabriel. Not a popular figure amongst the rest of the men, and Gabriel had no qualms about killing him, should it be necessary.

He nodded silently as he walked past him, turning the corner beyond the angle of the watchtower to where the control wheel was set. Quickly now, Gabriel squatted and began turning the wheel furiously, thankful the mechanism was kept well-greased, for the portcullis began to rise silently.

Marcus Levillus, though not the best soldier in the Ninth Legion, was alert and noticed that Gabriel had not reappeared on the other side of the watchtower, and so, he came along the perimeter wall to find out why this was so. "What are you doing there?" he called out, causing Gabriel to look up.

Quickly, Gabriel whistled shrilly to give Lucifer the signal, and he heard the snap of the reins as the leather cracked on the horses' backs, spurring them to movement. Marcus Levillus assessed the situation rapidly. "Ware the gate!" he cried out loudly and drew his short sword to rush upon Gabriel who was still hauling up the portcullis.

The chariot was closing the gap quickly as Lucifer spurred on the horses. Gabriel had no choice but to release the handwheel as the centurion came at him. Drawing his own short sword, he met Marcus Levillus full on, sword against sword, and was beaten quickly back by the former's heavier body weight.

Pushed back against the wall, he met the sword thrust with deflection as he tried to use his greater skill with the blade to overcome the other's weight advantage. At closed quarters like this, Marcus Levillus had the upper hand, for Gabriel's lighter bone structure was a distinct disadvantage in such a contest.

The portcullis was starting to descend now as Lucifer spurred on the horses, the chariot closing the distance rapidly. Cries of alarm were coming from the rest of the perimeter as Marcus's cry had alerted them that something was amiss.

Gabriel cursed as the other's short blade sliced his forearm and quickly changed hands with his sword, taking Marcus Levillus by surprise, for ambidextrousness was unheard of. He dropped quickly, slashing out at the other's leg, and Marcus fell, crying out.

Lucifer called out to his friend as the chariot began to pass beneath the descending portcullis, and Gabriel leaped from atop the perimeter wall to land on the back of one of the two horses, laughing wildly and using the short sword to slash at the control rope of the portcullis as they passed, letting it drop more quickly behind them as they thundered off into the dark forest. Pursuit would be delayed long enough for them to return Boudicca to her own people, and then let the Romans beware ...

Chapter Six

Four years passed after Boudicca was finally defeated, and the Second Legion consolidated its forces, pushing West into Wales, intent on putting all the Druids to the sword. Emperor Nero had decreed that all other religions be outlawed, and the Druids were perceived as a powerful threat to Roman conquest of these lands. In an attempt to curry favour with their persecutors, some of these Druids began telling strange tales of winged men who lived in the far north of the island, men whose blood made one immortal. Small flasks of this blood were offered in exchange for their lives by the more unscrupulous Druids. When one such Druid wounded himself to prove his claims and his wound healed in days, credence was given to his claims, and a small expeditionary force was sent north into the Pictish Wilderness.

This force was a scant one hundred men led by Centurion Cassius Marcus Branca, who was charged with the task of proving or disproving the Druids' claims. They set out for the wilds of Northern Britain and the lands of the fierce Picts, under orders to avoid contact with the Celtic tribes in between.

A week later, the small force began to approach the known lands of the Picts and decided to change their method of travel. They no longer felt safe to travel by day, as no treaties were signed with any of the warlike tribes of the north, who usually attacked strangers on sight.

So it was that they slept hidden in woodlands by day and ventured out only by night, skirting the obvious encampments of the Pictish tribes under cover of darkness and avoiding all contact. If their presence was noted this far north, and so isolated, then they would surely be attacked.

Once in the highlands, Branca took note of the landscape, seeking out the high places where he imagined such creatures as had been described were likely to frequent. Watching from refuge during the day, he and his men were amazed to notice large birdlike creatures occasionally soaring high overhead, and his search narrowed as he followed the patterns of their flight.

Remaining in hiding for days, he and his men noted where these strange creatures came to earth for food and for water. He noted the patterns and timings, eventually deciding where best to lay and spring his trap.

A small brook near the edge of a wood seemed a favourite place for these creatures to come for water in the early morning and dusk, when they thought themselves safe from predator man. Branca set his men to weaving nets and found positions where three of them could lay in wait for the opportunity.

It came on the third day, near dusk, when his men had their chance. Going early to their place of concealment, Branca and two of his men lay in hiding, late enough so that there was little chance of the Picts coming upon them and early enough to conceal themselves before the strange winged men showed themselves.

They swooped to earth in twos and threes, ever wary. But Branca had counted their numbers and noted the straggler who was always last to leave. Tonight, he would not leave at all.

From their hiding places in the thick underbrush, Branca listened to the strange hybrids communicate with each other. The language was high-pitched but seemed to have some stricture to it, along Celtic lines. Branca was not fluent in languages other than his native Latin and some Spanish he had picked up among earlier campaigns, so he didn't really understand what they said to one another.

As the last winged man bathed himself at the water's edge, Branca and his two men silently rose from beneath their well-manufactured concealment and threw their nets high as the creature reared back in surprise. The immense wings flapped back and down as he attempted to take to the air, but the weighted nets slowed him down enough for the three men to attack him.

His cries were almost human as the three soldiers clubbed him senseless. The rest of the expeditionary force came running as they heard the brief scuffle, and the strange being was trussed, his wings tightly bound. A wood and cloth travois was used to carry him as the soldiers wanted to be far away from here come the dawn, and Branca had his men quick march southwards.

The next day, they lay up in a deep forest, the creature gagged lest he somehow call out to his winged brethren who could be seen flitting back and forth across the skies more frequently than the day before, for they realised one of their number was missing, presumably taken by the humans. Though which humans, they knew not.

They fed the creature nuts and berries when it would not eat their own rations of dried meat. It took water as readily as they did amongst themselves but refused to talk, even when ungagged briefly. Some of the men were ready to abuse it as a freak, jostling it and prodding it with their spears as they made it walk, ankles and wings bound, but Branca frowned upon such behaviour. He was under orders to bring the beast back alive, as strange as it was. It was his duty to his emperor …

Two brief skirmishes with the Picts reduced Branca's force to less than sixty men by the time he made his way back to the relative safety of the Celtic lands. They seemed even more savage than normal upon seeing the nature of the captive the Romans had within their midst and fought ferociously to seize him from them.

He marched his captive, looking slightly the worse for wear, back into the fort to stunned silence from the rest of the Roman soldiers, who did not know what to make of the strange being.

Branca told tales of others of the winged race, which they luckily avoided by keeping to the woods and forests and travelling by night. The creature was weighed down by heavy chains to prevent him trying to fly off whilst one of the captive Druids was called for to begin the tests which would prove whether or not the stories he had told the commandant were true or not. Kept apart from other Celtic slaves who were obviously in awe of the strange hybrid, it and they were eventually sent back to Rome for Nero to make his own judgement on the freak.

The many weeks in a small cage as they transported him across the width of the Roman Empire proved hazardous to the angel's health as was the diet of slops fed to keep him alive. Needless to say, Nero did not believe all the claims made about the strange sorry-looking birdman and had him put into the arena, to be attacked and slain by wild beasts as a sacrifice to the gods, to prove or disprove his unique immortality. "Only we Gods are immortal …," Nero scoffed as they dragged what was left of the angel's body from the sand.

Inside the catacombs, captured Celtic slaves surrounded the partially dismembered body, lapping away like dogs at the many open wounds before being beaten away by their Roman guards, disgusted by their behaviour. "Savages … bloody heathen savages."

Watching from behind other bars were other slaves of the newly founded Christian cult. They watched with interest the behaviour of the Celts and were quick to question them about their beliefs. Was this actually one of their heralded angels come to Earth, only to be slaughtered by these Romans?

A time of change was coming to Rome. Nero persecuted the Christians in his own country as he did the Druids in Britain. Only Roman Gods could be worshipped, yet the cult of Christianity was slowly spreading from the east. It washed like a tide across known civilisation.

Sooner or later, even Nero must bow to the will of the people, for the mob made or broke emperors. The mob *was* Rome. A Christian emperor was not unthinkable in times to come. Emperors lived and emperors died. Nero's time was surely coming. Only faith lives on …

Ireland 1929

Chapter Seven

"Guinness, is it, Father?" asked Sean Reilly behind the bar of the Pig 'n' Whistle pub as the young priest called in for his evening drink and socialize with the regulars. It was a way to invite acceptance into this rural community and show that beneath his robes, he was a man, just like them.

"Aye, Sean. As usual," the priest confirmed with a smile. The tall dark figure of the young priest was a common sight in the bar most nights during the week, calling in just after nine o'clock and staying till closing time, to socialise. Newly arrived in the village less than a year before, after old Father Gilhooley had passed away, Father O'Brien had quickly been accepted by the small community. He had a kind friendly manner and was easy to talk to, not the usual fire-and-brimstone old-school priest that the village had become accustomed to during Father Gilhooley's time. The village regulars joked that the drink was a match for his attire of black cassock and white dog collar. He could only agree.

Father O'Brien paid for his pint and took a refreshing sip, letting the suds settle on his upper lip as he enjoyed the cool liquid's passage down the back of his throat. He turned back towards the interior of the bar, leaning back on the bar rail, when he was beckoned over to join a couple of the "lads" he had grown to know over the last year. "Come join us, Father. 'Tis a hot one, to be sure," Kenny Cassidy commented. Kenny was one of the new breed. Fresh out of school and working on one of the local farms. His family, like others, had suffered under the British occupation, and he was an easy recruit for the Republican Movement.

The dark bumfluff on his chin was his attempt at trying to look older than his years, and he was failing miserably.

A seat was pushed back for O'Brien at the small table to one side of the dartboard, where two youths who barely looked old enough to drink legally were playing pretty awfully, the odd dart ricocheting out to land point first on the floor. He accepted the seat graciously, though made a point of moving it slightly as the men chuckled at his caution.

"Not relying on the Lord to keep you safe, Father?" asked Big Jim Kennedy, a heavyset redheaded man in his midforties. Kennedy ran a small haulage company, which came in handy as what was hauled wasn't always what was on the manifests. Father O'Brien laughed as the others enjoyed their little joke at his faith's expense.

"The Lord himself couldn't help those two," O'Brien joked back. "Their dart-throwing is awful." Davey Brennan slapped him playfully on his back. A slap from Davey hurt, as he was quite a heavyset, well-muscled man in his early forties.

They could let their hair down with this priest, talk to him as an ordinary man, when he wasn't in his church. They felt at ease with him. O'Brien had been drawn into their company some six months ago. When he had first started frequenting the Pig 'n' Whistle, the locals were a bit distant, not used to the sight of their priest at the bar. But over the months, gradually, O'Brien had won them over.

Kennedy was involved with the IRA, O'Brien knew, and he had singled O'Brien out, obviously knowing about the previous members of O'Brien's family who had fought and died for the cause at the hands of the British. O'Brien's father had pushed the boy in the direction of the church after his two uncles had both been killed, one shot in a raid on an army barracks and the other arrested and publicly executed for his known affiliations. Although O'Brien had honored his father's wishes, his own sympathies lay with the movement too, which Kennedy slowly drew out of him in late conversation.

O'Brien didn't allow himself to get drunk in public, but his tongue loosened with the Guinness. Gradually, O'Brien became aware that he was being sounded out, as Kennedy slipped the odd reference to his IRA affiliations into their conversations. The secrecy of the confessional made him privy to lots of things about lots of people, though most of the IRA men in the village made a point of not discussing such things even at confession. But some did, and one only had to look at their known affiliates to realize who the "boys" were.

Ireland was still occupied by the British, and the scumbag Black 'n' Tans were allowed to run rampant over decent folk—nothing better than uniformed criminals. Supposedly sent over to keep the peace between the native Catholics and the Prods, they were all Protestant to a man and did nothing but persecute the Catholics and foster further unrest in the communities. They were stationed everywhere, even here just a few miles outside the village, where it was thought they could run the roost over several small village communities. They were known to saunter through the village on occasion, though not when off duty. Not all of them were that stupid. Just liked to let everyone know they were here and that they were in charge. Old Clooney, the local policeman, had little to do these days. He just kept his head down like everybody else.

O'Brien finished his Guinness, and Kennedy bought him another. The conversation was being drawn deliberately down a dark and possibly dangerous road. Kennedy explained, "You sympathize with us, Father. You know you do. You've felt British 'justice' first hand with the murder of your own kin. You could be of great help to everyone in the movement," he stated simply, keeping his voice low.

"And how do you see that, Jim Kennedy? The church would not look kindly upon me taking any sort of active role on your behalf," O'Brien complained, though part of him longed to offer some sort of support for his own people against an occupying army of oppression.

"It's not active support we need, Father. More of a sanctuary of sorts for some of our guns." There, Kennedy had said it at last. "There are a number of old crypts falling apart in the church cemetery, Father. One or more could be used to store some of our arms and munitions. I'm sure the dead wouldn't mind. The British wouldn't think or dare to look there," he went on as O'Brien thought seriously on the proposal, trying to ratify his loyalties with his religious beliefs.

Just then, the sound of hobnailed boots was heard outside the pub, and the door to the bar was quickly thrown open as a big man in a sergeant's uniform entered with his Webley revolver already drawn as a precaution. As the occupants of the pub froze into immobility, four more troopers followed the sergeant inside, rifles shouldered but instantly accessible. "Good evening, Mr. Reilly," announced the tall imposing figure, turning to survey every occupant of the bar with cold calculating eyes. Hostile eyes glared back. O'Brien was caught momentarily flustered, though Big Jim Kennedy and his two friends remained calm, brazening it out, well used to such intimidation from the Black 'n' Tans. "There's a black bicycle with a handbasket parked outside. Who does it belong to?" he asked to no one in particular.

Straight away, one of the two youths playing darts began to visibly pale. From slightly drunk, he sobered up very quickly indeed as the sergeant noticed his fright and rounded on him straight away. "Yours is it, son?" He smiled cruelly. "Farmer Fitzpatrick says he saw a poacher off on his land just around dusk, and he rode off on a black bicycle just like yours."

"It wasn't me," the lad blurted out. "I've never been anywhere near his farm today." The four squaddies surrounded him. "Honest, it wasn't me," he complained. His friend was backing away from him slowly, looking more worried now than the lad who was originally being questioned as he then looked towards him, realizing who it was that had borrowed his bicycle earlier that evening.

"Take him away. His friend too," ordered the sergeant, and the four squaddies went to apprehend the two youths. In the brief struggle that followed, one of the youths was floored by a rifle butt smashing into his face. O'Brien stood up from his chair, horrified at the calm brutality of the Black 'n' Tans.

"There was no need for that, Sergeant. He's just a boy!" he protested. The sergeant looked at him coldly, the Webley now aimed in O'Brien's direction. There was silence for a few seconds as the rest of the pub held its collective breath. Then the sergeant spoke while the two youths were dragged out of the bar.

"If you have any complaints, Father, take them up with Brigadier Stewart. I'm not interesting in hearing them. The youths resisted arrest and were duly subdued with a minimum of force. I would have been quite within my rights to have shot the thieving little bastard." He grinned mirthlessly. "I do my duty, Father, and you had best learn to do yours and shut your fucking face!" With that insult, the sergeant turned on his heels and exited the bar quickly, following close behind the four squaddies, and everyone in the bar let out their breath once more.

"English bastards!" cursed one of the regulars.

"Mostly Scottish and Welsh, if the truth be known," Sean, the landlord, explained as he pulled himself a pint from his own pump to calm his nerves.

"Whoever the fook they are, they just waltzed in here and carted off two of our lads!" protested another. 'So who cares if they helped themselves to a chicken or two off Fitzpatrick's farm? Times are hard."

"Are they with the movement, Jim?" O'Brien asked the older man. He shook his head.

"No, they're not. But they probably will be in a month or two, once the Brits get through with them. They don't seem to realize they do all our recruiting for us. People flock to us from all walks of life," he explained. "You can't treat a people like they treat us and expect to get away with it! We don't forgive, and we certainly don't forget!" He grinned coldly.

"You know, I never heard any truck pull up outside," said Davey Brennan as he looked out into the darkness through the lace curtains. "If they're walking them back to barracks, it's a four-mile walk, and they'll have to go around Dilby Wood." The three IRA men slowly grinned, and as one, they turned towards O'Brien. "It's a nice dark night out there," He grinned.

"Do you feel up for some fun 'n' games, Father?" asked Big Jim Kennedy, smiling amusedly.

Chapter Eight

The darkness in the wood was almost complete as O'Brien struggled to keep up with the other three men, careful to follow close behind as they seemed to know the pathways even on a night as dark as this. Kenny and Davey both carried Enfield rifles after a brief stop at a small cottage where a small arms cache was secreted, and Big Jim himself carried a revolver. He had handed a second revolver to O'Brien, who found himself accepting it, the weight heavy in his hand as he ran, asking himself just what the hell it was he thought he was doing. The confrontation in the pub had sent his blood pounding, and he wasn't thinking with his brain, just his heart. Was that wrong?

Around them, the night air was alive with the sounds of nocturnal animals and insects, momentarily quieting at their passage and then resounding again behind them. The wood was scarcely a mile across, yet the road around was a good three miles or more, and that was the way the small troop of Black 'n' Tans had chosen to march their prisoners on their way back to their barracks. They would head them off a mile or more before they reached their destination.

Suddenly, the darkness lessened, and O'Brien could see the moon overhead once more as they cleared the edge of the wood. Big Jim whispered rushed instructions to Davey and Kenny, who separated and took up positions near the edge of the tree line but inside the wood itself, using the inner darkness for cover. "You come with me, Father." He led O'Brien forward and to the same side of the road, making sure he was not in the line of fire. O'Brien crouched down beside him, breathing hard. Jim gave him a smile, which showed his crooked teeth in the moonlight. "Nothing to it, Father," he reassured the priest. "It should all be over in a matter of seconds, and then we'll all be away sharpish, in case the sound of the gunfire carries to their barracks." O'Brien found himself looking at the gun in his hands once more. "You might not even need to use it, Father. But if you do, just point and pull the trigger. Cock it first, like this," he demonstrated and then carefully lowered the hammer once more. "Don't think about it or try to aim. Instinct is best," he assured him. "Just point and pull."

They settled down to wait in a dip in the ground behind some bushes, the sound of their breathing unusually loud, thought O'Brien. They were going to kill those men, he thought to himself, partially horrified yet equally partly excited at the prospect. Could he bring himself to fire the gun? The mere weight of it in his hands was unnerving. He could feel the sweat cooling on his backbone and shivered. After some five minutes or more, the sound of hobnail army boots on tarmac and gravel could be heard in the distance. O'Brien's breathing became harsher, nerves starting to get to him. If anything, Kennedy looked more relaxed the louder the stomping became.

Gradually, in the distance, O'Brien could make out the approaching band and could now hear the whimpering from the two youths they had in custody with them, each flanked by two of the squaddies. "When do we shoot?" O'Brien asked nervously. Kennedy just smiled reassuringly.

"Let the front rank pass us, Father. Davey will take the first shot. As he fires, so will Kenny, taking out the front two soldiers. We'll take the rear two, one each. If you can't make the shot, don't worry. I should be able to take the other one too before he knows what's going on. There's just that ogre of a sergeant to worry about. If he's good enough, he might get a shot off. So whoever first chambers a round will take him as their secondary target. I don't care how many of us end up shooting the bastard as long as he's dead at the end of it. Try not to hit the wee 'uns." He grinned coldly.

O'Brien crouched in the bushes, forcing his breathing to become shallower, calming himself. The two pints of Guinness were making themselves felt, and he badly needed to relieve himself. Closer and closer the unsuspecting soldiers came. O'Brien offered a silent prayer. The moment approached. The crunching boots became louder, passing him, as the small column frog-marched the two frightened teenagers. All of a sudden, the night came instantly alive as one, no, two shots rang out, almost as one, and echoed in the night air. Instantly, Big Jim rose up alongside him, leveling and firing his own revolver. O'Brien's body was pulled upright, matching his movement to Kennedy's. O'Brien looked down the length of his own arm as he pointed the gun and awkwardly pulled back the hammer.

It went off seemingly all by itself as his finger barely touched the trigger, the shot going high in the air. Shouting now as both of the two surviving soldiers realized what was happening. Kennedy cursed as one of the remaining soldiers pulled one of the youths in front of him as a human shield, only to go down from another rifle bullet from Davey, their best marksman. The sergeant was good enough to fire off a couple of shots at the flashes of gunfire he saw and then went to seek cover, charging off the road ... straight towards O'Brien and Kennedy in the darkness.

The big man stumbled in the undergrowth as Kennedy fired, the bullet narrowly missing, and the frightened sergeant returned fire again hurriedly, Kennedy screaming as the bullet struck him in the thigh. The man came on as Kennedy fell, and as he staggered back to his feet, he stood staring at the priest with the gun in his hand, momentarily shocked into immobility as was O'Brien himself. The sergeant's gun rose and tracked towards him too late as O'Brien hurriedly cocked the hammer, and his finger tightened on that hair trigger once more. From that distance, he couldn't miss. The bullet took the sergeant centre chest and flung him back to fall, motionless on the ground. "Good shooting, Father," congratulated Kennedy through gritted teeth as he sought to tie a handkerchief around his thigh to control the bleeding. O'Brien just stood there looking dazed. He had just killed a man. Oh God, forgive him ...

Chapter Nine

Father O'Brien was recalled to Rome in 1932. The telegram gave no explanation, except to say that his presence was urgently required by Cardinal Zola, one of the powers behind the Holy See. Another priest was being organized as a replacement, but he was instructed to leave immediately. "Immediately" meant something different in Ireland, and so a few days later, Father Patrick O'Brien caught the ferry to Liverpool, en route for Dover and a ship, which was bound for Italy. It was the earliest ship he could get a passage on, and the journey was expected to take between one and two weeks, depending on the weather.

Arriving finally in Italy after a rough sea passage, he took a train north to Rome, leaving the train at the Rome Termini station. O'Brien took a taxi to a hotel near the Vatican City and checked in, going up to his allocated room to make himself more presentable. After showering and changing, he walked on foot to the Vatican, asking directions to Cardinal Zola's office, and reported to the curate in the office antechambers. He was then instructed to take a seat and wait.

Four days later, he was still waiting as an endless stream of other clergy and obviously more important visitors was ushered in and out of the inner chambers. O'Brien was getting frustrated and prayed for inner patience. He puzzled over the reasons for his summons.

Finally, when he thought his patience must surely snap, the curate summoned him and bade him to enter the inner chamber to finally meet the cardinal. Looking up from behind his oak desk, the portly cardinal rose to greet him cordially. "Ah, Father O'Brien. Patrick, isn't it? Please take a seat." His English was heavily accented but a lot better than O'Brien's Italian. He shook O'Brien's hand firmly, and O'Brien took a seat across the desk from the slightly older man.

"Your Eminence. I'm at your service but a bit puzzled as to why you requested this meeting. Surely a priest, particularly a foreign one, is not usually summoned to the Vatican?" O'Brien expressed his honest bemusement. Zola smiled benevolently, though his eyes seemed to see right through O'Brien.

"A delicate matter, Patrick. One best not discussed over the phone or written down in a telegram which might, say, be intercepted by the authorities. Particularly the British authorities," he emphasized. Ryan was instantly on guard, his back stiffening noticeably as he sat straighter in the chair. "I understand they're paying you a bit of attention these days." Zola smiled. *What did he know?* wondered O'Brien.

"The British Army is still occupying Ireland, if that is what you mean, Your Eminence. They are still laying down 'their' law and generally making life uncomfortable for every Irishman."

"I was, in fact, speaking of you personally, Patrick," he said, pulling out a thick folder from within his desk. Its cover bore Patrick O'Brien's name, and Zola opened it to pull out the uppermost sheet of paper. "It seems the army considers you a destabilizing influence in the northern provinces." He passed the letter to O'Brien, who read it with open astonishment. "What have you been up to, to annoy them so much?" Zola's eyes twinkled wickedly, as though he already knew the answer to the question he had just asked. The letter was from Brigadier Peter Stewart to the Home Office, asking for permission to put O'Brien under surveillance.

"How did you come by this?" was the first question that O'Brien could think of, and he handed the letter back as Zola reached for it.

"Oh, we have our contacts. Needless to say, this letter was never received in London. But I think your departure from Ireland has come at a rather opportune time, wouldn't you?" He smiled. "The Catholic Church, as such, officially frowns on the action of terrorists, as the British care to call your friends in the Republican Movement. But unofficially, good Catholics are being persecuted for their beliefs, and the church's sympathies will always lie with the oppressed. I've been led to understand you lent them a little more than just your passive support?" Now he was coming to it. O'Brien said nothing, just stared at Zola as he went on. "Your activities are hardly in keeping with a priest, Patrick. Not a normal priest, anyway. But your rather diverse skills may be of benefit within other areas of church activity. Tell me, have you heard of the Sword of Solomon?" Zola stood up and went over to his wine cabinet.

"The sword King Solomon was alleged to have offered to slice a baby in two with when two women claimed the child as their own?" O'Brien asked. Zola smiled, taking out a carafe of red wine and bringing two glasses back over to the desk.

"A rather unique solution to a seeming dilemma, wasn't it?" He poured the wine, and O'Brien graciously accepted as the cardinal continued. "The Catholic Church is often faced with many dilemmas in this modern world, Patrick. Some decisions aren't easy to make. Sometimes that sort of unique solution is called for when no other will do. When justice fails, there is always the sword to fall back on. A sad but inescapable fact." Zola took a deep draught from the wine glass, savoring the taste fully before slowly swallowing. "The church has its own Sword of Solomon these days, Patrick. We would like you to take up that sword on our behalf."

"I'm not sure I catch your meaning, Your Eminence." O'Brien was perplexed and took a comforting sip of wine himself as Zola began to expand on his statement.

"There is a special branch of the church, whose activities must remain secret from the rest of the world." Zola went on, "They have existed for many years, acting behind the scenes to further the faith in areas where religion alone has needed a little help. This is our Sword of Solomon, Patrick. We would like you to become one of its agents, and if you agree, you will be taken from here and will then learn more. You will be given a new identity, a change of name. All links with your past will be severed. If you do not wish this, then we will talk about it no more, and you will never hear of it again. We will simply find you a remote posting somewhere where your friends in the British Army will be unable to find you, don't worry. The church looks after its own. But let me stress that I think this is a chance you should not miss. Your 'talents' would be of immense use to the church, and your work could take you anywhere in the world, perhaps even back to your native Ireland—under another identity, of course. Something not too dissimilar to your old name," he added, laughing, and then took another drink of wine whilst O'Brien just sat there, mulling over what had just been offered to him.

O'Brien thought over his position. Ireland was now no longer his home if the British were onto him. He'd be arrested and shot; priest or no priest, those bastards didn't mess about. They'd just haul him off one night and make it look like a sectarian killing. A remote posting abroad somewhere else might be of interest but not as interesting as the offer Zola had just made him. His curiosity was piqued, no mistake. He made his decision. "If it pleases Your Eminence, if I can be of help to the church in this regard, then so be it." Zola smiled, draining his glass and then reaching for the carafe to refill it.

"Good, Patrick. Excellent, in fact. Let us make a toast to your future success. I am sure you will go far, working for the power *behind* the throne, so to speak." Zola laughed and clinked glasses with O'Brien, who was now only just getting an inkling of what Zola had meant. "I'll organize transport to one of our Monasteries in the north, where your indoctrination will begin. Needless to say, the secrecy of this particular branch of the church is dependent upon its operatives not discussing its work with outsiders."

"You'll have no worries on that score, Your Eminence. My friends in the IRA shoot people for talking out of turn," O'Brien admitted.

"So do we, Patrick. So do we!" Zola added, straight-faced and deadly serious.

Rome 1941

Chapter Ten

The shadow of the swastika reached even further than the shadow of the Holy Roman Church, encompassing all within the grip of twin tyrants Hitler and his puppet ruler Mussolini. The church lived in fear of the Fascists and strove to maintain a low profile while doing what it could to further its own aspirations.

Gabriel had come to Italy under an American passport—one of many—yet the safest nationality in these troubled times. For all the rumors, America had not officially entered the war, even though it was common knowledge many of their civilians had volunteered to join the Allied forces.

Lucifer had not been in touch for some months, and Rome was where his enquiries had led him. Under the guise of a war correspondent for the wire services, Gabriel began making discreet enquiries.

It was the American embassy where he met her, referred by one of the senior clerks to a young woman in the immigration section, who handled all missing-person enquiries. She was busy with some paperwork when he was first ushered into her office, and he waited patiently as she finished filling in an innocuous form.

The perfume invaded his nostrils, for he was gifted with a very keen sense of smell. A perfect match for her unique body chemistry and very pleasant. The nicotine was there too. A pity humans did not have the benefit of his own special "healing factor," which allowed regeneration of damaged tissue. Even so, he had had no desire to flirt with addiction to any drug, either old or relatively new.

As he mused, she looked up; those deep green eyes met his, and he felt an intangible hand reach into his chest and lightly solidify around his heart. He caught his breath as he imagined a ghostly whisper close to his ear. "Gotcha …," it said.

He stared momentarily at the simple small gold crucifix around her neck, fighting the inherent revulsion at the symbol. Most humans had no idea of the amount of blood that had been spilled in the name of "religion" over the centuries.

"Can I help you?" she asked as he tried to compose himself, smiling slightly at his obvious bemusement. Gabriel forced himself to speak with difficulty. He noted the name on the nameplate on the desk—Mrs. Laura Donovan.

"Mrs. Donovan?" She smiled again.

"Yep, that's me. What can I do for you, Mr. …?" she queried.

"My name is Angell. I'm looking for my brother, and I believe he is somewhere in Rome." He was finding it hard to concentrate. It had been a long time since he had felt any attraction towards a human female. Yet he couldn't deny the instant and extremely powerful attraction that sparked as their eyes met. Love at first sight? It had happened to him twice before, just like this. His memory wasn't yet dampened by the centuries. *I don't need this*, he thought to himself as the realization hit him.

Sadly, he wasn't meant for such relationships. It wasn't fair on the human women, watching them grow old while he just didn't. "Do you always stare at women, Mr. Angell?" she asked amusedly. She knew men found her attractive, yet she did not go out of her way to court such attention. Gabriel gasped as he realized he was doing just that.

"I'm so sorry. Only the beautiful ones." He smiled in apology. She laughed, breaking the tension momentarily.

"Good save. I'll take that as a compliment, Mr. Angell," she chuckled. She'd heard similar chat-up lines before, though she was quite taken with the man's classic almost timeless features. "Now, what can you tell me about your brother? Let's see if we can trace him for you. We like to keep tabs on all American citizens in these troubled times."

The next hour flew by as Gabriel recited all he knew of his "brother's" whereabouts, and Mrs. Donovan dutifully recorded all the pertinent details and quizzed him for more background information, which caused a bit of on-the-spot fabrication, as Gabriel did not want to give too much information away. Making small talk came easily between the two of them, and she was good enough to recommend a good hotel when he revealed he had only just arrived in Rome himself. He left, albeit reluctantly, with Mrs. Donovan promising to do all she could to trace his brother for him.

Chapter Eleven

A couple of days passed as Gabriel toured the city, making his own careful investigations in quarters best kept unknown from officialdom. Il Duce's Fascists and Nazi advisors were everywhere. Luckily, his papers were excellent forgeries. He called again at the embassy to see Mrs. Donovan for an update on her official enquiries and found himself asking her to dinner once she had let slip in conversation that she was a widow, albeit a young one.

For dinner that evening, she took his breath away in a long black silk evening dress, the bodice cut low enough to reveal the swell of her bosom. The cool evening breeze and the clinging material of her dress made it hard to keep his eyes on her face. But of course, being a woman, that was exactly why she had chosen to wear that particular dress.

"My husband Jack liked to fly. Unfortunately, the plane didn't," she explained with a rueful smile. "He used to do some barnstorming shows at the county fair, fancy acrobatics to thrill the crowds. One day, they got more than they bargained for." She paused, taking a sip from her glass of water. "It was a couple of years ago. Life goes on. I needed a new start, something to put the memories behind me." A mixture of sadness and relief came over Gabriel at the news.

He had fought for a woman many years ago but was glad he would not have such a conflict thrust upon him again. She was indeed beautiful—long blonde hair tied today in a braid, which hung down her back between her shoulder blades. This was a woman worth the fight. The attraction was there between them, but just how strong it was with her, he did not know. Too early to say, and he could not imagine she felt the emotions as strongly and as instantly as he himself did.

A fine meal followed the small talk, accompanied by an even finer wine. "Your brother arrived by ship some two and a half months ago, checking into a small hotel on the south side of the city. He registered his presence at the embassy in line with immigration procedures before hiring a guide to show him some of the vineyards in the countryside. The guide's name was Grimaldi. He is known to the embassy, and we had no hesitation in recommending him to your brother. That was the last time we saw him, but here's a list of Grimaldi's known haunts. You can catch up with him yourself. I'm sure he'll be able to tell you where your brother got to." Laura passed him a folded piece of paper, slightly scented with neat delicate handwriting, listing a number of addresses. Gabriel nodded and pocketed the information.

"Thank you. I'll look him up," he promised. Lucifer had indeed been over here on a wine-buying expedition, though Gabriel saw no reason to reveal that to her.

Gabriel then concentrated on enjoying the rest of the evening in her delightful company. He hired a horse carriage to enjoy a moonlight tour of Rome by night as she delighted in pointing out the various tourist and historical spots. She was obviously quite knowledgeable on architecture, and he refrained from revealing his own views on the subject, for she was enjoying playing the teacher, having imbibed slightly too much wine.

The evening ended as he dropped her off at her home, a small villa. The carriage waited discreetly while he walked her to her door. Impulsively, she turned and embraced him, kissing him lightly on the lips. Gabriel returned the embrace automatically, the feel of her body against his awakening his senses. He had not felt a woman's body against his own in many years, and it felt so right. She made to pull away instinctively but only for a second. "Thank you for a wonderful evening." She smiled, her eyes holding his own.

As he loosened his hold on her, she pressed herself further into his arms, the kiss hungrier, losing herself in the moment till at last, Gabriel forced himself back in control, against his own obvious desire. The two of them stood there, still holding each other. Laura was breathing quite heavily, the ample bosom rising and falling within the black silk bodice.

Gabriel spoke first. "This night has been too short." He smiled. "I can't remember enjoying myself so much in years."

"Me too …," Laura added, getting her breath back as the cool evening air helped to sober her up slightly. Those eyes were slowly mesmerizing him, and he fought to break their hold as he turned away, not wanting to, yet also not wanting to take advantage of her. He wasn't sure if her desire was fired by the wine, but he could taste the desire on her lips. Her skin was hot, even in the cool night air.

"I'd better go …" He was lost for words. She started to speak and then bit her lip. *Do all human relationships start off so hesitantly?* he asked himself. I want her, and she wants me, yet neither of us is going to say so. "Good night." He kissed her once more, lightly on the forehead and then turned and retraced his steps up the short path to where the carriage waited. Laura stood in the doorway, smiling strangely, waving briefly as he got back into the carriage and the horse started off, hooves ringing on the cobbled street. Strangely saddened, she opened the door and went inside.

Chapter Twelve

The next day dawned with a tinge of regret as Gabriel dwelled on the previous evening. He forced himself to put Mrs. Donovan to the back of his mind and concentrate on the search for his "brother."

Once, a very long time ago, they had all lived together—Gabriel, Lucifer, Michael, and all the others of the Elohim—high among the mountain peaks. So long ago that even Gabriel's memory failed him at times. Brain cells regenerated at the same rate as the rest of their bodies, yet the sheer input of experience over the years was too much for their brains to keep track of, and occasionally, memories got filtered out and replaced by others deemed more relevant or important.

As human evolution progressed, the humans feared the race of "angels" less and turned their fear to hate. Soon, the humans began hunting them down, and there were far more humans than "angels." Michael, even Michael, mightiest of them all, must have finally fallen before the humans' relentless rage.

The ancient Druids learnt that draining an "angel" of blood and imbibing that blood themselves would greatly prolong the lifespan of an ordinary human, though not to the extent of the seemingly immortal "angels" themselves. Once word spread, the semiorganized religions helped organize the genocide that followed.

Hunted to the far ends of the earth, Gabriel had fled with the others, driven out of their lofty homes in the mountains as they were hunted down one by one. Some, like Gabriel and Lucifer, were maimed, their wings destroyed in flames. Others, like Michael, must have died in battle, attempting to rescue their captured brethren from the humans. Now their once proud race was reduced to just two, maybe even one, for he and Lucifer were all that remained of a once lofty race as far as he knew.

Over the years, Gabriel had tried to trace any of his people who might be still kept as captives by the humans. He had been unfortunate on two occasions, where he had found dewinged angels being bled of their life's blood to provide the "Blood of Christ" that would prolong some undeserving human's life. He had arrived too late to save his people and had administered a final act of kindness upon them both, spilling blood other than theirs in the process and earning himself the enmity of the Holy Catholic Church in the process.

Technology marches on, and he knew the Holy Church was making a persistent and prolonged effort to find the two of them. He had advised Lucifer against coming here, but Lucifer had always been foolhardy, sure it was the last place they would expect him to be.

Now Gabriel found himself here too, possibly walking into a trap. Yet he could not allow Lucifer to suffer as he had seen the last two of his people suffer. If a trap it was, it would be sprung, and even though he may fall in the process, the humans would know the Angel of Death had walked among them!

Chapter Thirteen

"Forgive me, Father, for I have sinned." Laura bowed her head in the confessional, talking through the darkened screen to the priest, whose silhouette she could see through the latticed screen work.

"How have you sinned, child?" A comforting voice answered her through the anonymity of the confessional. The voice was warm, patient, waiting for her to answer in her own time.

"I met a man, Father. I had dinner with him last night," she explained, feeling awkward.

"Sure, and that seems a little enough sin," the priest chided almost amusedly, his lilting Irish accent more noticeable talking English than it was when he spoke Italian.

"I haven't been with a man since my husband died, Father." She blushed in the shadows. "Yet last night, even though I've only known him a few days, I wanted him so badly," she admitted. There was a moment's silence, and then the priest spoke to comfort her.

"Is he a good man?" the priest asked.

"He isn't married if that's what you mean, Father, at least I don't think so. He's only just come to Rome in search of his missing brother. I know so little about him." The response from the other side of the screen took longer this time.

"Why don't you tell me a little more about him, my child?" the priest spoke, his interest suddenly piqued.

"He's American like me, Father. His brother came to Rome about two months ago to look at the vineyards, and he hasn't heard from his brother since. Understandably, he seems quite concerned for him."

"You would expect him to be concerned for his brother's welfare, child. But do go on, describe him to me," the voice coaxed gently, well used to this form of gentle persuasion with parishioners.

"He's tall, Father, dark hair, suntanned skin, and so handsome …" Laura paused, remembering the previous evening. "Well-spoken, very polite, something different about him. I mean he's not like anyone I've ever met before. He seems older than his years, if you know what I mean," she tried to explain.

"I think I know exactly what you mean, child," the anonymous voice replied.

"Last night when he kissed me, Father, was I wrong to feel the way I felt about him? I mean I hardly know him, but it felt so right, so good, so natural." Laura was confused about her own feelings for this handsome stranger, who had just walked into her life. She sat there with head bowed, fingers kneading the hem of her skirt nervously.

"Such feelings are normal, my child. You are no longer married, and neither is he. I suggest you see him again, and perhaps in time, with God's help, both of you may understand more about your feelings for each other."

"Oh thank you, Father, thank you." Laura was relieved at the priest's blessing. She walked out of the cool church into the hot midday sunlight with a spring in her step. Talking to Father Ryan was always a comfort, so easier to talk to than one of the Italian priests.

As she walked away, Father Ryan came out of the confessional. He was a tall man, who walked lightly for his fifty-three years. His silver hair and thin frame were deceptive. His eyes were sharp and focused. He had aged little since living a different life under a different name in Northern Ireland. Life in Rome had been good to him.

He walked into the vestry and picked up the telephone, winding the handle to charge the thing. He spoke softly into the mouthpiece. "Gabriel is here. Tell Cardinal Montpelier to have the Donovan woman at the American Embassy watched from a distance. Watched only, you understand?" he reiterated. "Gabriel is the prize, and he must take the bait. I want no mistakes!" he replaced the receiver sharply.

Chapter Fourteen

Gabriel found Grimaldi in a small tavern after a few discreet enquiries. The man was eating a meal, washing it down with cheap red wine as Gabriel entered. The bartender pointed him out and sat in the corner booth. Grimaldi waved him over.

"Signor Angell, you join me, yes?" He laughed heartily. Gabriel allowed the man to pour him a generous mug of wine as he introduced himself. He was a middle-aged man of average height but a less than average paunch. He obviously liked his wine and his food. A thin moustache tried to compensate for the balding pate. Once black hair was starting to turn grey.

"I am trying to find my brother," Gabriel explained. "I believe you acted as his guide to show him the vineyards locally?" he quizzed Grimaldi, taking a drink of the wine, more for appearance's sake than a desire for the lukewarm brew.

"Yes, your brother," Grimaldi recollected. "I show him all the good vineyards in Rome. He know wine, your brother." He laughed and then burped noisily. Wiping his moustache with the back of his hand, Grimaldi continued to devour his pasta. "I take him to nine, no, ten vineyards … and then one day, he does not seek me out. I assume he is happy with what he has seen and has contacted the owners of the vineyards direct to conclude his business here. He paid me in advance, so I think nothing of it. If you want, I take you to the same vineyards."

"I'm very interested in the vineyards you took him to see." Gabriel was to the point. "And anywhere else you might have taken him." He leaned forward in his seat. "I'll pay you double what my brother paid you." Grimaldi smiled at the offer and then chuckled.

"How you know how much your brother pay me? Do not worry, I will not cheat you, Signor Angell," he reassured Gabriel. "I have other matters which demand my attention today, but tomorrow I will take you to the vineyards," he promised. Gabriel saw no reason to be pushy and risk the man's ire, so he settled on tomorrow. He finished his wine and left Grimaldi to finish his lunch.

Time on his hands, and Laura's face on his mind. Gabriel didn't feel so guilty thinking of her now that he had made a start to tracing Lucifer. The embassy was on his way back to his hotel. Perhaps she would agree to have dinner with him again.

Chapter Fifteen

He found her by her perfume, following his nose through the musty anterooms until he came across her sifting though some files. She blushed momentarily as she looked up and saw him. "Oh. You startled me." She smiled, part of her delighted that he'd sought her out.

"Laura, about last night …" He wanted to say so much, but the words were stuck in his throat. He felt awkward talking over such personal things as emotions. Distinct lack of practice.

"It was a wonderful evening," Laura interrupted, relieving him momentarily. "I enjoyed it so much I didn't want it to end," she admitted. Gabriel took her hand, enjoying the feel of the soft skin, the bones and tendons underneath. Anatomy was so complex and yet so wonderful—male and female so basically the same and yet such delightful differences.

"Would you think me too forward to extend another dinner invitation for tonight? I mean, I know we've hardly met, but I enjoyed last night too." Her hand stayed within his. She made no attempt to remove it, instead moving closer. Her perfume was intoxicating, and he found his peripheral vision was starting to blur. If there was someone else in the room, Gabriel was unaware of their presence, for she was all he had eyes for.

"Yes, I'd like that very much." She smiled softly. The moment was becoming dangerous. Any closer and he would not be able to resist taking her in his arms. He forced himself to step back, breaking the contact with a palpable start. She withdrew her hand, enfolding it within the other.

"Is it okay if I call for you, about eight?" he asked.

"Yes, that would be fine," she answered, slight tremor in her voice. Gabriel smiled, relieved.

"Eight it is then." He nodded courteously, and then he turned and left the anteroom. Laura stood there, shivering slightly despite the warmth. She was pulled back to reality by Emily Ward, one of the other clerks, who had been assisting her in her search through the musty old files.

"Laura. You dark horse!" she chided. "Who is he? He's gorgeous. You've got to tell me all about him." The two of them broke up into a fit of the giggles, and the girl talk continued.

Chapter Sixteen

Laura waited nervously for the taxi to arrive, having taken a second shower of the evening because of the humidity and nerves. She chose a dark blue evening dress, more modest than the one she wore last night, perhaps as an unconscious admission of a little guilt over how the evening had ended and thoughts of how the evening could well have ended.

Eight o'clock came and went with no sign of any taxi arriving. She was starting to worry when, about fifteen minutes late, the taxi arrived with an apologetic Gabriel. "Laura, I'm sorry. Some sort of disturbance in the main square. The Nazis are out in force tonight." She took his arm and got into the taxi with him.

The taxi driver laughed and offered his opinion without being asked as do taxi drivers the world over. "The Nazis, hah. They are nothing," he scoffed. "The Cosa Nostra runs Rome. Forget Il Duce, forget Il Papa. For all the people they arrest or shoot, they will never rule Rome!" He spat out of the window, having delivered his sermon. Gabriel and Laura looked at one another, deciding laughter was not in their best interests at the moment, though it was hard not to wear a wry smile on their faces at the driver's outburst.

They drove to a restaurant which was surprisingly nearby, though one Laura had not frequented before—a small cozy bistro in a secluded street which looked out onto a small square, where a fountain glittered in the moonlight. They left the taxi and went inside and were quietly ushered to an upstairs table on the balcony, which looked out over the fountain.

"You look lovely tonight." Gabriel found the words tripping off his tongue without thinking. Laura blushed demurely.

"Thank you." She smiled wistfully, a faint blush coloring her cheeks. Gabriel always found the behavior of women to be most confusing. It was as though their brains functioned on a different level altogether. Just when you thought you understood them, they did completely the opposite of what you expected.

"Tell me about yourself," he spoke, curious.

Laura laughed. "What do you want to know? I'm a widow, I told you already. I met Jack six years ago in Boston. My folks live there. My dad works for the State Department. Got married, got pregnant. Then Jack died, and I miscarried." She looked away, her voice tinged with sadness for a moment. "That's me in a nutshell."

"I'm sorry to bring back such unpleasant memories. Truly …," he apologized. Laura looked up.

"I'm over it. Time is a great healer, they say." She forced a laugh, though he could tell the memory still hurt.

"Yes, it is," he remarked simply.

"My dad got me this job out here just before all this silliness started with Hitler and Mussolini. He wanted me to come home, but hey, I'm a big girl! Can look out for myself," she added with steel in her eyes.

"You're American Irish by your voice then? I can still make out a faint accent at times," he explained.

"My branch of the Donovan family hailed from County Cork originally, some six or seven generations ago. Never been there but guess I picked up the accent from all my folks and relatives. We're a big family. Enough about me, what about you?" she chided, poking an accusing finger at him. "Mr. tall dark handsome stranger, where do you come from?" she asked. Gabriel paused, looking at her over the rim of his wineglass …

"Oh, I come from an old, old family …," he answered vaguely. "But we moved around a lot," he explained. "My family originally hailed from central Europe, I believe. Records are confusing and incomplete." He told her as much as he thought safe, for now.

"I know what you mean," Laura agreed. "Hard to keep track of friends and family. Particularly when there's a war on and there's been a few of those over the years."

"Yes, indeed," Gabriel agreed, peering at her intently over the rim of his glass. Laura caught his stare and flushed slightly, avoiding his eyes. The waiter interrupted their conversation by bringing their meal, and they resorted to small talk as they consumed their fare. Isolated gunshots could be heard in the distance, ringing out clear across the night sky. Laura shuddered as she heard them.

"The Nazis think they own this city," she stated. "Mussolini is just a puppet, though he can't see it yet. Don't know what he could do about it if he did." She chuckled amusedly. "The Mafia prefers to stay in the shadows, running the crime syndicates. They like to avoid open confrontation with either the Nazis or the Fascists."

"And every once in a while, one or the other decides to crack down on them, eh?" Gabriel mused at the "politics" of the holy city. "Good for morale."

The meal progressed well, the two of them feeling at home in each other's company. More wine flowed, and the two of them held hands across the table, the flickering candlelight reflecting in each other's eyes. It was a special night. They could both feel the electricity between them.

Chapter Seventeen

Two in the morning found them walking along a cobbled street as Gabriel escorted Laura home. Time had just seemed to melt away in each others' company. It was a clear night, and all the stars were out and shining brightly above. They still held hands; truth to tell, he didn't want to let go of her. She leaned against him as they walked, enjoying the cool evening air. Shots still rang out in the distance, though they had tried not to dwell on them.

Gabriel knew that tonight, if she wanted, he would stay. He ached to make love to her, but he would not force himself on her. He didn't want to rush her into anything she wasn't ready for. All he knew was that it was a physical pain to be apart from her. Was this love? Could fate be so cruel yet again?

Lost in his thoughts, the sound of running footsteps suddenly brought him back to reality, and Laura gasped as a loud shot rang out close by, and a rushing figure suddenly turned the corner and crashed into Gabriel, the collision knocking him back across the street as though hit by a car. Laura screamed as the intruder struggled to his feet, breathing hard—a young boy barely in his teens, though tall for his age. He stood there frozen for a moment, and Laura looked at his arm, which was dripping blood. "Scusi, signora … scusi …," the boy blurted, obviously terrified, and started to run off again down the street, when all of a sudden a German soldier appeared at the street corner.

"Halten!" the soldier bellowed, leveling his rifle as the youth continued to make his escape. Laura opened her mouth to scream, when all of a sudden a shadow passed over her, and Gabriel fell on the soldier from a height. The rifle went off as Gabriel forced it back, the bullet whistling high into the night in the brief struggle, and then a dull crack accompanied the fall of the soldier's lifeless body to the floor, his head now lolling at an unnatural angle.

It was all over so suddenly. Laura stood there gasping, looking up to see where Gabriel had jumped from, wondering how he could have gotten back so quickly from the collision which had knocked him clear across the street. There was nothing above them—no balcony, not even an adjacent external staircase. She was at a loss to explain what she had just seen. She turned, seeing the frightened youth leaning heavily against the wall. Then all of a sudden, Gabriel was taking her arm, ushering her towards the youth. "He was going to murder him," he explained. The youth allowed Gabriel to pull him upright. "Your villa is nearest. Do you have medical supplies?" Gabriel asked. Laura nodded, still partially in shock at the way events had unfolded so swiftly. "Quickly, we must go now before more soldiers come." Gabriel took instant charge of the situation, one hand on each of Laura's and the boy's arms, hurrying them along the street.

More shots could be heard in the distance. Rifle, and machine-gun fire. It sounded like more than just an isolated incident going down tonight. One party had seriously pissed off the other. They made it to her villa without interruption, and she fumbled in her purse for her key, finally letting them inside and locking the door quickly behind her. "I'll get the lights." Laura made to switch on the electricity.

"Rear of the house only. No lights near the street." Gabriel quickly took charge of the situation, giving orders as though he expected them to be obeyed. Laura's mothering nature quickly overcame her shock at the situation she found herself in, and she quickly broke out iodine and bandages from the kitchen as Gabriel tore open the boy's shirt to expose the bullet wound in the fleshy muscle of his upper arm. "It's not serious," he announced as Laura prepared a swab of iodine. "Just a flesh wound."

"This will hurt," she said gravely as the boy gritted his teeth.

Chapter Eighteen

Later, as the boy lay asleep in one of the spare rooms, Laura sat by the fire which Gabriel had lit, nursing a drink a little stronger than the wine she normally drank. They sat in silence for a while. Gabriel decided to let the fire help ease the shock out of her system. He sat patiently with her, waiting for her to break her silence.

"You killed him." It was more of a statement than an accusation. There was no venom in it. She looked up over the cut glass goblet she was drinking out of.

"I couldn't let him kill the boy. I've seen too much senseless slaughter in my life," he explained.

"That's not what I meant." Laura took another sip of brandy. "You made it look so easy, as though you'd 'practiced' it." Gabriel felt the need to defend himself.

"I suppose I have become proficient at it over the years, though it's not something I enjoy," he added. "I've fought in too many wars to enjoy the bloodshed any more. Sometimes it's just *necessary* ..." Laura could feel the man's sincerity. Her feelings and emotions were in conflict. She was still in shock, more drunk than she should be, sitting here drinking with a self-confessed murderer. She should be horrified, yet she knew she had never been so wet in her life!

Every inch of her body wanted him. Her skin felt so sensitive that she shuddered. Her mind was still arguing but fast losing the argument. She drank the rest of the brandy hurriedly, shivering as she felt the fiery liquid burning its way down her throat. She looked at him as he sat there—the firm thighs, chiseled dark face so handsome and so pained, the hands so delicate. He was what she imagined an angel must look like. So divine as to be untrue.

Putting down the glass, she stood up, the fire flickering away behind her. Her eyes betrayed her desire, and she reached back to unfasten her evening dress. It fell away, leaving her naked, silhouetted against the flames, a vision of temptation. Gabriel stood up, eyes losing themselves in her beauty as she reached for him.

"I need you. Oh God, I need you …," she sobbed as she fell into his arms. "Make love to me, Gabriel," she moaned breathlessly into his ear as she pressed herself against him.

Their lovemaking was hurried and intense. Discarded clothes soon formed a bed in front of the flames, which cast amorous shadows on the walls. Each was so hungry for the other, devouring each other's body. Laura's fingers and tongue marveled at the golden sheen and salty taste of Gabriel's skin.

Limbs intertwined, and passions were fulfilled as the lovers rested in each other's arms. Gabriel gasped as her gently raking fingernails tormented the soft hairs on the inside of his thighs, quickly raising his passions once more.

Soon, after a brief rest, their lovemaking resumed, more measured this time and in control. Laura marveled at how light Gabriel felt on top of her as his sculpted body took her to new heights of passion. She had never known a more tender lover, one so aware of her body and how to please her. Mouth hot on her nipples, tongue so expert between her legs.

She pleasured him in return, wanting—needing—to repay his passion with her own. "I like it better when you come …," she moaned, holding him as he gasped and shuddered against her.

"I like it better when I come too." Gabriel laughed. The burning embers glowed warmly as their lovemaking finally was over, and Gabriel carried the sleeping Laura to her bed.

Chapter Nineteen

Laura awoke to the sound of the birds twittering away with their early morning wake-up song in the tree outside the bedroom window, the curtains fluttering in the light breeze to allow bright shafts of sunlight to slowly approach the bed from across the floor. The window had been left open, and the air had that good-to-be-alive taste to it. Laura turned her head, pleased to see the dark head on the next pillow. She was half afraid she would not find him there still. If such a dream it was, then please don't let it end.

She remembered their wild passionate lovemaking, and she reached out a hand for him, lightly stroking the back of Gabriel's head. He remained asleep as she lightly caressed his broad shoulders, down to his back. The feint scars that were on his shoulder blades puzzled her.

She gathered he had probably been a soldier and had fought in wars. Yet he seemed too young, and the two scars seemed so symmetrical. She had never seen anything like them. Her fingers touched featherlight, across and down, and further. He fidgeted in his sleep as her hand delved lower, and Laura giggled. Then she decided to let him sleep on, as she remembered the boy they had nursed last night.

Slipping quietly out of the bed, she padded across the room and pulled on her dressing robe. Tying the belt loosely around her waist, she stepped into her slippers and then went off to seek the guest bedroom they had left the boy in last night. The bed was empty, slept in, to be sure, and there were blood stains, but the boy was gone, probably alarmed and frightened at waking up in a strange house. She couldn't blame him. Still, they had helped him last night, and that was enough.

She needed no thanks from the boy for what they had managed to do for him, mainly what Gabriel had done.

Looking back on the incident, she felt no remorse for the death of the German soldier, a stranger in a strange land. It was the suddenness, the expediency with which Gabriel had carried out the act. She shuddered, drawing her robe closer around her as her mind's eye relived the brief yet fatal encounter.

She gathered up the sheets, carrying them out onto the landing to place with the dirty linen. The next wash would erase all trace of the boy's visit. In the bathroom, the ornate tub luckily had a shower attachment, which she preferred to the actual tub itself, and slipping out of her robe, she turned on the faucet, adjusted the water temperature till it was just right, and then stepped into the tub and under the cascading water. She groaned lightly with pleasure as the rivulets of water streamed down her skin. She turned to and fro, soaking herself as she reached for the sponge and the bar of soap she had managed to get on the black market. She soaped herself thoroughly, luxuriating in the pleasant tactile sensation as she rubbed the soapy sponge over her skin, teasing her nipples deliciously. Her eyes closed as she soaped her sleek belly.

The bathroom door opened lightly, making no noise she could hear. Gabriel stood there, watching her. Steam filled the bathroom, partially obscuring the delightful vision. Laura's head dipped fully under the spray, golden hair matting down her naked back as the water ran through it, and she moaned. "Ohhhh," she gasped, startled as she felt his hands on her shoulders. He was suddenly standing there in the tub with her as naked as she herself as he pressed up against her, and she felt the urgency of his renewed passion, hot and hard against her wet, soapy buttocks. Arms entwined instantly as she turned to face him, and Gabriel's lips locked against hers in a passionate kiss. The water beat down relentlessly, making their bodies sleek and slippery.

Gabriel's head dipped down to her breasts, mouth kissing and licking deliciously as she hung her head back under the water, biting her lower lip and groaning as she felt his mouth on her nipple, suckling and then biting hard just as she liked it, making her gasp. The water went up her nose, and she suddenly stiffened, spluttering as Gabriel rocked with laughter. "You …" She took a playful swipe at him, almost slipping on the soapy porcelain floor of the bathtub, his laughter infectious, and then she threw herself into his arms once more, kissing him hungrily.

Her hand reached for him, found him, guided him as she raised one leg to rest high on his hip. Gabriel entered her easily, groaning into her ear as he did so, the cooling water having no effect upon the heat of their passion. They made love slowly, their mouths hardly ever off each other. Gabriel buried his face in her wet hair, enjoying the smell, the taste, kissing and nibbling the nape of her neck just below the ear. Laura gasped, thrusting her hips against him, impaling herself so deliciously. "Yessss. Ohhhh yesss …," she moaned into his ear.

They rested in each other's arms on the bed, the sheets still damp beneath them. The sunlight streamed in through the window, warming and drying their bodies. "I have to go …," whispered Gabriel as he leaned forward to kiss her damp hair. "There's a man I must meet, who will help me to search for my brother," he explained and turned to slide off the bed.

"Grimaldi?" she asked. Gabriel nodded. Laura drew the tousled sheets around her as she lay back against the pillow and watched him dress. "Can I come with you?" she regretted asking the question, even as it left her lips. "I could take the day off from the embassy. They owe me some free time." She frowned, feeling guilty for asking.

Gabriel's face darkened slightly as he shook his head. "No, it might be dangerous. Grimaldi is expecting only me, and I think he knows more than he told me. I may have to be careful, and I wouldn't want to take a chance on any harm befalling you. You've come to mean a lot to me in such a short space of time." He reached out to lightly stroke the side of her head, and she reached out for him to embrace him once more.

"Be careful …," she warned. "This city is beautiful, but it has its darker side." Gabriel kissed her once, lightly, on the lips, and she relaxed her embrace, settling back down on the bed.

"Two or three days should suffice." Gabriel fastened his tie as he spoke. "I'll be back by the weekend at the latest," he promised.

"Do you really think you'll find him?" Laura asked, knowing the city's reputation for "losing" people.

"I won't know till I try"—Gabriel half-smiled—"but I have to try," he added resolutely. "We came from a large family," he started to explain. "As far as I know, he and I are all that's left of it," he added sorrowfully. "Grimaldi knows something. He'll tell me," he added, that steely glint coming back into his eyes momentarily. Gabriel put on his jacket, not bothering to button it. "I have to go. Luke would like you," he added. "One day I'll introduce you to him, that's a promise." He smiled and then opened the bedroom door, blowing her a kiss as he left.

Laura remained wrapped in the damp sheets as she heard his footsteps retreating down the staircase. She tried not to dwell on it, but she had a dark foreboding that things would not go well for Gabriel in his quest. There had been times in the past when she had these types of feelings, and when she got them, she was rarely wrong. There had been rumors of witchcraft in her ancestry, and some claimed the dark gift to be hereditary. She hoped against hope that her feelings would turn out to be wrong.

As she heard the heavy door close downstairs, she jumped up out of bed and went to the open window. She watched as Gabriel went out through the wrought iron gate, closing it behind him. The cobbled street passed in front of the surrounding wall of her villa, and then one of the tributary streets ran off at ninety degrees, and it was down this street that Gabriel reappeared, walking off into the distance.

As she watched, a priest passed in front of the wrought iron gate, pausing momentarily at the corner of the street and then taking the same route as Gabriel. Laura thought nothing untoward about the occurrence at first, but then, also appearing at a distance behind the priest was the young boy with the bandaged arm.

The boy paused, looking up at Laura framed in the window as she hastily drew the curtain around her body. With a flash of white teeth, the boy grinned up at her and then turned away. He appeared to be following the priest. Laura shook her head. She hadn't expected to see the boy again at all. What was he doing?

Chapter Twenty

The sun was already beating down by nine o'clock as Gabriel left his hotel after a moderate breakfast. He had gone back there to change clothing and prepare a rucksack to take with him on his trip. A tooting of a car horn alerted him to where Grimaldi waited in a dusty black covered sedan, which had obviously seen better days. He waved acknowledgement and crossed through the intermittent traffic to the other side of the road.

"Buon giorno, Signor Angell. A fine day to visit the country, no?" He smiled, opening the door for Gabriel. He took his seat up front with Grimaldi and threw his rucksack into the rear of the car, where another satchel was already deposited. Grimaldi had warned him to expect a walk to get to the remote monastery vineyards, and so he had come prepared. "And now we go, eh?" the Italian laughed, checking his mirror as he pulled off into the traffic. He smiled as he noted the car pulling out some distance behind them and shook his head knowingly. "It will take us maybe two hours drive, plenty of time to get to know each other better, yes?" He smiled a knowing smile, which Gabriel puzzled over momentarily.

Gabriel was looking at the old map that was on the dashboard of the car, studying the route they would take to the monastery marked on the map. "Shouldn't we be heading north of the city?" he enquired, wondering at the direction Grimaldi was heading.

"In a little while, signor. I must take a little shortcut first." Grimaldi smiled again, once more checking his mirror carefully. Gabriel was nothing if not observant and, within a mile or two, had noticed the compulsive checking of the view behind them. He started to turn in his seat to look back himself, when Grimaldi put his hand on his arm. "No, signor, it is nothing to worry about."

"We're being followed, aren't we?" Gabriel asked the obvious.

"Yes, signor, but not for much longer. This was not unexpected." Grimaldi chuckled. He turned the wheel, heading for the piazza down a one way street; the following car turned with them and then came screeching to a halt as a lorry and another car came out of a junction in the road ahead of them, one colliding into the other and effectively blocking the road. Grimaldi laughed, enjoying the view through his rearview mirror.

"Friends of yours?" asked Gabriel, puzzled.

"Si,"—Grimaldi laughed—"and fortunately, now friends of yours also," he added with a knowing grin. "Now we take a different road, and we talk a little, yes?" The car speeded up somewhat, putting distance between them and the arranged accident behind them. Grimaldi turned off the road, skirting the inner city before turning off at right angles, heading out towards the countryside.

An hour later, they were clear of the city proper and heading up into the hills. Gabriel had travelled in silence, enjoying the countryside and checking the route they travelled against that shown on the map, waiting for Grimaldi to speak, for he obviously knew a lot more of what was going on than he did himself. "Your silence is commendable, my friend. You contain your curiosity well," he complimented Gabriel, taking one hand of the wheel to mop his perspiring brow.

"I figure you'll tell me what you want me to know in your own time. I've learned to be patient over the years," Gabriel explained.

"The people in the car were Nazis," Grimaldi stated.

"Why would Nazis be following me?" Gabriel asked, feigning innocence. He could not recollect leaving any sort of clue as to his identity near the dead soldier's body. He knew of no other reason they might be interested in him. "Do they follow all Americans? We're not involved with this war. It's strictly a European thing."

Grimaldi laughed, scoffing. "Hahhhh … You go on deluding yourselves, you Americans. Hitler and Il Duce will not be content with just Europe, my friend. They are madmen, truly." He shook his head. "I have seen what has become of Italy since the war started. The Fascists and the Nazis, even the church collaborates." He spat out of the open window of the car as they drove along the bumpy road.

"I've seen the martial law that governs this place since I first arrived. It can't be pleasant. Is there nothing you can do about it?" Gabriel asked.

"Oh, we do, signor, we do." Grimaldi laughed knowingly. "Last night, we tried to do something about it. We were ambushed by the Nazis. You know some of this already, I think?" He looked at Gabriel out of the corner of his eye.

"The boy was with you?" Gabriel asked.

"Si. You saved his life. He is known to me, this boy. We are in your debt. We pay our debts," he stated simply.

"*We* being ...?" Gabriel grinned back at Grimaldi.

"Very funny, signor. You do not strike me as stupid," Grimaldi grunted. "The Cosa Nostra is almost as old as the church itself and far more honest in its dealings. You gave us back a life at risk to your own. You made our fight your fight, and now we offer the same to you. We will help you find your brother," he stated simply.

"What can you tell me about what happened to my brother?" Gabriel asked.

Grimaldi frowned. "Nothing happened to him, at least until he visited the monastery I am taking you to see. That was the last time I saw your brother." He wiped the sweat from his brow with handkerchief as he drove.

A couple of hours later, Grimaldi pulled the sedan off the road and drove it some way between the trees in a thick copse. It would keep the car in the shade for when they got back and also away from prying eyes. They would walk the rest of the way to the monastery, which was only a few miles over the hills, Grimaldi assured Gabriel.

"You have been watched and followed for the last couple of days at least, my friend," Grimaldi explained. "The boy was eager to leave the signora's house, when he noticed the priest on the corner. We do not expect all our priests to be saints, you understand ... but the boy thought it odd to see one loitering in that place in the early hours of the morning. So he waited, watching the priest who watched the house … and then followed the priest as the priest followed you," he explained.

"You have a name for this priest?" Gabriel enquired as they walked.

"Father Paulo reports to the Vatican City, where the boy could not follow. But he waited and saw him collected by a staff car with a German officer in it an hour or so later. They only enter the place by invitation. All part of their deal with the church."

"You think the Germans could be holding my brother?"

"Who knows? The last I heard from your brother, he phoned to tell me of his intention to revisit this monastery. He asked me to pick him up at his hotel after the weekend. A few days later, when I attempted to collect him, I found he was booked out of the hotel. I called at the monastery to ask about him. One of the brothers denied that any American had been there. That is all I know." He waved both hands aloft in typical Neapolitan fashion.

They walked the rest of the way in silence till they came to the brow of one last hill. Scattered trees covered the slopes at a height below which cows grazed.

They remained at a height, skirting their way through the thick tree line until they got a clear look at the monastery. Grimaldi pulled out an old pair of binoculars, handing them to Gabriel, who used them to survey the place carefully. Nothing at first glance that would seem to indicate the place was anything other than what it appeared to be. The old road led all the way up to the large wooden doors, which were the only way in or out of the place, and the tire tracks within the courtyard looked fresh. The old stone walls which surrounded the place were made of rough unfinished blocks and looked about twenty feet high.

Within the monastery itself, a few of the monks wandered about. The vineyards ran up the slope of the hill behind the monastery. Gabriel looked at his watch. It was nearly midday. "We'll wait till nightfall, and then I'll do some scouting around," Gabriel suggested. Grimaldi shrugged his shoulders.

They broke open their rations. Bread and cheese, a nice red wine, which Gabriel enjoyed, though left most of it to Grimaldi. They settled down in the shade, taking turns with the binoculars to keep a watch on the place.

Chapter Twenty-one

Grimaldi waved away a fly as he concentrated on using the binoculars, wondering what it was that didn't look right as he studied the monastery. Something he'd noticed but would not make itself obvious. It was nearly two in the afternoon, when they both heard the sound of an automobile approaching.

It came into view around the bottom of the hill, slowly negotiating the potholes in the poorly kept road leading up to the monastery, the engine laboring. There were two people inside the car, one in plain clothes. The other man seemed to be a priest.

At a blast from the car horn, the main doors were opened, and the car drove inside the courtyard. Further inner doors were opened, and the car disappeared from view as it drove into what appeared to be a stable, or could even have been a storage area. Moments later, two figures reappeared. Some of the monks gathered around them, standing stiffly to attention and saluting the man in plain clothes.

"Basta!" Grimaldi cursed, now realizing what his eyes had seen but his brain had not understood. Some of the monks were moving far too agilely for their supposed advanced years. They were not monks. "It is a trap," he said as he handed the binoculars to Gabriel.

He put them to his eyes, adjusting the focusing ring to zoom in on the courtyard. "Father Paulo, I take it?" he queried.

"Si. That is him. The other, I am not sure. He does not look Italian."

"German then. So too are some of the monks. Looks like they are indeed working together," Gabriel mused.

"I have never heard of the church collaborating to such an extent with the Nazis. It is unheard of." Grimaldi scratched his balding head, exasperated.

Gabriel had his own ideas about the partnership. He had heard of Hitler's interest in the occult and magic. If word had gotten back out from the church about the true "Blood of Christ" as they called it, perhaps Hitler himself was planning on prolonging his pension. Perhaps the church was using it as a bargaining tool to keep the Germans out of the Vatican City. *What dark secrets did they hide within its confines?* he wondered. If they would share the secret of his blood with others, what lay within the Vatican must hold even more importance.

"I think we should have a word with Father Paulo, don't you?" Gabriel smiled a cold smile. Grimaldi nodded, feeling a new respect for the American.

Chapter Twenty-two

Grimaldi grew impatient as dusk darkened the skies. They had watched the monastery through binoculars from their vantage point within the tree line throughout the afternoon. Gabriel took out a dark sweater from his rucksack and put it on. His trousers were already dark grey.

It was dark enough by half past nine. "I'll go in on my own. You wait in the woods close to the south wall." Gabriel took command of the situation. Grimaldi took out the padded grappling hook and rope from his own rucksack, but Gabriel shook his head. "I'm a good climber. I won't need that."

Grimaldi huffed incredulously. "The walls are twenty feet high." He shrugged his shoulders and replaced the hook in his rucksack, slinging it over his shoulder. He then offered the old Webley revolver to Gabriel. "I wasn't expecting much trouble, but it's all I have with me. You may need it."

Gabriel shook his head. "As you say, my friend, if I need it, it won't do me much good against the firepower they've probably got waiting for me. You keep it."

They started down the hillside towards the waiting monastery, careful of their footing in the dark. Grimaldi muffled a curse as he stepped in something soft, praying it was only mud, but the smell said otherwise.

Gabriel chuckled, whispering, "They say it's good luck." Grimaldi's response was muffled again under his breath. In silence for the rest of the way, they approached the monastery. They had seen no outward signs of any guards being posted during the day, but still they made use of what cover there was, going out of the direct line of approach to stay within the trees.

Gabriel paused within the trees and took from his rucksack two sheathed throwing knives and strapped one to each thigh. Grimaldi nodded approvingly, though Gabriel did not notice. Italians appreciated knives. So much cleaner and more silent than a bullet. Such knives were only carried by people who could use them, and use them well. Knives were for close-quarter killing and used by men who were not afraid of a little bloodshed. *This Gabriel was turning out to be quite an interesting fellow*, he thought.

"Give me an hour," Gabriel warned. "If I'm not back by then, I won't be coming. Get the hell out."

"You think I'd do that? Run off and leave you like a little mouse? Hahhh!"

"You've gotten me this far, and that's all I ask. No need for both of us to get killed," Gabriel explained. "Besides, after what you've told me, I think someone needs to warn Signora Donovan, don't you?"

"If I must, I must. Just get back here within the hour, so you can warn her yourself." He took Gabriel's rucksack and crouched down behind the tree as he watched the American pad lightly over to the foot of the old stone wall.

Grimaldi gawped as he saw the ease with which Gabriel scaled the wall. True, the stones were old and crudely joined, but the gaps between them would provide scant purchase. Gabriel went up the wall like a human fly. Within less than thirty seconds, he had reached the top and then vanished from sight. Instinctively, Grimaldi made the sign of the cross and settled down to wait.

The wall had been relatively easy with his light body weight and strong muscles. His fingernails were also deceptively sharp and strong, and they provided a good grip where needed. Once at the top, he flipped quickly over and crouched down on the parapet at the other side, lest his silhouette be seen against the night sky, which was far too bright and clear for his liking.

He remained motionless for almost a minute, listening, watching, allowing himself to blend in with the shadows. Two nonmonks were huddled together in the courtyard. They carried rifles, military issue, and they were smoking cigarettes, probably illicitly, as they should no doubt have been patrolling the perimeter discreetly.

Confident they hadn't seen him, Gabriel scurried along the parapet towards the stairwell, which led down into the courtyard. That exit would leave him too exposed, so instead, he went up, scaling the wall again towards an open window in the tower.

Cautiously, Gabriel prized open the window of the darkened room. No sounds of breathing, so he quickly climbed through and into the empty bedroom of one of the monks. Sparsely decorated with just a bed, small table, and old wardrobe, Gabriel quickly pulled open the wardrobe, relieved to find the monk's spare habit hung up inside.

Quickly, he pulled it on, finding it a little short but otherwise suitable. He took a few minutes to transfer the knife sheathes from his thighs to his forearms, the baggy sleeves of the habit would provide better and quicker access should he need them.

Cracking open the door, he peered out into the inner stairwell, which lead both up and down. Down first then, he decided, quickly exiting the room and closing the door behind him.

The stone stairwell was dark, lit by odd flickering lamps at irregular intervals, which would serve its purpose if anyone should see him. In such cloistered communities, he would expect all the monks to know each other. He had to hope any such would think he was one of the Germans and vice versa. He paused at each door, listening momentarily. All was quiet. With luck, most of the normal monks would be in their beds by now.

The lower chamber was a mess hall, and one or two monks still sat there around a log fire, one of them stirring the embers with a metal poker. At the back, an open door revealed the beginnings of a kitchen.

Gabriel took the door to the outside, not wanting to pass close inspection by the monks. He had had a good look at the courtyard from the parapet and so showed no hesitation as he exited the hall, and the two nonmonks turned towards him.

They muttered softly and chuckled to themselves in German as he walked towards the chapel. Opening the door, Gabriel knelt and made the sign of the cross before he entered and then closed the door behind him. With luck, they would think him just a late worshipper.

Once inside, Gabriel had a cursory look around, though not expecting to find anything. The wine cellar was his best bet, and to get there, he would have to pass those two German soldiers.

He waited ten minutes, half hoping they would go to some other part of the monastery, but they remained in position. No other choice then. He opened the door and went back out. The two of them muttered again, and one of them looked up in surprise as this monk walked towards them instead of going back into the mess hall.

Tall for a monk, he walked gracefully, head bowed as they always did, hands in his sleeves. Something about him wasn't quite right as one of them looked him up and down. Then the guard noticed the shoes, where there should have been sandals.

He started to raise the rifle and opened his mouth to warn his less observant friend, when moonlight glinted on deadly twins, and Gabriel lunged forward with unbelievable speed, driving the sharp blades in below the breastbones of both men and up into the heart …

Death was instantaneous, and Gabriel held onto the knives firmly to lower the two bodies to the ground. Fortunately, the soldier had had the good sense to keep his safety catch on, and so the rifle hadn't gone off as it hit the ground.

Scanning quickly around and seeing no one, Gabriel opened the door to the cellars and dragged the two bodies inside. He went back for the rifles and closed the door. He would have to hurry, for he didn't know when the two men had expected to be relieved.

The smell of sour wine filled his nostrils as he descended the stairs. He took a torch from the wall to light his way down the rickety stairs. The flickering light illuminated long rows of huge casks, racks of bottles. There was no one down here, he could tell, save for a few rats. But a cursory search soon revealed leather straps hanging from one of the long racks of wine bottles. There were also old bread crusts and a broken earthenware jug. Someone had been kept here, in confinement. Probably Lucifer, but taken where? He needed answers, and he had three men who could possibly give him an answer. The abbot, Father Paulo, or the German officer? Decisions, decisions …

Time meant only one, and the choice must be right. Father Paulo it was then! Crossing the courtyard, Gabriel went back into the mess, finding it now deserted. In silence, he climbed the stairwell. He had expected to find all three men near the top of the tower. The abbot, naturally enough, would be in the uppermost room. Father Paulo and the German probably appropriating rooms near him.

He passed the exit to the parapet, pausing once more for a quick look out over the courtyard. Nothing moved, and all was silent. Finally satisfied, he went up the stone steps, pausing at each door, to listen and sniff the air …

The smell of leather and polish behind one door revealed the presence of the German officer. Listening, Gabriel heard the sounds of movement. He seemed to be alone, but then he heard voices …

"When do you expect him?" asked a cultured voice in recognizable Italian.

"It might even be tonight. Are your men posted discreetly? We don't want to frighten him off, Keisel," answered Father Paulo.

"My men are patrolling in pairs every hour. The other four are out of the way in the kitchen, available at a minute's notice." *A lucky decision to leave the kitchen alone then*, thought Gabriel as he eavesdropped. Still, when did the "hour" start? He checked his watch. Twenty past ten. Logical to do it on the hour or every half hour?

"We need him alive. Have your men been told to shoot only if necessary and then only to wound?" Father Paulo enquired.

"Ja, my men are well-disciplined. Also well-trained. Six of them should be sufficient to take this "demon" of yours. You worry too much. Here, have some more wine." Keisel poured another measure into the priest's goblet and again into his own.

"Have your scientists made arrangements for the delivery of the equipment we need? It's vital to our research. Working together, we may be able to analyze and synthesize the blood successfully."

"And then your Ubermensch will be expendable, ja?" Keisel laughed.

"Precisely," the priest agreed. "You have no idea how dangerous this Lucifer is. Even in chains, he killed four of our brethren."

"Keep him drugged and happy as we planned. Till we have no further use for him." Keisel burped and reached for the wine bottle again to refill his goblet.

Gabriel put his hand on the door latch. Fortunately, none of these doors was built with thoughts of security. Slowly, he swung the door inward.

The priest saw him first, dropping the goblet and spilling his wine. Keisel whirled around, surprisingly quickly, reaching for the Luger stuffed in his belt.

Gabriel's knife cut the distance between them in a split second with a sudden backward flick of one wrist, taking him in the throat. Gurgling, he dropped to the stone floor as the priest backed up against the wall, eyes wide with terror.

"You should never wish too hard, Father. Sometimes wishes come true." Gabriel smiled as he closed the door behind him.

Chapter Twenty-three

Grimaldi saw the figure leaning over the top of the wall, hurriedly beckoning to him. He ran up to the foot of the wall to hear Gabriel whispering, just loud enough for him to hear, to throw him the grappling hook.

Gabriel looked around as he waited for the Italian to throw the padded hook up to him. Checking his watch again, he found it was ten thirty-five. Fortunately, the German army ran predictably enough on time and stuck to the hour for changes in their routine.

He caught the hook in midair as Grimaldi threw it up to him. Heaving the unconscious priest onto the edge of the wall, he hooked the metal claw into the makeshift bindings around his body and began lowering it over the side.

Grimaldi accepted the limp body, thinking it at first Gabriel's brother and then recognizing it was the priest that was all bound and gagged; he let the body drop the last few feet to the ground. "Sorry, Father," he chuckled.

Gabriel jumped from the top of the wall, silhouetted like a falling spider for a second against the night sky, dropping unaided the full twenty feet and only rolling lightly as he hit the ground. Grimaldi shook his head. What was he? Some sort of circus acrobat?

The priest was quickly slung over Gabriel's shoulder. "We have about twenty minutes to make ourselves scarce," he warned. "Let's get out of here." Gabriel started off up the sloping hillside, making good speed even with the weight of the priest. Grimaldi huffed and puffed a bit as he sought to keep up with him.

They drove by moonlight only till they were some miles away from the monastery. "Somewhere quiet and deserted, I think," Gabriel suggested to Grimaldi as he stole a glance at the priest, who was starting to come around. "Time for a little chat with the good Father here." He grinned coldly, teeth white in the moonlight.

Close to midnight, in an old, deserted, half-demolished factory, Father Paulo sat on a battered oil drum. Hands still bound behind him, he looked from side to side as if a condemned man seeking a last minute reprieve.

Grimaldi had risked a fire made from gasoline, rags, and bits of old wooden packing crates. He was warming a length of angle iron in its flames, the end starting to grow cherry red. He smiled knowingly at the priest, who was starting to sweat, though at a distance from the flames.

Gabriel stepped in front of him, silhouetted by the flames. His eyes burned with a fire of their own as he glared at the priest. Father Paulo's eyes widened as did Grimaldi's, when Gabriel began to speak to him in fluent Latin.

The dialect was stilted, not heard for hundreds of years, but Latin nevertheless. "*You know who I am …*" It was a statement, not a question. "*I am your worst nightmare …*" Father Paulo nodded once hesitantly. "*Your kind has been hunting mine for centuries. You've all but wiped us out,*" he admitted sorrowfully. "*As far as I know, Lucifer and I are the last of my kind, but we're not ready to die just yet.*" He tore the gag away from the priest's face roughly. "*Now you're going to tell me where it is you've got Lucifer. You're going to tell me who is organizing this, what the connection is with the Germans, everything you know,*" he promised. "*If you won't talk to me, you can talk to him …*" He indicated Grimaldi. "*He's Mafia, and his love of the church is close to my own.*" He let Father Paulo see Grimaldi tending the length of angle iron lovingly. As he watched, the older man lifted it out of the fire and spat on the reddened end, the spittle hissing and crackling as it touched the hot metal. With a grin, he replaced it in the fire. "*Now, talk. I don't have time for niceties …*"

One look into Gabriel's eyes was enough. Father Paulo talked, his Latin more modern but nowhere near as fluent as Gabriel's.

Father Paulo gave them all the information he knew. As expected, his knowledge of the inner workings of the Holy Catholic Church were only skin deep. Grimaldi suggested a little more encouragement with the hot iron but, although not adverse to its use if the circumstances determined it, thought the priest had told all he had knowledge of.

They had left the priest still bound in the abandoned factory, though Grimaldi had argued against it. Cold-blooded murder would bring him down to their level.

As they drove back towards Rome, Grimaldi argued strategy with Gabriel. "Forget about Signora Donovan, my friend. Your face is now marked, and they will expect you. I will send one of my own people to her."

"You're probably right," Gabriel reluctantly acknowledged. "What do you know of this Ryan and DiMatteo?" he asked.

"DiMatteo, I know something about." Grimaldi chuckled. "He is high up in the Vatican hierarchy. Ryan, I know as well. Irish, I think, though speaks Italian well. Tall, grey hair, in his forties at least. The church welcomes many foreign priests in these troubled times," Grimaldi revealed. "His church is close to Signora Donovan's house."

"I think she's a Catholic too, so they probably know each other." Gabriel realized the implications. "No, I don't think she knows what's going on. Most of the Catholic Church doesn't know what's going on." He fretted for a moment, rubbing his knuckles against his forehead in frustration.

"All the talk between you and the priest ..." Grimaldi continued, "The Latin was a nice touch. I only understood a few words. There was a reason, yes?" He looked at Gabriel accusingly.

Gabriel wondered just how much he could trust the man, and he deliberated for long moments before replying. "We all have our secrets, don't we?" he queried. Grimaldi nodded, and then Gabriel continued, "Very well. Lucifer is not my brother but my friend," he explained. Perhaps half-truths would suffice. "We share a very unique blood group. In fact, it's so unique I think that only we two have it. The blood has certain 'properties' which would be very valuable to the medical authorities and other groups." He told as much of the truth as he thought Grimaldi would understand.

"So the church and now the Germans hunt you for this blood? They really *are* bloodsuckers," Grimaldi commented.

"They would literally bleed us dry for it," Gabriel answered. "From what I learned, it seems that my friend is being 'experimented' on in some hidden laboratory under the Vatican, even as we speak." His voice hardened, trying to blot the thought from his mind. A cool head was needed, not a rush of anger. "I have to get him out of there."

"My friend of many talents, I still think you do not tell me everything, but that is good. Every man must keep his own counsel. As long as there are no lies between us. We trust each other, yes?" Gabriel nodded his head. "Then I can still be of service to you. There are still maps of the old catacombs before the church took them over and closed off many of the tunnels to public access. My people have the resources you need, never fear."

Chapter Twenty-four

Later that day, Laura Donovan received a visit at the Embassy from Father Ryan. "Why, Father … what brings you here?" She smiled in greeting, looking up from the visa applications she was processing. She did not normally see the man outside of his church.

Ryan was smiling and affable as always. "Good morning to you, child," he greeted her. "I have some news for your friend. Do you know where I might find him?" he asked innocently enough.

Laura was nonplussed for a moment; she hadn't thought to actively seek help from the priest, though obviously the church would have its contacts. "That's great news, Father. But I don't know where he is at the moment. He only told me he would be in touch by the weekend," she explained.

"I see, child …" Ryan appeared to ponder for a brief moment then came to a decision. "Well, I suppose if we can't find this elusive friend of yours, it'll be best if I took you to his brother." He smiled. "Then when he does get in touch, it'll all be one big happy reunion, won't it, child?" He grinned broadly.

"Why, Father, that's great news … You know where he is then?"

"Yes, my child. But he might not be there much longer. It's best if I take you to him right now …," he said casually and gently taking her arm, betraying a hint of urgency.

"All right, Father, just let me get my jacket and bag." Ryan released her arm, and she nipped back into her office, reappearing moments later. Excited, she accompanied the old priest out of the Embassy and into the midmorning sun.

In the streets outside, helpless eyes watched her exit the building with the priest. The watcher had not expected the priest to visit Signora Donovan at the Embassy. All that could be done was trail the car. But he knew its probable destination already. He started up his car and pulled out into the traffic behind the priest's car.

Half an hour later, the car passed into the Vatican City proper, Swiss Guards, all purple and gold, at attention and saluting as the car went by. Laura's head was swimming with the news Father Ryan had just given her.

Lucifer, as Ryan had explained, had apparently been in Italy a lot longer than the couple of months Gabriel had suggested and had joined the church as a novitiate two years ago. Whilst in Rome, he had then suffered a severe brain seizure and was even now undergoing radical treatment in a special facility within the Vatican. All this had been unknown to Father Ryan until he had begun to make enquiries on her behalf.

"Father, it all sounds so incredible ...," she expressed her disbelief. "Gabriel isn't like the picture you ..." And then she paused, remembering the skilful way he had dispatched the German soldier that first night.

"He is a mercenary, my child. One laboring under the wild misguided belief that the church is responsible for his brother's medical condition. His reputation precedes him, I assure you. Even I found this hard to believe, but I checked my sources with other members of the clergy in Spain, where he was remembered from the Civil War, with notoriety, I assure you. Gabriel is still sought there for 'crimes against the state' as I understand they call it. He is not the sweet soul he appears to be, my child, but a cold-blooded killer who believes the church are torturing instead of trying to help his brother." Ryan told his tale well, blending half-truths with blatant lies, but then he was skilled at this sort of deception. "I fear for his soul. He is a desperate man. Who knows what action he may take?"

Laura fretted, head down as she pondered the events since their meeting. Could it be true? She had known the gentle side but also witnessed Gabriel's other side, a side she knew so little about. It was starting to frighten her.

"We'll soon be there, child, and you can see for yourself just how well we are taking care of Gabriel's brother." He smiled inwardly.

Half an hour later, Father Ryan and Laura were being escorted below ground, into a recently built facility beneath the Vatican by a Cardinal DiMatteo, a large rotund man with a large face, whose sagging jowls bespoke of too much claret.

"As you will see, Father and Signora Donovan, this special medical facility is maintained with all the latest advances in medical science. It is a joint effort between the church and a few research laboratories. The church aids in funding their research and, in return, benefits from the treatments available," he explained. Father Ryan nodded as though learning the knowledge for the first time. "When Brother Angell's condition became known, it was decided to house him in this facility, where some of the best medical minds available can work on his case. I believe some sort of radical blood-filtering process is being tried, but this latest attempt at a cure is in its early stages."

He led them along long corridors, seemingly deserted, their footsteps echoing around them. The walls maintained the roughness of old, though the floors had been smoothed somewhat. Electric bulbs and cables ran along the corridor walls.

Before long, the narrow passageway opened out into a more spacious area filled with desks and cabinets, some electrical apparatus Laura was unfamiliar with. Two priests busied themselves within, one noisily using a typewriter.

Down another long corridor, through two larger chambers, the corridor twisted and turned with numerous forks and cross connections being ignored by the cardinal, who obviously knew his way around. One corridor held a number of doors along its walls. One of these doors was ajar, and through it, Laura glimpsed a priest, his back to her. The room contained a bed and some other furniture. Laura assumed the rooms were for patients, or visitors?

At length, the cardinal ushered them into a much larger chamber, where three priests scurried back and forth checking dials on machines. A large generator hummed away in the corner, attracting her attention at first. Then two of the priests moved aside, and she got her first glimpse of Gabriel's brother.

She gasped, hand flying up to her mouth, at the scene before her. What looked like a large steel bell stood in the middle of the floor, and out of the top of this bell protruded Lucifer's head. The hinged segments of the bell completely encased his body all the way up to his neck, where surgical tubes had been inserted into his arteries, one either side of his neck, one draining, and one replacing his blood, long scarlet tubes which connected to some large machine with some sort of glass-enclosed large rubber diaphragm, which was slowly pumping the blood from his body.

Lucifer's eyes were unfocused, staring blindly into space. She could see the resemblance in his features, but Lucifer was blond where Gabriel was dark. "It's horrible," she said.

"But necessary, my child. The drugs kill his pain, and within a few more weeks, the blood-filtering process may cure or improve the brain disorder," the cardinal explained.

"It's still horrible." The wet suction noises from the diaphragm were making her nauseous. It looked like he was being bled dry, his face so white.

"This is making you ill, child." Father Ryan comforted her. "Come and we'll go into one of the anterooms, where the cardinal has had prepared a little refreshment." He stood back as one of the other priests began to escort her out of the main chamber and turned back to DiMatteo. "Did you drug the food as I asked?"

DiMatteo nodded. "I agree … keeping her here may prove a valuable bargaining ploy if this Gabriel is as resourceful as you say."

"If Keisel were still alive, I'm sure he'd vouch for Gabriel's resourcefulness." He smiled grimly. "We're lucky he let Father Paulo live. His compassion may yet be his undoing," he added.

"Luckier still, that a good Catholic managed to find and free the good father so promptly."

"Very lucky," admitted Ryan. "At least we now know that he knew everything Father Paulo knew, which wasn't much, so we can make an educated guess as to how he will make his next move. His new friends may prove a problem. Our German allies will have to assist us." Cardinal DiMatteo nodded agreement.

"I will make the necessary arrangements, never fear. Now if you will excuse me, I have our other 'guest' to see to. He's been a little 'disruptive' lately …"

Chapter Twenty-five

The room above the restaurant was obviously used for parties or the like. Chairs were currently stacked on tables, except the one around which they were all gathered. Gabriel was introduced to the other men in the room by Grimaldi. He nodded acknowledgement to them all, noting the individuals to whom Grimaldi gave great deference.

Grimaldi, it seems, was quite high up in the ranks of the Cosa Nostra. Only three men in the room seemed to hold greater influence, though Gabriel did not know whether this meeting had been contrived to give that impression.

They spoke English, in deference to his nationality, though Grimaldi suspected (and he was right) that Gabriel's Italian was just as good as his Latin. The room was filled with cigarette smoke, which Gabriel tried to ignore.

One of the men spread an old, weathered map of the catacomb system, which had existed under Rome since the days of the old Roman Empire. Red crayon marked various passages, which had been sealed off to the public since the turn of the century. As they ran under the Vatican, they were deemed the property of the church itself and so claimed in the Holy Father's name. Crosses marked large chambers underground, large enough to house the sort of facilities Gabriel had described. A second map, obtained from a source at the Power Ministry, was a schematic of the installation works carried out for the Vatican in the years since. Comparing one with the other, there were four possible chambers which seemed likely candidates for exploration.

"This operation is rushed … too many unknowns." One of the old Capos shook his head worriedly.

"Don Giovanni," argued Grimaldi, "the boy was your nephew. Would you refuse this man our help?"

The older man shook his head dismissively. "You mistake reluctance for caution, Luigi … I merely point out the limited resources we can supply at such short notice," the older man explained. "The dynamite and guns are nothing without men to wield them, and after the betrayal at the munitions factory the other night, our people have scattered to the countryside till things quieted down. We could raise no more than a dozen men by tonight, if tonight it must be, but if necessary, I will be proud to accompany your friend into the catacombs myself. A debt is a debt. I may be old, but let no one doubt my courage." He looked sternly at Grimaldi, who looked justifiably chastened.

"Forgive me, Don Giovanni … I did not mean to suggest such a thing …" Gabriel then interrupted him in an attempt to save Grimaldi's face.

"Twelve good men should be enough. I do not plan on starting a war. The action has to be carried out tonight though. The faster we move, the greater the chance of surprise," he explained, using the map to point out his strategy. "We use the dynamite here," he said, finger pointing out one of the red crosses. "Blow the wall at this point, between these two chambers. We split two ways, each group checking out one of these chambers. If no luck, we regroup here and continue on down this corridor to the next possible site."

"How much resistance do you expect from the priests?" one of the other capos asked.

"Not much at all from the priests," Gabriel explained. "But with the Nazis involved, I daresay they have more of their own people in the catacombs to oversee the scientists. Maybe half a dozen or so," he conjectured. "The catacombs are mainly narrow, and any large group would only hamper itself. That's why a small group stands a better chance of success."

"Don Giovanni, have your men assemble here at this public access gate tonight at ten o'clock," said Grimaldi. "Myself and Signor Angell will lead the two teams of six, once we blow our way through one of the sealed-off sections." He pointed again to the map. "With luck, we should be in and out within ten minutes." Grimaldi looked to Gabriel for confirmation, glad to see him nodding. "Before the Germans realize what is happening," he added.

"We may need medical supplies just in case. Do you know a doctor we could use at such short notice?" Gabriel asked. Some of the men looked around at each other. One of the younger men there—relatively younger, anyway—spoke.

"I know someone. He has a villa on the outskirts of Rome. I will tell him to expect you. His name is Maldini. I will mark the location on the other map for you. It is less than ten minutes by car. Your friend will be in good hands," he assured Gabriel.

Grimaldi offered Gabriel his choice of weapons from his own personal arsenal in the cellar beneath his home. Gabriel accepted a couple of stick grenades and a serviceable Luger with a couple of clips of ammunition. Besides this, he again had his two favored knives fastened to his thighs.

Preferring heavier armament, Grimaldi took a submachine gun in addition to his old Webley revolver. He too carried a knife, British commando variety. It had drawn blood before.

As night fell, they drove close to their rendezvous point, parking the car a few streets away. Once organized and introductions quickly made, Gabriel was introduced to the other Mafiosi who were to help rescue his friend Lucifer. Some were older than Grimaldi, some mere youths, but they all had that look in their eyes—half-sorrow, half-anger. He knew they were no novices at this game, if game it could be called. The small group then made their way by foot for the last few hundred yards, vanishing inside the normally closed entrance gates as one of their accomplices beckoned them to hurry. He closed the gate behind them so that to outward impressions, it still remained locked.

Across the street, a curtain moved in a darkened window and then was still. Within the room, the crackle of an old shortwave radio could be heard as it warmed up its transistors. At length, once the thing was fully operational, a finger depressed the "transmit" button, and a German voice spoke.

Chapter Twenty-six

Inside the weathered tunnel entrance, one of the younger men handed Gabriel and Grimaldi gas masks. "For the smoke, and dust, signor," explained the man.

"Grazie." Gabriel thanked him and fastened the mask around his neck. Grimaldi quickly assigned the men to their respective teams. Six would go with him and six with Gabriel. Torches were handed out, and one man led the way, navigating from a mini version of the map, copies of which all of them carried, in case bearings were misplaced.

It took ten minutes to locate the passageway they wanted, newish cement blocking any further way forward. It was one of the younger Mafiosi who carried the dynamite. Six sticks wrapped together with tape. He attached the detonator expertly and began unwinding the fuse wire back to the junction of the corridor. "Get back beyond the next bend, and cover your ears," the youth ordered as he lit the fuse, which sparked and burnt brightly, the hissing flame running back along the length of wire towards the obstruction.

Outside the catacombs, in the cobbled street, a truck screeched to a halt. The tailgate dropped instantly and jackbooted soldiers launched themselves out of the back of the truck. "Lauss! Lauss! Faster, you excuses for soldiers …," the German officer bellowed at the Italian conscripts as he organized them into positions. The call had given them hardly any notice, scattered as they were, keeping watch on the likeliest entry points to the catacombs, for Ryan had guessed correctly that that was the way Gabriel would choose to come. Half his contingent of men was made up of the lazy Fascist conscripts, who were slow to follow his orders. His regular men hurried into position, eager to show up the sloppiness of their so-called allies.

Two tripod-mounted machine guns were positioned at either end of the narrow cobbled street, setting up a lethal crossfire. The house that contained the radio was entered, and troops took up their positions behind the windows. The *kommandant* took up position in the house also. "Shoot to kill, Leutnant. Relay the orders. Even those peasants shouldn't be able to miss such easy targets." He chuckled. "If the Amerikaner is lucky enough to get out of the catacombs alive, well …" He chuckled. "We'll take him alive if we can. If not, those damn priests had better be quick with a bucket and sponge, eh, Heinie?" He laughed to his underling. "As for the rest of them, those surviving the crossfire are to be shot out of hand. Verstammenzie?"

"Ja, mein Kommandant. I will tell the men." As he spoke, he heard a low rumble of noise, feeling the vibration beneath his feet. Less than a minute later, smoke came billowing out of the catacomb entrance.

"Tell the men to be ready," the kommandant spoke, a confident smile lighting his face.

Chapter Twenty-seven

Cardinal DiMatteo consulted with Father Ryan in one of the spare offices in the underground complex. "My friend, a complication has arisen with the American woman ..."

"Oh? In what way?" Ryan asked. "Didn't she take the drugged food?"

"Yes, eventually she did. But before that, she complained of feeling slightly queasy, probably because of seeing Lucifer confined like that, but I asked one of our medical staff to humor her with a brief clinical examination."

"And?" Ryan asked.

"Without a thorough examination, he could not be sure ..." DiMatteo paused, whirling around at the noise of an explosion far off below ground.

"Sound the alarm. That's got to be him!" Ryan reacted quicker than the overweight DiMatteo, hitting the button which made alarms ring throughout the complex.

"I'll look after Lucifer," DiMatteo said, face flushing with sudden exertion. "You organize the German troops. Prevent him from reaching his friend." He rushed off along the corridor while Ryan quickly picked up the phone, winding furiously to activate the direct line to the troops' quarters.

The explosion was deafening in the confined space of the tunnel. Gabriel remembered to open his mouth and not hold his breath, the pressure shockwave knocking all of them back a pace. Then as the smoke and dust came billowing around the corner, gas masks came down over their faces.

Torches came on, and men were running rapidly into the thick smoke, not wanting to lose any element of surprise the explosion had caused on the other side. Gabriel ran alongside Grimaldi, eager to take charge of the operation within the Vatican laboratory complex.

"Knock … Knock …" Grimaldi laughed under his mask as he fought his way through the smoke and dust. He moved fast for his size, Gabriel noted, already alongside him. "Left or right?" Grimaldi asked him as their team reached the juncture.

"I'm right-handed …," lied Gabriel lightheartedly. "You take your team left." In the distance, alarms could be heard ringing along the corridors. "Let's move." He led the way through the thinning smoke, Luger primed and ready. Six men were at his back, eager to follow. He gave no thought to Grimaldi as he concentrated on the job at hand.

They came to a corridor full of doors, smashing open each one in turn, wasting no time on niceties. All offices of some description, a couple obviously vacated in a hurry once the alarm had sounded. "Keep going. Don't stop," Gabriel urged.

Within minutes, they came upon the large chamber wherein they found four priests cowering in fear at the sight of the armed party, trying to hide behind a large bulky piece of equipment, whose purpose Gabriel was puzzled to determine.

"Don't shoot us. Don't shoot us … please …," they pleaded. Gabriel walked up to them as he pulled off his gas mask. One priest's eyes widened as his face was revealed, and Gabriel turned on that one.

"That's got the introductions over. You obviously know me, and I don't give a shit who *you* are." He raised the Luger to the man's temple. "Where is he?" he asked, finger tightening on the trigger.

Grimaldi's party had similar bad luck. The chamber, when they came upon it, was used as a storeroom for medical supplies and quantities of unknown chemicals. He waved his party back. "Regroup with the American. Hurry, time is not on our side here!" He pushed his men back into the tunnel.

Gunfire rang out up ahead, and Grimaldi pushed his men faster till they came into sight of Gabriel's party, firing around a juncture in the tunnel network. "Two Germans. They hold the next corner!" Gabriel shouted over the fusillade of bullets.

Grimaldi risked a quick look around the corner, ducking back quickly as bullets drifted towards his head. He pulled one of the stick grenades from his belt and pulled the pin.

"We stole these from the munitions dump. Time we gave them one back, eh?" He grinned, stepping quickly out into the line of fire and hurling the smoking grenade down the tunnel, where it bounced off one wall and around the corner.

Brief screams of panic could be heard seconds before the detonation, and more smoke and debris filled the corridor. Gabriel led the way through, putting his gas mask on once more. They stepped through the blood and bits of bodies, impossible to avoid in the close quarters of the cramped tunnels.

The next chamber was a few minutes away, and as they'd just seen, the German troops were mobilizing to answer the alarms. "Which way?" asked Grimaldi, pausing his men. "We must keep the men together now," he warned.

"Agreed. We go right!" Gabriel insisted.

"Why so sure?" Grimaldi queried as they started along the corridor, guns leveled. Two of the men covered their rear.

"I had a little talk with one of the priests we found. You could say I put the fear of God into him." Gabriel smiled grimly beneath his gas mask. Grimaldi found time to laugh.

"You are rather good at that, my friend," he agreed, motioning his men to follow as he and Gabriel quickened the pace.

Gabriel's band of Mafiosi came under fire again as they were approaching the large chamber where he expected to find Lucifer. Bullets zipped past in both directions as both sides were surprised by the sudden encounter. Gabriel flung himself to the floor to present the least target, returning fire with the Luger.

Behind him, men died, caught by the fusillade of bullets in the narrow passageway. Fortunately, there were only a handful of German troops ahead of them, rushing to hold up the invading force till reinforcements arrived. They died just as quickly as the Mafiosi. Grimaldi pushed his men on, their number now reduced to eight.

Gabriel changed clips in his gun as he kept pace with Grimaldi, noting the older man's bleeding shoulder. "It's nothing …," he said, obviously pained. Gabriel stuffed the Luger into his belt.

"Give me the machine gun. You won't be able to hold it with that arm." Grimaldi reluctantly gave the weapon to him, taking out the Webley revolver, and Gabriel slung the strap over his shoulder. "Quickly now," he urged them on, the lights of the large chamber brightening ahead of them.

Rushing into the chamber, they found priests scattering before them. The room was filled with generators and strange machines the like of which Gabriel had not seen before. Some, their purpose he could guess at; others, he had no idea.

Amid the panic, his eyes were drawn to one side of the room, where a large steel bell-shaped object was surrounded by numerous apparatus, red tubes running to and fro. Lucifer's head stuck out from the top of the bell.

"One more step and he dies," cried the fat cardinal now holding a pistol to Lucifer's head. Gabriel held up his arm to call his men to a halt. "Nice try, Gabriel, but it all ends here," he gloated, turning his head at the sound of running jackboots approaching from one of the far corridors.

"It does for you," said Grimaldi as he stepped around Gabriel, leveling the Webley and fired one clean shot, which sent the shaven head back, with blood, bone, and brains scattering over the equipment behind him. DiMatteo dropped like a stone.

Gabriel's eyes flashed like dark fire as he rounded upon Grimaldi. "That was risky," he warned, feeling his cheeks flushing darkly as he controlled his anger.

"You would not have taken the shot, and then where would we be, eh? We argue later," he said. "Spread out and hold positions. Don't let them into the chamber." He gave orders while Gabriel got a grip on himself.

Gunfire exploded deafeningly within the chamber as the first of the German reinforcements arrived, trying to force their way inside. Gabriel took cover behind a generator, trying to work his way over to where Lucifer still remained helpless confined in that strange apparatus.

Bullets sprayed the chamber, hitting generators and equipment. An overhead light shattered, and Gabriel ducked as he was showered with broken glass. He returned fire with the machine gun, raking the entrance to the corridor with a deadly fire.

"Grenade!" yelled an Italian voice as a smoking stick grenade was hurled into the chamber by the attacking Germans, and Gabriel flung himself behind a large piece of equipment as the blast went off against a generator, his ears deafened by the blast. He hoped the steel bell would save Lucifer from the force of the explosion.

More gunfire verified his allies were still on their feet, as the generator went wild, its inner workings damaged by the explosion. The humming became louder by the second. Gabriel got to his feet. He had to free Lucifer.

Ducking and weaving, he got out of the line of fire, running over to the large steel device. Lucifer's eyes were vague and unfocused, tubes bleeding him from the neck and pumping God knows what drugs into his system. He had no time to waste, so he ripped the tubes away, blood spurting from Lucifer's neck. "Forgive me, my friend," he pleaded as Lucifer went into some sort of spasm, head shaking violently as he tried to mouth some words but making only sad gargling sounds. He was barely aware of what was happening around him.

Hurrying, Gabriel tried to find a way of opening the shaped metal enclosure, ducking instinctively as another explosion ripped through the chamber. Stray gunfire was raking the bits of apparatus, causing electrical discharges. Spilt chemicals were catching fire all over the place.

Gabriel grunted with effort as he managed to release the hinged segments and heaved back the first of them. Yet more intravenous tubes were attached to Lucifer's body within the steel housing. He began tugging them free, when a shot rang out, the bullet careening off the steel bell.

He whirled around, leveling the machine gun, finger already tightening on the trigger as he caught sight of Laura through the smoke. She was being used as a human shield by another of the priests …

"Gabriel … Gabriel …," she called, staggering as Ryan held her upright before him. She was still too drugged up to walk unaided, and it was all the priest could do to keep her upright in front of him as he pressed the revolver to her temple.

"Put it down, Gabriel," Ryan ordered. "You can't save both of them, as good as you are. Save one and the other dies, I promise you!" he gloated, wincing as another explosion sent blazing chemicals amongst attackers and defenders alike. Screams echoed through the chamber as Gabriel looked frantically around. Grimaldi's men were pinned down. He was on his own. "Give it up. The Italians mean nothing to you. Let the Germans kill them, and I guarantee no lasting harm will befall you. Your blood is valuable, Gabriel. We need to examine it, test it, synthesize it. Once we've done that, we'll let you go free," Ryan implored.

"Your kind will never let mine go free!" Gabriel accused, trying desperately to think of a way out of this.

"Gabriel ..." Laura held her hands out to him. "What's happening here? This is wrong ... You shouldn't ...," she rambled, her clouded perceptions leaving her remote from events.

"It's okay, Laura. It's okay ...," he tried to reassure her, guessing that drugs had been used on her.

"I'll kill her, I'm warning you," Ryan sneered, making Laura cry out as he forced the gun against the side of her head. Gabriel wanted to leap forward, but daren't. Grimaldi was right. He wouldn't have taken the shot.

"You kill her, and there's nothing stopping me from killing you!" he said defiantly. "Make no mistake, I *will* kill you," he promised the priest. Ryan looked flustered. Things weren't going as planned. He looked around. Gabriel's force was down to six men. But the fire from the Germans was diminishing.

In desperation, another stick grenade was hurled into the chamber, the explosion setting off a chain reaction as it rocked the floor as drums of chemicals were ignited one by one. Laura fell to the floor, and for one second, Ryan faced Gabriel.

His attention drifting to Laura's slumping body, Gabriel was slow in bringing the machine gun to bear on the priest. Ryan fired his gun, once, twice... Gabriel cried out as the first bullet whirled him around, out of the path of the second, which hit Lucifer a glancing blow to his exposed head.

Falling to his knees, Gabriel swung back, raising the machine gun, intending to empty the magazine into the priest. Six bullets raked Ryan's body, sending him flying back into another of the overloaded generators, some bullets passing through and into the equipment itself.

The magazine fell silent, and in frustrated rage, Gabriel threw the gun at the priest's body. He struggled to his feet, one hand examining his wound. An exit wound told him the bullet had passed straight through his side, just above the hip. Nonfatal but would need treatment to staunch the loss of blood.

"Gabriel!" Laura cried out to him, trying to stand. He began to stagger over to her, when another tremendous explosion rocked the chamber as some of the chemical drums exploded together, this time with enough force to cave in part of the roof.

Laura looked up through the falling dust, in time to see the steel girder and tons of rubble falling towards her. "Gabriel!" she screamed his name once more, and then, even as he tried to reach her, the debris descended with such force as to knock him over once more.

Coughing and spluttering without his gas mask, Gabriel found it hard to see in the dust and forced himself to rise. "Laura!" he cried hopelessly, fighting his way through the debris, lifting chunks of masonry and flinging them aside till he saw the one bare leg sticking out from beneath the rubble and knew it was hopeless.

Inside him, something died. He screamed her name once more to the heavens, sobbing as he turned away from her. There was still a chance for Lucifer, but time was running out. Chemicals were igniting all over the place.

Two of the other Italians helped him open the rest of the steel shell, and Lucifer was pulled free, the head wound quickly bandaged with a field dressing.

He was unconscious, thankfully, and two of the men supported him between them. "Can you walk?" Grimaldi asked Gabriel, seeing his condition.

"Yes … Yes, I can walk."

"We must hurry." Grimaldi took charge of the situation, ushering the wounded to the front as the remnants of his force held the rear against the few remaining German troops. "Two minutes! Then leave the dynamite and run like hell!" he ordered.

Gabriel ran painfully along the corridor with them, hearing the gunfire behind. Minutes later, they heard another loud explosion and then running feet and cries in Italian behind them.

He gathered the booby trap had succeeded; the dynamite sealing off any pursuit behind them. Breathing hard, he forced himself on.

Outside in the Via Catenza, a German soldier listened intently at the entrance to the catacombs. At the first faint sounds of running feet, he whirled abruptly away from the entrance, signaling furiously to the watching officer in the darkened window.

Inside the house, the kommandant chuckled to himself. "On my signal." As he raised his hand, at either end of the street twin machine guns were cocked and loaded, and as the weary party began to exit through the gates, the Kommandant's hand fell.

The night air exploded in a cacophony of screams and death as the twin machine guns opened fire.

Chapter Twenty-eight

The machine guns opened up as Gabriel and what was left of the Mafiosi started to exit the wrought iron gates, and he instantly flung himself back to escape the hail of death as the bullets began to fly. Cries and confusion echoed and surrounded him as more gunfire came from the house opposite, and he and his men returned fire where they could, one body falling through the shattered window.

More screams were coming from the streets, and Grimaldi and his men wondered what was happening. Gabriel chanced sticking his head back outside for a quick look as he realized the two machine guns were firing on each other.

Taken by surprise, the gun manned by the German troops was quickly silenced, and the deadly fire then turned on the remaining troops, surprised at the Italian conscripts' treachery. They were mowed down as they tried to fall back, bullets taking no prisoners.

A deathly silence fell upon the street as the guns finally fell quiet. Gabriel, and now Grimaldi, looking towards the machine gun manned by the Italian conscripts.

"You can come out now, Uncle Luigi ...," a voice called from among the uniformed troops.

Grimaldi laughed as he came out into the moonlight. "Marco, you save my fat ass tonight for sure." The two of them embraced each other.

The rest of the group came out of the catacombs, and all, save for the two supporting Lucifer between them, joined in the momentary celebrations.

The Italian conscripts had been infiltrated by the Mafia long ago. For some, it was a living, providing a wage and food on the table for their families in these troubled times. But blood always came first, and no Italian would fire on another at a German's behest.

"You had better go quickly, Uncle," the boy warned. "More troops were called and will be here shortly. We will rearrange the bodies a little, and everyone will think we were outfought."

"Good thinking, boy." Grimaldi slapped him on the back. "You kiss your mother for me, eh?" He laughed and then turned to his men. "Bring the American to the car. The rest of you, scatter. You know the routes." Shadows vanished into the night, and Gabriel walked slowly with them to where they had left the car.

Behind them, the Italian troops were stage-managing the scene of the slaughter. Some of the German bodies were being stripped whilst some of the Italians were undressing to clothe some of the bodies in Italian uniforms. "A good boy, that Marco," Gabriel commented to Grimaldi wearily.

"Can you make it?" Grimaldi asked, noticing Gabriel's unsuccessful attempts to staunch the flow of blood from his side.

"I'll make it ...," he promised.

Smoke still filled the large chamber, though the dust from the cave in was settling now. Father Ryan crawled slowly, agonizingly, across the rubble-strewn floor. He was dying, and he knew it ... in shock and losing too much blood.

One chance for life, and soon it would be too late. He crawled desperately towards the steel housing wherein they had kept Lucifer confined. Discarded tubes hung down, their open ends dripping his salvation onto the floor.

His hand reached out, flailing for the plastic tube ... tried again as he lurched closer. Desperately catching hold and bringing the open end to his mouth where he sucked and sucked and sucked, the remnants of Lucifer's tainted blood filled his mouth and throat with their unique coppery flavor.

He drained the tube dry and then fell back. If only it would still be enough. He had no practical experience of the tainted blood's efficacy, if or how quickly it would react with his body's own regenerative system. Mentally, he prayed, finally collapsing onto the laboratory floor.

German troops began putting out the fires, and more priests began reappearing now that the battle was over. Bodies were removed on makeshift field stretchers, and the wounded offered on-the-spot treatment by the church's doctors and scientists.

"Quickly. The father's alive. Get a stretcher over here!" called one of the priests, seeing that Ryan still breathed, though badly injured. He heard groaning behind him and turned to see the bare leg sticking out from under the rubble.

He went around the thick steel girder, which had half-crushed the desk behind which the woman lay as she groaned in pain, face all bloody and most of her lower body covered with rubble. "Shovels. Quickly, get shovels … The American woman is still alive!"

Maldini was up late, expecting Grimaldi and whatever wounded he brought with him. He ushered them through the large gates, bidding them to drive round to the rear of his house while he closed the gates behind them.

Helping them from the car, he led them into the darkened house. Despite protests from Gabriel, he tended to him first in the surgery he maintained in his cellar.

He was surprised when told the bullet wound was fresh, as it looked to be healing on its own, yet the wound definitely needed cleaning, and this he did with swabbing alcohol, which stung enough to make Gabriel swear.

Aching, Gabriel got up off the surgical bench and helped Grimaldi as he lowered the semiconscious Lucifer onto it. Maldini quickly removed the bandages and examined the head wound, the flesh still gaping to display part of the man's skull with a deep crease in the thin bone.

"I am no neurosurgeon and cannot tell if your friend has suffered a serious injury," he explained as he swabbed the wound and then reached for needle and thread. "I can only make running repairs. The Germans will be searching wide for you, I think. All surgeries are registered," he explained his concern, starting to stitch the head wound.

"Just do what you can," Gabriel implored. The doctor's skilled fingers did their work. The small wounds in Lucifer's neck had healed after a fashion already and needed little treatment, though the flesh looked raw.

Grimaldi was the last to be treated by the doctor, removing his sweater to expose the torn flesh of his shoulder. "Just like old times, my friend." Maldini and Grimaldi shared a joke, and then the older man cursed as the sting of the alcohol cleaned the wound.

As the doctor tended to his arm, Grimaldi advised Gabriel of his plans for their escape. "We drive south once we leave the city. There is a merchant ship leaving tonight for Greece. The captain is known to me, and arrangements have been made for you to slip aboard. Once you are in Greece, you are on your own, my friend," he explained.

"I thank you for your help …," Gabriel said sincerely. "If my friend were conscious, he would thank you as well. I am only sorry that in helping me, some of your men lost their lives." He was honestly saddened, and Grimaldi could see this.

"One war or another, what is the difference my friend?" he shrugged resignedly, much to Maldini's annoyance as he tried to bandage the wound. "At least we killed some of the Germans in the process, and I finally settled with that old bastard DiMatteo." He grinned.

"Just what was the bad blood between you, anyway?" Gabriel asked out of curiosity. Grimaldi shrugged once more, and the exasperated Maldini threw up his hands.

"Many years ago, when he was just a priest, he performed the ceremony at my wedding to Maria. I never forgave him!" he said glowering and then, seeing Gabriel's confusion, burst out laughing. He could contain himself no more. "You Americans … so serious … Hah …," he added, and even Gabriel managed a smile as he cradled his semiconscious friend. Whatever the reason, Grimaldi seemed intent on keeping it to himself. Vendettas were very personal things in Italy.

Lucifer's eyes flickered open at Grimaldi's coarse laughter. "Gabriel …," he gasped, weak from his ordeal and still feeling the drugs in his system. "Is it over?" he asked.

"Soon, my friend. Soon …," promised Gabriel.

Chapter Twenty-nine

Days later, as Gabriel and Lucifer were approaching the coast of Greece, back in the catacomb complex beneath the Vatican, Father Ryan was managing to sit up in bed. Once the bullets had been removed, his recovery had astonished the medical team. He was still weakened but felt that he would eventually make a complete recovery. His body felt like a stranger's to him. The very skin itself seemed more alive and sensitive, hot now to the touch, as inside his improved regenerative system worked hard to effect repairs.

"How is Mrs. Donovan?" he asked one of the members of the medical staff. He remembered vaguely seeing her being stretchered away from the half-destroyed laboratory chamber.

The doctor was frank in his answer. "Her condition is stabilized. The head injuries were not as bad as first thought. Some broken ribs, again not a real problem, but whether she will walk again unaided is another matter entirely, Father. The bones in her leg were badly crushed by the debris. We were considering amputation …," he explained. Ryan's face saddened.

"The news saddens me," he admitted. "She was a good woman." He shook his head slowly. The entire debacle was Gabriel's fault. That damned demon! All their plans ruined. His collaboration with the Mafia had been unexpected, and they had not moved quickly or thoroughly enough to counter it.

The worst of it was half of what he'd told Gabriel had been true. If the church scientists had been successful in synthesizing the blood, there would have been no great necessity to keep him in captivity, save for purposes of security. At least, that was what he had been told.

All the scientists had succeeded in doing in the few months they'd had Lucifer to play with was to somehow deteriorate the original blood in Lucifer's body, some flaw in the filtration process. The German scientists had refined the process, but they had come too late, and the damage had already been done, and they couldn't undo it. The escaped angel would soon find his body's regenerative skills were no longer what they were, though the flawed blood was still enough to help Ryan recover from otherwise fatal wounds. That made the capture of Gabriel all the more important. One not-quite-human guinea pig was never enough.

Ryan's attention drifted back as the doctor continued to discuss Laura's condition. "And then of course there are the internal injuries and the beginnings of a pregnancy that will have to be terminated …," he went on.

"Her what?" Ryan's attention snapped back to full awareness. "What did you say?"

"Why, we examined her to ascertain the extent of any internal injuries. She's bleeding slightly," the doctor explained. "We found the woman to have been recently impregnated, the eggs barely days old. But we decided to wait till some of her other injuries had cleared up before putting her through more surgery …," he explained.

"My God …," Ryan exclaimed, a thousand and one thoughts and ideas rushing through his mind. "We've never had an opportunity like this." He talked to himself, though the doctor had no idea what his patient was going on about.

Ryan started to get out of bed. The doctor went to try to force him back down. "Are you mad? Get back into bed. You're lucky to be alive." Ryan reluctantly did as the doctor advised.

"I need to see Cardinal Montpelier. Immediately!" he ordered.

Chapter Thirty

"Come in, Cardinal Montpelier," a warbling voice ushered the fearful cardinal into the obscenely affluent and grandiose chamber beneath the Vatican. He looked around the table at the men sat there, all of them staring at him. He had only been inside this chamber twice before, and he hadn't liked the experience.

It took a great amount of arguing from Father Ryan to get him agree to make the plea on his behalf. Dark hungry eyes watched him as he walked slowly into the chamber, to stand before the large table. Not many people knew of this strange grim council that held sway beneath the Corridors of Power above. For this was where the real power was. The current Pope was at best an unknowing puppet of darker forces. Forces which had held such power for longer than was imagined.

"You're looking well, Cardinal. Something must agree with you," joked Romanus, sitting around the table. The laughter was taken up by a few of the others. It failed to put him at his ease.

"Your Reverences ...," he began. "Father Ryan has alerted me to a rather unique opportunity," he started to explain but was interrupted.

"Ryan? He drank some of the tainted blood, did he not?" queried Guillaum de Grimoard. "I trust he is recovering from his injuries?"

"Yes, milord." Montpelier nodded his head. "As you know, even the tainted blood greatly increases the human regenerative processes. It's just that its effects are not as long-lasting as that of the pure untainted blood," he explained.

"Indeed," acknowledged Sisinnius, the eldest around the table, examining the skin on the back of one hand for more detrimental effects. He had noticed the odd blotch blemishing his skin lately.

"And so we come to the crux of the matter, milords," Montpelier went on. "Father Ryan has requested a vial of the untainted Blood of Christ." Hushed whispers went around the table. Montpelier continued, "We have a rather unique opportunity as Father Ryan has pointed out. The American woman is critically injured, and without the blood, she may die."

"Why should we waste our precious stock on this American woman, my good Cardinal? A good catholic she may be, but that is no reason to …," Alonso Borgia interrupted the cardinal.

"She is also pregnant with Gabriel's child." Montpelier stunned them all into silence, gazing into their eyes for once. The revelation gave him power, however fleeting, and he savored it.

"I see," stated a voice, and more whispers went around the table.

"An angel-child of our very own to play with," mused Grimoard.

"An angel-child born of a human mother already *with* the Blood …," enthused Alonso Borgia. *What would such a child grow to be?* he wondered.

Alonso, though not the "eldest" of those sitting here, was the de facto head of the council, as ruthless in his "afterlife" as he had ever been before his "rebirth." His scheming mind was already working out ways he could turn this situation to his advantage.

Some of the other council members stared at Borgia from the shadows. They knew the way his mind worked. Yet should he succeed in raising this angel-child, to what use would he put it in the future; how would it be used against its father?

It had been a shame that none of the earlier known angels' children had come into the hands of the church. Rome had taken care of Michael's whelp from his brief liaison in Bethlehem. Still, the earlier children had been born of normal human women … Never before had one been born of a woman whose regenerative system had already been fortified with Blood of Christ …

The Nazarean had possessed more than human powers, the seeming Resurrection a case in point. Perhaps of a match with those of his father, minus the wings of course. Gabriel's child could be a useful tool, or weapon if need be. Certainly, the child would be unique.

Alonso Borgia spoke, and no one shouted him down. "You have our permission, my good Cardinal, to administer a vial of the original Blood of Christ to the woman." Montpelier bowed his head.

"His Reverence will not regret this kindness," Montpelier spoke glibly, but Borgia was not fooled.

"His Reverence had better *not* regret it, good Cardinal," he warned. "I place the woman's recovery fully in your hands." He let the cardinal know that by doing so, he lived or died with the woman. So be it, the cardinal nodded gravely. "Tell this Father Ryan that upon his recovery, he is to seek audience with this council. There are matters of great import to discuss."

"I will do as you say, your Reverence." Montpelier bowed once, briefly, and turned and left the chamber and the men within, who continued to sit amidst the shadows.

Chapter Thirty-one

Cardinal Montpelier and Father Ryan met in one of the anterooms adjacent to the surgical facility under the Vatican. Montpelier seemed most concerned for the American woman in his charge. "It's not her physical well-being that's my concern, Father, but rather her mental state," he explained.

"How so, Cardinal?" Ryan queried. "As you say, since she ingested the blood, her physical injuries have showed tremendous recovery. I have seen the X-rays of her leg myself, and far from amputation, she'll be walking on it again in weeks."

Montpelier still shook his head. "Since she understood about the pregnancy, she has had great difficulty in reconciling her situation," he explained. "Her memory of events during the attack on the facility were necessarily clouded by the drugs we gave her at the time. Her last memory of Gabriel is of him trying to kill you and leaving her to die in the rubble. Hardly surprising really that she is not too keen on having his child."

"You think there's a chance she might injure herself deliberately to miscarry? Is that what you're saying?" Ryan was indeed starting to worry now.

"It's a possibility that should not be overlooked," the cardinal warned.

"Very well, increase the dosage of her medication, and double the medical staff in attendance on her. I want her watched around the clock," Ryan advised.

"There is of course the added complication with our German friends to consider as well," Montpelier went on.

"Now that America has entered the war you mean?" Montpelier nodded. "As far as they are concerned, the American Laura Donovan died in the cave-in. It should be little trouble to create another identity for her, perhaps using her Irish descent, in a similar manner to that which the church did for me when I first left Ireland." Ryan reminisced momentarily. "Southern Ireland has always allied itself with Germany against England. I foresee no problems there if we're careful. Once her mental state has been satisfactorily appraised, and after the child is born, we can look to move her out of Italy, to somewhere she can get the rest and relaxation she needs."

"It will be as you say then, Father. The council has placed you in full control of this operation." His words were a two-edged sword, Ryan noted.

"They have not misplaced their trust, Cardinal." He smiled grimly. "Nothing must be allowed to get in the way of the birth of this child."

Modern Day

Chapter Thirty-two

The tall man walked nimbly despite his obvious age. Dressed in a plain black suit and black shirt, it looked like he had broken down somewhere, for he carried a jerrican of petrol, seemingly headed back to fill up his car wherever he had been forced to abandon it. Walking past the fenced off derelict warehouse, he took note of the Alsatian dog patrolling around inside the grounds. Casually looking about him, he walked closer along the fence line and turned off along it, away from the nearest road. Spotting an opening in the fence where one could slip through quite easily, assuming you were on friendly terms with the dog, he crouched down close to it.

Ryan reached into his pocket, taking out the couple of bacon sandwiches he had got from the roadside stall earlier. He threw the first one over the fence as the dog tracked him around the corner. Eagerly, the animal went to the sandwich and wolfed it down, long tongue lapping its chops as it enjoyed the morsel. Ryan ducked to fold aside the loose piece of fencing and crouched as he slid through, holding the second sandwich out as the dog padded forward. Gingerly, the beast took the offering out of his hand as Ryan smiled. "Good dog. That's a good dog. Eat it up." He reached out to ruffle the fur on the dog's thick neck.

The sandwich was still lodged in the dog's throat when Ryan's hands took a firm hold, and he lunged forward, twisting, to snap the dog's neck cleanly and swiftly. The animal fell to the floor dead, and Ryan stood up, dusting off stray dog hairs from his dark suit.

He used the wire cutters from his pocket to open enough of a hole in the linked fence, to allow him to bend it back and slip through. Dragging the dog by the collar, he hid the body behind some of the rusty old oil drums that were stacked against one of the walls and then took the jerrican of petrol and gingerly opened the nearby door, looking into the open space of the old warehouse.

A light was on in one of the upstairs offices that looked out onto what was once the working area, but the windows were too grimy to see in or out. Ryan picked his way across the floor, trying to avoid the many pools of water. Holes in the roof had let rain in, and a damp smell of cement mixed with other chemicals was quite strong.

An old forklift truck stood rusting by one of the walls, its hood up and engine parts were noticeable on top of a ripped tarpaulin, spread over an old packing crate by the side of it. Other oil drums lay against a far wall. The place hadn't been used for its proper purpose in years since the recession had kicked in, and O'Donnell had commandeered the place for his own use.

Billy O'Donnell and four of his gang were sat divvying up the day's takings around a table in one of the offices on the first floor of the abandoned warehouse in one of Dublin's run-down industrial estates. Billy was a former enforcer for the IRA, now running his own little operation using unemployed youths to peddle drugs and the odd break-in to finance his new lifestyle. The office above the warehouse was still habitable, and another of the offices had been turned into a comfortable bedroom. It wasn't Billy's main home, but it was useful when he was in town.

His frequent absences were not liked by his wife, but she was wise enough to know her lifestyle came at a price and so kept quiet. At forty-three, she was not likely to find a better catch than the forty-four-year-old Billy O'Donnell.

Parts of the warehouse, mainly the upstairs offices and storerooms, now stocked his disposable assets and stolen goods. All his utilities were now free of charge, thanks to threats to local councilors, and he paid the right people to ensure the police left him alone.

The mainly teenage "employees" were easily impressed, and he used his former reputation to maintain a fear factor, which left them all kowtowing to him and easy to manipulate. A little money, a few drugs, and they did what he wanted without question or remorse. "Which do you think was more profitable, lads?" he asked, stuffing his hands in the pockets of his sheepskin jacket to keep them warm. "Peddling drugs or shagging that nun's arse?" He laughed, reminding them of the recent assault he had allowed on that busybody nun who was trying to interfere with his drugs sales.

"I know which was the more enjoyable." Jimmy chuckled, pulling up the hood on his top against the cold in the warehouse. He had been a virgin before hooking up with O'Donnell, whose contacts in the seedier side of life had put all sorts of women his way. The women would definitely not have chosen him by choice—overweight and with that horrible moustache that definitely didn't suit him. Yet money talked, and knickers dropped. O'Donnell kept him well salaried and ensured the women were in easy supply.

"Next week, let's make her wear that habit while she's giving us all blowjobs!" suggested Seamus. "She'll mind her own business now we've got that tape of her. Just threaten to show it to the abbot, and she'll do anything we want. Won't have to drug her next time." He chuckled. Seamus was a pervert's pervert. Into everything, and he'd shove his dick into any hole going. Three previous arrests for indecent assault had warned to keep his dick in his pants until Billy told him he could take it out if he wanted to keep working for him.

"There'll be plenty more videos of her before we're done with the bitch," promised Billy. He handed Jacko a ten-pound note. "Off you go, Jacko. Get the fish 'n' chips, and hurry back. I'm bloody starved." Jacko was Billy's nephew and just learning the ropes. He'd dropped school last year, and his young looks and a school uniform that still fit made him a valuable asset on some of Billy's stings. His old school contacts made him ripe for selling drugs in the school yards.

"Plenty of vinegar on mine, Jacko, lad," advised Kenny, the other member of the gang. "Make sure they're still hot by the time you get back here." He pulled up the zip on his parka a bit more against the cold. Kenny was an old friend of Billy's from his IRA days, a former "dicker" who moved the way the wind blew.

Jacko shrugged. The youngest member of the gang, he still got to do all the runaround work. He still needed to prove himself in the eyes of the older men. He moved his chair back from the table and stood up, and then he froze in place. "Fuck me, Uncle Billy. We've got company," he pointed out, and the other two men turned around to see the tall elderly man who had just entered from the top of the flight of stairs. There had been no barking from the guard dog downstairs to warn them of his presence.

"This place is getting really popular with the clergy!" Billy laughed, nonplussed by the sudden appearance. The others laughed too for a second, and then they stopped, noticing the stern look in the older man's eyes, and they all began to slowly step back from the table. The man just stood there defiantly, eyes sweeping back across the open spaces, from the table to the scattered beds and sundry items of obviously stolen furniture. A pair of silk knickers and some pornographic Polaroid photos were pinned up on the wall above the video recorder and TV. Souvenirs of their four days and nights with Sister Catherine. Kidnapped off the streets, drugged and abused by Billy and his gang.

"You're Billy O'Donnell, I take it?" Ryan accused Billy, who remained calmly at the table, his attention returned to counting bills. His gang kept looking from Billy to the older man and back again as the atmosphere thickened.

"So what if I am?"

"I've just come from the hospital," Ryan said coldly. "I've been talking to Sister Catherine."

"She got there okay then, did she?" Billy sneered. "She was walking a bit funny when she left here. Kinda bowlegged, like." A few of them chuckled as Billy tormented the old man. "A real naughty nun was Sister Catherine," Billy goaded. "I hope she hasn't forgotten our date next week. I told her to come back for another shagging next Thursday night." He laughed, setting off the others with his joking remarks.

"Do you have any idea what you did, you little shit?" asked Ryan, not really expecting an answer.

Billy turned to regard him for the first time. Tall, over six foot, but almost skinny. Too old to give them much trouble, even if he was a mind to try it on. Still, his attitude showed he wasn't cowed by the presence of Billy and his associates. "We fucked a nun, that's what we did," he boasted. "She fucking loved it too, Father," he added. "A few stiff cocks after all those years of wanking with candles in the nunnery.

Did her a world of good. Turned her into a right old hoor." He laughed. "If you don't believe me, I'll give you a free copy of the videotape," Billy taunted.

"No remorse at all then?" Ryan asked, temper rising. The rest of Billy's gang took up a defensive posture, spreading out around the table in case the old man tried to start anything.

"Remorse?" sneered Billy. "What the hell for? Emptied me balls into the good Sister a few times, and so did the rest of the lads," Billy taunted him. "That Catherine was some goer. You want to try her yourself. She knows a few tricks, that one." He chuckled. "Sucks like a Hoover. Takes it up the arse too. Couldn't get enough," he cackled. The old man looked from one to another, failing to rise to the bait. All of them grinned defiantly back at him, emboldened by Billy's bravado.

"You're all going to hell!" he announced. Billy just laughed in response, setting them all off.

"Calm down. You'll give yourself a heart attack." He laughed. "If hell is where I'll end up for fucking a nun, I think I'd just repent on me deathbed then, to be sure of going upstairs." He chuckled.

"Who said you were getting the *chance* to repent?" the priest asked, wide-eyed. "I meant you were going to hell *now*, ye little bastard!"

"And what are you going to do about it, eh? You're just an old man. Who gives a fuck what you think?"

"I may be old," Ryan admitted, "but I used to be with the movement, and I still have my connections. Plenty of people besides me are not happy with you, Billy O'Donnell. You've brought unwanted attention to certain people. Those same people were happy to help me out when I told them what you'd done to Sister Catherine."

In one swift movement, Ryan pulled the Luger out from within his jacket and shot Billy O'Donnell point-blank in the face. The loud and sudden boom of the gun reverberated through the warehouse. The rest of the gang looked on horrified, watching it all as if in slow motion, hardly believing what they had just seen. Billy's body fell back over the chair and slumped lifeless to the ground.

"Oh, fuck ..." was all Kenny had time to say when the echo of the loud gunshot faded and just before the still-smoking Luger turned in his direction. Then it was all screams and more gunshots as the old man blasted them coldly and deliberately, one after the other, as some of them tried to rush him. As he was between them and the only exit, they had no chance of escape. None of his bullets missed. By the time the clip was empty, Ryan was the only one left alive in the warehouse turned *abattoir*.

Stern-faced, Ryan put the Luger back inside his jacket, into the special holster he had had fitted there, and he turned and slowly walked back down the staircase to where he had left the gallon drum of petrol. Coming back up the stairs, he began splashing the petrol all over the place, being careful not to step in any of the rapidly forming pools of blood.

Satisfied, Ryan went back over to the staircase and took a box of matches from his pocket. He struck a match and threw it down into the petrol, which ignited easily. Watching the flames spread, the grim-faced figure went back down the stairs, and he could hear the crackling and roaring above him as he exited on the ground floor.

A window shattering in the floor above caused him to turn and look back. The warehouse was now well alight, and the flames would destroy most of the evidence of the crime he had just committed and the reason behind it. Forensic procedures wouldn't do much good in a fire of this magnitude. "Burn in hell!"

Ryan stepped over the dead body of the dog, squeezed through the loose piece of fencing, and walked calmly away from the scene before someone rang in the fire to the emergency services. They were slower in response these days with the cease-fire more or less holding, but they'd be here eventually. Best be away, sharpish.

Turned up his jacket to conceal the white dog-collar, and then went calmly along his way. One or two people came out onto the streets, attracted by the noise and flames. No one gave him a second glance.

Chapter Thirty-three

Hunched over his computer in his villa a few miles outside Buenos Aires, Gabriel studied meteorology reports for the United Kingdom. Lucifer had dropped off the map, and he had had no contact with him in over a week, which was unusual. Forecasts of a severe weather front heading north from the Bay of Biscay were causing lots of changes in air pressure over the United Kingdom, and that was one of the things that were always likely to trigger one of Lucifer's amnesiac attacks. He had suffered from them since being experimented on by Nazi scientists during the Second World War. They had left him with a blood disorder, and he had suffered cranial damage during his rescue.

"Still no news, sir?" asked Manuel, his faithful retainer. Manuel put the tray of coffee on the desk to one side of the computer. Gabriel could already smell the heady flavor of those coffee beans. Manuel poured, filling the cup.

"No, Manuel. It's been a week now. I know I shouldn't worry. He's had these attacks before. Sooner or later he'll snap out of it once the weather changes. Sometimes it can take a while, and UK weather is famous for its unpredictability." Gabriel picked up the cup and took a sip of the hot coffee, taking it black and unsweetened.

"I'm sure we'll hear from him soon, Master Gabriel," his old manservant reassured him.

Chapter Thirty-four

On the other side of the world, in Stockton on Tees in the United Kingdom, Luke was up in his room again, busy on his computer, when he heard the car pull up outside. At ten years old, the boy had developed quite an aptitude for computers. Encouraged by his father since he was old enough to sit upright on his father's knee, the boy had been well supplied with educational software and the latest computers to run that software on. Now he was interested in programming and was ahead of his game, academically speaking.

Half-interested in the noise outside, Luke picked his way across the bedroom floor, which was idly strewn with discarded homework and magazines. He just managed to avoid standing on one of his dad's CDs. Where did that CD case get to? His room was turning into a jungle, but he could never be bothered to do much about it despite his mother's threats.

He heard the sound of a car pulling up outside the house, and the boy glanced out of his bedroom window to see the figure of a man disembarking from a taxi at the drive of the vacant adjoining house. Luke remembered something his parents had been discussing about the place finally being rented out. The taxi pulled away, around the kidney-shaped green, and off up the road, leaving the man standing there in the rain, struggling with a couple of suitcases.

The figure looked up at Luke, framed nosily against the lit bedroom window, and, a bit embarrassed at appearing to be nosey, the boy moved away, back to his computer. He heard next door's front door open and close as he engrossed himself in his latest project. The house next door had been stood empty ever since the family there had moved away nearly six months ago. The husband had to move where his company wanted him, and his family had to go with him. The company had agreed to rent the property on his behalf, still fully furnished, but there had been no prospective takers until now.

Luke was far more interested in his latest computer project. It had started life as a hacking program he had originally gotten off one of his dad's former friends and then been modified to include a few utilities he had filched off various websites. He had been testing it whenever he got the chance, whenever his dad would let him on the internet, which wasn't as often as he would have liked. He didn't know why his father wouldn't get a network installed; dial-up was a pain.

The program was a sort of cross between a super search engine and a password-hacking utility designed expressly to find out what other people didn't want him to know. He was getting quite good at using it too. Though very careful to only view files so far, he had never dared to tamper with them.

Luke understood that as anonymous as the internet could be, there were ways and means of finding out who was doing what. You could always be traced. And until Luke solved that particular problem, he was content to just experiment and test the water. But it always helped to know just how much money Dad had in his bank account when you were trying to argue a case for a rise in pocket money.

His dad had gradually upgraded Luke's system to the point where it was even better than his own. At the moment, it was top of the range. Just a shame it wouldn't stay top of the range forever. Technology always marched on. There was always something else waiting just around the corner with computers.

Dad had said that was it. Anything else and Luke would have to find the money for it himself. That was why he'd bought him a CD writer—so he could make a bit of money for himself copying stuff for his friends. He could always get round his dad though if it came down to it. He would never refuse him anything for too long.

His dad wasn't as good at gaming as was Luke. He always accused Luke of cheating when he played him in Quake death matches, but then Luke was *very* good at those type of games, and he only cheated a *little* bit, even though he would never admit it.

Outside the window, Luke could see a brightening of the skyline over the rooftops to the east. About time. His mother always got depressed and bad-tempered by the seemingly endless rain at this time of the year. Kids didn't notice it as much, he assumed. Not in this part of the country, anyway. The north always seemed to get the worst of the weather, even here, sheltered as they were by the Cleveland Hills on the edge of the North Yorkshire Moors. They never seemed to get as much snow as other parts of the country, but they certainly got more than their fair share of rain.

Luke turned his attention to his pet snake in the vivarium, stepping automatically over a pile of clothes and schoolbooks without thinking about it. The snake was sleeping now, and Luke didn't disturb it. He took the water bowl out to refill it, carefully replacing the lid back on the tank. After already having lost one snake, he didn't want to lose another one. He never did find out what had happened to it.

Filling the small bowl in the bathroom, Luke returned to his bedroom to put it in the tank. He made a mental note to ask his mother to get a couple of pinkies from the pet shop next time she went down town.

Luke thought no more about his neighbor for a day or two, preferring to devote his time to annoying his sister, Emma. The two of them took it in turns to play their music too loud. "Emma, if you don't turn down that racket, I'll put a virus on your computer. I will," Luke shouted exasperatedly.

"I'll tell Dad," Emma counterthreatened, and so it went on. His sister was almost a year younger than him and was typically a royal pain. Daresay she had the same opinion of her brother. It was only rarely they agreed or cooperated on anything.

Chapter Thirty-five

The next few days were sunny, and Luke broke off from his computer studies and schoolwork to play football with some of his pals. He loved the game, playing it more than watching it. His local team had been kicked out of the premiership the previous season for not fulfilling a fixture, and it still rankled. He got quite aggressive on the pitch sometimes. His dad had always told him that you never went for a ball unless you intended to win it, and he tackled hard accordingly. He was the first to admit he was only an average player though. He played it purely for the enjoyment and the exercise.

Luke overheard his parents talking about the new neighbor, whom his mother had been talking to in the garden as he had been starting to do some work in the back of the house, which had been left to run wild since the previous occupants had moved. His name was Angell, and his first name was Luke too. *Strange coincidence*, the boy thought.

Luke heard noises from the back lawn one Saturday afternoon and went into his parents' bedroom to look out of the window. Mr. Angell was there digging some soil with a spade, trying to clear out some weeds in what used to be a vegetable patch.

The man was stripped to the waist, and Luke was surprised to see the large scars on the man's back, where his shoulder blades were. The scar tissue was quite pronounced too, almost looking as if some sort of growth had been amputated from his shoulders. As Luke stared fascinated, Mr. Angell turned around, looking up at the window as Luke stepped back quickly. Had he seen him?

Luke carefully crawled along the carpet out of the bedroom, not wanting the man to see him and think he was being nosey. In the garden, Mr. Angell smiled as he looked up at the window. Lightly, he shook his head. He wiped his forehead with the back of a hand and then returned to his weeding.

Ordinarily, Luke would have thought nothing much more about the scars he had seen on his neighbor's back, for lots of people have accidents, leaving some with more scars than others. But that week in Religious Studies, Mr. Henderson was going through the Old Testament, telling the story of God's holy host and the fall from grace of the Archangel Lucifer, which culminated from the War in Heaven, wherein Lucifer and his followers were cast out of heaven and given the antithesis called hell to rule over.

Luke frequently used the internet to help him with his school projects and had been amused to find that his own name, Luke, was a variation on the Old Testament name Lucifer. The name Luke Angell seemed both coincidental and intriguing, bringing to the forefront of his mind what he had been learning about in Religious Studies. Curiosity finally got the better of the boy, who had determined that it was time he put his homemade search engine to work and find out a bit about his new neighbor. He switched on his machine and logged onto the internet. Then he booted up "Rover," his pet name for the search engine he had put together.

A simple name search to start with, but that yielded a few hundred entries. He tried narrowing it down with amputee, country, sex, race, and off it went again. Rover warned him that cookies were being sent to his machine, which was odd, as that normally didn't happen until he actually logged onto a site. Bloody Windows. It was always doing that with Internet Explorer. Unfortunately for Luke, he thought nothing more of it as he concentrated on the six possible links left on his screen.

Rover was an extremely sophisticated program, able to dip into highly classified sites to search for its information, leaving no trace of its presence. Police databases, government classified sites. He had never left a trace before on any of his visits and so had a false sense of security with regard to his own abilities, considerable though they were. He no longer bothered to check just which sites he was logging onto to get his information.

He pulled down the first file, almost discarding it as he realized the dates were wrong, but then the photo popped up on screen, old though it was. Luke's jaw dropped. It was him or maybe his father. No, the photo was older than that.

This man had apparently died in 1897 according to the attached file. *Must be a relative of some sort*, thought Luke. The photo was a bit grainy as old photos sometimes are. If it was a relative, there was a terrific resemblance. Luke noted the file reference and called up the next one. No, not him. Neither was the next one. Then the photo hit him again, more modern, prewar, but him definitely. No, the dates were wrong again. What was this? Died 1943? This must have been his father. Luke checked the next entry.

Luke finally found him. This time he was sure of the photo. That was him all right. Strange how all three photos showed a man of about the same age. Angell, Lucifer. Lucifer? There it was. The Old Testament name. He hadn't heard of anyone called Lucifer these days though. Luke, Lucas maybe, but Lucifer? No way!

Then a weird expression crossed the boy's face as he connected the first and last names. Angell. Angel. Lucifer. The other two photos bore an uncommon likeness to the man. He knew records could be falsified. What had he stumbled onto here? It was too weird to give serious thought, or was it? All of a sudden, the boy remembered the two bits of scar tissue on the man's shoulder blades, and a chill went through him. Quickly, he typed in more keywords, impatient to learn more. Lucifer, Angel, War in Heaven. All sorts of associations flagged up on his screen, and he spent the next few hours going through them one by one.

Lucifer was originally one of the hosts, God's lieutenants who questioned God's will, and for this "sin," he and his followers were cast out of heaven. Popular belief held that Lucifer "became" Satan and ruled over hell, which was the antithesis of God's heaven. All of a sudden, his mother's voice intruded into his concentration.

"Luke! I've shouted for you three times. Your tea will be getting cold!" His mother's shrill voice echoed from the landing. Luke reluctantly logged off, promising himself he would do more research later that night as long as his dad wasn't using the internet. Cursing quietly, he switched the machine off and went downstairs for his evening meal. It would have to wait till later that night.

Chapter Thirty-six

A couple of days went by with Luke sending Rover off through cyberspace to fetch back sticks. The boy loved a mystery, and he thought he was onto one here. Mr. Angell behaved as you would expect any new neighbor to behave, bit of DIY'ing here and there, tidying things up.

Luke was out in the garden one afternoon, cleaning the pond out for a bit of extra pocket money, when he spotted the new neighbor taking in his washing. The man smiled at him in greeting, and Luke found himself responding with a wave. "So you're the other Luke?" the man asked half-laughing pleasantly enough. "I've met the rest of the family, so it was about your turn." Luke came over to the garden fence, getting over his reluctance somewhat. "Have you been avoiding me on purpose?" Mr. Angell asked with a knowing twinkle in his eye.

"No," Luke answered rather too quickly, feeling embarrassed about spying on him. "Just been busy, that's all," he explained.

"Yes, your mother told me you're always on your computer. Fun hobby?" he asked.

"Yes, it is. You have one?" Luke enquired and then noticed the studious look that came over Mr. Angell's features. He looked genuinely puzzled for a moment.

"Think I might have done at one time," he explained strangely. "Not now though." Then he noticed the way the boy was looking at him and explained further, "I don't always remember things too well these days." He smiled and brushed aside some of his hair to reveal more scarring on his skull which the hair almost concealed. "I was in a war somewhere. Got too close to something that blew up." He laughed off his injury. This close, Luke could make out some other smaller scars on the man's neck.

"You can't even remember which war?" Luke asked incredulously, thinking back to the research he had already done on Mr. Angell. The soldier with the remarkable resemblance in the First World War who had "died" of a head injury.

"Nope, some things just elude me. Can't be important. A war's a war, right?" Angell chuckled. "Seen too many," he added, seeming to drift off somewhere as his concentration lapsed. Then suddenly pulled his thoughts back into focus again.

"Excuse me for asking, Mr. Angell, but is your first name Luke or Lucifer?" He just had to ask the question. Mr. Angell seemed to consider for a second or two.

"I use Luke these days." He chuckled. "Don't hear of too many people called Lucifer now, do you? Lucifer's an old name, but it's the name on my passport, so I guess that's me," he added, again with the strange twinkle in his eye. "Well, got to get on with this laundry and stuff. Folks lived here left this lovely house in a bit of a mess." He continued to take down clothes from the line. "Nice talking to you, young Luke." He grinned.

"See you later, Mr. Angell." Luke nodded as he turned away.

Later that evening, Luke began to go over the research he had done so far. It kept poking away at him. Something really strange about all of this, but it was so unreal. If only he could actually call up Mulder and megababe Scully and ask their help on this one. Real life was just so weird at times.

He broke off momentarily as his dad came up the stairs to remind him that he expected to see Luke's homework finished on time for a change. Reluctantly, the boy got his school bag out and got stuck into it. Homework never seemed that important, and he sometimes forgot to do it. Detention was a pain.

Finally, he got his work finished and then went to switch on his computer. E-mail was waiting for him. The boy was instantly alarmed as he read the text …

Very interesting program you use but not as clever as the one I used to trace it. You don't know me, and I don't know you. But you appear to know a friend of mine. For his sake, please stop all your Internet activities in connection with him. If I can trace you, it won't be long before others do too. Both your lives would be in very great danger, should this happen.

Gabriel

Luke was shocked by the message, not so much about what it had implied, but the fact that someone, somewhere had managed to discover Rover. Not only that, but that same someone was clever enough to backtrack and reach him here. He didn't understand how they'd done it. At ten years old, he wasn't yet vain enough to think he was the fastest gun in the west, where computers were concerned. He was good, but there were people out there who were better. This Gabriel seemed to be one of them. *Gabriel*, another biblical sounding name, and who were these "others" he mentioned?

Luke accessed the next e-mail message as he pondered the significance of the first. Some sort of junk mail asking if he wanted to be put on the mailing list for free trial software. Personal details form to fill in, name, address, etcetera, and details of the types of software interested in. Might be something worthwhile after all, so Luke decided to fill it in later.

Internet time again. This time the boy started researching Gabriel's name. If there was any sort of connection between the two men, he intended to find it. Biblical again—Gabriel—also one of the host known commonly as the Angel of Death. Without a second name to go by, Luke's inquiries were limited, even using Rover, and the e-mail address was routed through a server in Australia. He was tempted to send an e-mail back to the mysterious Gabriel. He hit "reply" to the first e-mail and started typing.

On the other side of the world, the owner of the palatial estate was swimming in his private pool as he did most days at this hour when he was in the country. The lean athletic figure cut the water gracefully through an even twenty lengths, no more and no less. Then he got out of the water to dry himself with the towel previously laid out on a nearby chair near the sunshade. Almost swarthy skinned, dark hair matted to his forehead as he toweled himself dry. His body was that of a man in his early forties, though in fact, he was much, much older. Scar tissue on his shoulder blades the only remaining signs of any disfigurement.

As he put on a light robe, breakfast was served by his manservant of many years, Manuel Estevez, who was privy to most of his "young" master's secrets. He and his family had been well rewarded for his loyalty and, more than anything, for his friendship. Estevez loved the man as though he was his own son. He had known him most of his life.

As he left his master to enjoy breakfast, Estevez went back inside the mansion and up into the electronic nerve centre that kept control of the huge financial empire that very few people were aware all belonged to this one man, for a series of fronts, blinds, and aliases served to disguise and conceal the man's activities on the stock market and on the wider world stage.

He kept enough for his needs and contingencies. Many funds ended up as mysterious donations to worthy charities and the like, for his master wasn't a greedy man, never carried away with his affluence. He liked to maintain a low profile, and he had his reasons.

The wealth of computer equipment he had in an upstairs suite wasn't much to look at, but on closer inspection, it was the sort of apparatus most techies would kill for. Top of the range stuff, personally modified with technology few, if any, people had ever seen. He could afford to buy the best, and what he couldn't buy, he could manufacture in his private little workshop in the basement under the mansion.

As he did every day, Estevez collected the printouts from the e-mail, glancing at them as he did so. His master was not going to be pleased. The reply from England was not unexpected, but there was also a communication from "them." Manuel would never understand how his "young" charge could permit any form of communication with "them," even one as secure and firewalled as was set up here. Alonso Borgia was too resourceful a foe. He put the printouts on a tray and went back downstairs to deliver them with the morning papers.

The printouts were read impassively, with just a flicker in the dark eyes. He almost smiled as he read the one from England

Who are you, and who are we talking about? How did you backtrack Rover? Ekul.

"Naive or unknowing, this *Ekul* could get us all killed." He smiled grimly and put the printout down on the table.

"Or worse, sir," Estevez offered with a well-worn smile. For he knew the way his master's mind worked.

"Yes, or worse," he agreed. Then he went on to read the second e-mail.

We are closing in on him, Gabriel. Once we have him, we will have you. It is only a matter of time. A true statement or just an attempt to panic him into action? They knew he wouldn't let Lucifer fall into their hands again.

He crumpled the printouts up in his clenched fist. "Poor Lucifer, are you to be damned forever?" he asked himself. Estevez could only look down, for he knew what was going through Gabriel's mind. "Only the two of us left, and still they're not satisfied!" He cursed mentally. "If only ..."

"You blame yourself too much, sir," Manuel interjected. "My memory is still quite good unlike Lucifer's. I remember only too well how you rescued him from their clutches many years ago. You could have been killed yourself."

"Better that than knowing I was the last of my kind." Gabriel's head lowered. "I was too late as you know. The treatment had gone on too long, and Lucifer's mind was affected. Who else is left to blame but myself?" he tortured himself unnecessarily. "It was all a trap from the beginning." His mind was dredging up memories he had tried to forget—the catacombs under Rome, his last friend Lucifer imprisoned, helpless in that ... that abomination, and the tubes, those red tubes ... The memories pained him.

"History is rewriting itself again, sir. Surely, it is another trap?" Manuel asked, worried.

Gabriel looked up. "You have no idea just how many times history *has* rewritten itself, old friend," he stated, matter-of-fact. "But if it is a trap, they know it is a trap I must spring. I will not let them take him alive a second time. Mayhap this world is best rid of us," he added somberly. "Now, I must 'talk' to this *Ekul*."

Chapter Thirty-seven

Lucifer dreamed strange dreams. He didn't always understand them. Flight, soaring over plains and canyons, yet he had no honest recollection of being a pilot. He couldn't even remember ever having been in a plane, but then there were some things he couldn't remember at all.

The panic attacks came on quickly and quite unannounced. What had caused his head wound, anyway? His memory played tricks on him. Strange he still bore the scars, for he realized that he was a fast healer. Most minor cuts and grazes disappeared within hours. He noticed other things about himself that made him wary. His body weight, for instance, was considerably less than that of a normal person, yet he looked no different. Was healthy enough as far as he knew, but he had been reluctant to seek medical advice.

He had papers which identified him as Lucifer Angell. The passport was British, one of the old black ones, and it bore a lot of stamps from around the world—South America, Africa. He had obviously travelled a fair bit. The driving license bore the same name. Yet when he had tried to research his past, he didn't get very far before the trail had come to a dead end. It was as though he bore a made-up identity. Was he a criminal? He didn't know. The debit card he had on him gave him access to an account in "his" name, which held nearly a hundred thousand pounds. It was just as well the PIN number was written down on a card inside his wallet; otherwise, the card would have been useless to him. The number was certainly not memorable in his present state.

He was worried at first, thinking there must be something of a criminal connection. Yet, desperate, he had drawn money from the account. A few days later, he had found the debit had been replaced in his account. Queries to the bank only gave him an account number in the Cayman Islands as the source for the transfer. He had no idea how he would be able to track down his mysterious benefactor from just that one account number.

Surely, if the account was fraudulent, it would not be replenished, so he used the money where he needed to yet was inclined to travel the country as discretely as he could, in the hope of finding something or someone to jog his memory. Caution was somehow instilled into him.

He woke up to another windy day in the northeast of England. He liked the wind, the wild untamed weather, and they certainly got enough of it in this part of England. He found it hard to describe to himself just what he felt as the wind buffeted him, threatening to blow him off his feet at times. Elated and yet saddened at the same time. He didn't understand those conflicting emotions.

Clearing his head, he went for his morning shower, the smell of recent paint still clogging his nostrils. He had completely redecorated the inside of the house since moving in. Though some rooms were already furnished, he had not been happy with the color schemes, preferring muted indistinct colors, almost austere. He found such more relaxing.

From the bathroom, he heard the two children next door as they cleaned the leaves out of their little pond. The centre of their garden was designed in Asian fashion, lots of pebbles and stones, broken up with a few grasses and plants. Not a style he was used to, but it was pleasing on the eye.

There was still a bit of work to be done in the back garden of his new home, but today he would go and hire a car with which to explore the area. He never considered actually buying a car, for all the insurance procedures that were involved. Just so much easier to hire, and let somebody else worry about running repairs, etcetera.

It was a Saturday morning, and Luke was a late riser. He always stayed up later than he should, his father usually catching him still on the computer after midnight unless he was very quiet about it. It was one of the advantages of having a bedroom in the extension that was built above the garage, which his father now used as a minigym. You had two doors between you and the rest of the house to drown out any noise.

His mother rarely came into his room these days, refusing to tidy it up. Dad was always on at him to keep the place tidy, but Luke just couldn't keep it that way for long. He had already lost his first snake somewhere in this artificial jungle, and his Nana, upon hearing the news, flatly refused to come in the house these days. Luke found that mildly amusing, though annoying, that there was still no sign of the snake even after many months. Where could it have gone?

Eleven o'clock came and went before Luke stirred in his bed. He had to go into town to get some new pinkies for his latest corn snake, which he kept in the perspex tank in the corner of the bedroom. It would still leave him nearly seven pounds out of his pocket money. He let his computer boot up as he was getting dressed. Then he went into the bathroom to make himself look as close to human as he got these days. He was getting spots everywhere. Puberty sucks!

Coming back into his bedroom, he found an e-mail waiting for him. He opened it up and found another message from the mysterious Gabriel.

I need to "speak" to our mutual friend urgently. He is suffering from partial memory loss, so he may not remember my name. Call me on the following number ... 07720-467-4929. It's a mobile, which I can pick up anywhere in the world. Do not give the number to anyone else. Be very careful with any e-mails you may receive ... Gabriel.

Luke reread the message. Should he phone the number? He wanted to, and yet he decided to think it over while he had breakfast.

The phone call was forgotten till after he had got back from town later in the afternoon. Dad was still working away, and his Mom was off doing a shift at the supermarket, so he had the place to himself till Emma came back from the cinema with her friends. He gave one of the pinkies to his snake, Ka, and then decided to make the call.

The number rang, and he could hear connections being made to redirect the call. Then a voice came on the line. "Hello? Who is this?" Luke paused momentarily before answering.

"This is Ekul," he answered, feeling slightly awkward.

"Ah yes. Luke, isn't it?" The voice chuckled at the other end. "So you share the same name as my friend?" he stated. Luke was taken aback at how the unknown voice knew his real name then realized it wasn't too hard to work out from his nom de plume.

"Is Gabriel *your* real name?" he asked. The voice chuckled again, not in any sinister way.

"It's close enough," he replied.

"As in 'the Angel of Death' …?" Luke asked, feeling compelled to after the research he had done. There was a long silence on the other end of the phone.

"Well, now that's a name I haven't used in a *long* time," he answered, again with a touch of humor in his voice. Luke gasped audibly. "Come now, Luke, I'm sure you've been doing your research on me as well as on my friend. Hopefully you won't have found out that much. I keep a much lower profile, fortunately."

"Are you really Mr. Angell's friend?" he asked.

"Yes, you could even say we're family," he explained. "But since Lucifer's 'accident,' he gets these panic attacks, and his memory goes, sometimes for months at a time. A lot to do with the weather systems. I've been trying to find him since he went missing in the south of England some time ago. I see from the location of this call, he's still there," he added. Luke realized he must be tracing the call, but as he seemed genuine enough, he wasn't too bothered.

"How long before you've traced this call?" he asked, wanting Gabriel to know that he knew what he was doing. A small chuckle was heard at the other end.

"Already done, my young friend. I can be there in a week or so. But is it safe to come?" he asked. Luke wondered at the strangeness of his question.

"What do you mean?" he asked, doing some quick calculations. A week seemed a long time to get anywhere in this modern world.

"As I mentioned, there are other 'parties' interested in our whereabouts. Have you noticed anything unusual in the last few days?

Anything out of the ordinary? The same faces in a crowd or on the street? Parked cars that have only appeared recently? Any strange or unusual e-mails?"

"No, not really. Just run-of-the-mill stuff." He didn't think the software questionnaire was worth mentioning.

"In that case, I'll make arrangements. It's probably best if you say nothing to Lucifer. Once he sees me, everything will be okay. I'll call you later, now that I have your number." The line went dead, and there was a faint "click" on the line, which Luke didn't hear as he was already putting down the handset.

Across the Irish Sea, in a nondescript village church, Father Patrick Ryan smiled and switched off the tape recorder. He picked up the phone and dialed an overseas number. "Our local agents have been in touch. Gabriel has made contact." He spoke in fluent Italian. "It is time I supervised the operation directly. Please ask His Eminence to make arrangements to cover my absence. I leave this afternoon. This time there will be no escape for Gabriel. His love for his friend will be his undoing."

Chapter Thirty-eight

Gabriel made last minute preparations for his trip to England. It was safest to expect them to know he was coming. He had learnt from bitter experience just how far the shadow of the Holy Roman Church fell. His own allies were few these days, and the church had thousands upon which they could draw.

The flight was arranged into Faro, Portugal, and assuming all cross-channel routes would be watched, Gabriel was arranging to drive south to a small coastal resort, where he kept a small yacht. His appreciation of the winds had benefited him when he had learnt his seamanship, and he handled a small boat quite skillfully, needing no other crew than himself.

His internet enquiries had yielded a *Tees-net* site, which revealed quite a lot about the area where both Luke and Lucifer currently lived, including the details of the marina at Hartlepool, where he was making arrangements to berth in three days time. From there, it was only a fifteen minute drive to the boy's address, but he would take longer to make contact.

The boy had no idea what he had let himself in for with his enquiries. He was sure the church would avoid causing any harm to the boy and his family, but it wouldn't be the first time innocents had been caught up in his holy war.

Chapter Thirty-nine

The old Irish pub had changed names long since, obviously. The sign outside which proclaimed "The Wheatsheaf Arms" was old and weathered. Modernized now, it looked rather sterile, even amongst the signs of prosperity that EEC money had injected back into the farming community. A new extension had changed the original shape of the place on one side, but he still recognized it. *It had all been so different back then*, thought Ryan. He peered around through the open car window as Sister Mary drove slowly through the village, pandering to an old man's whim to revisit part of his youth.

The village was a little out of the way, requiring a detour of nearly two hours, but they were still in good time to catch the ferry to Liverpool. He couldn't resist the opportunity, having never been back here since his abrupt departure so many years ago. It was not as if there were anyone left alive of an age to remember him. His appearance had changed a lot since then, though not as much as might be thought. The change of name had been forced upon him by circumstance.

Dilby Wood came upon them so suddenly as to take his breath away. Not quite so dense but still as dark and foreboding, and he was of a mind to bet still used by the poachers as it was in his day, when he was the priest of this parish and known by a different name. He recognized the spot, even though it had been dark that night. The dip in the ground, just there behind the bushes. The place where he had sworn a second allegiance to a cause and a belief his forefathers had fought for, his family had died for. A cause which at times was at odds with the previous allegiance he had sworn to the church and which sometimes, in moments of solitude, caused him rare heartache.

"Would it be rude of me to ask what you're thinking, Father?" Sister Mary asked as she changed down the gearbox, steering easily around the bend and accelerating slightly along the narrow winding road. Ryan smiled wryly and shook his head.

"No, Sister. It's all right. Just reminiscing about my misspent youth. This was my first parish," he explained. "A place where a lot of things changed for me. A crossroads of sorts," he mused. Sister Mary took the answer at face value, though she had known Father Ryan for many years, a lot of his past was veiled with time. He didn't talk much about himself. No mention of family, but then again, she herself didn't like to dwell too much on the past either. The past was the past, and no amount of regret would ever change it. Time marched on, and you had to march with it. *Onward, Christian soldiers*, she thought, a sudden smile on her face for once. *Is that what we are?* she asked herself.

She had questioned her role in the Catholic Church many times over the years, the things she had done in its name. We are what events make us was the only answer she could come up with. It was so difficult trying to determine your own course in life, when it was forever bound and restricted by events and people around you. You just had to make the best of your lot in life.

The church had helped her through tragedy, and she now found a purpose to her life in her current role as Ryan's assistant. She still had normal human frailties and weaknesses. The thought of revenge was hard to deny once she had been told of their current assignment.

It was a sin, but prayers could not remove that thought from her mind. It was a nice thought. A thorn in her side which had long needed to be plucked, for it would not go away by itself. She had felt that pain for far too long. You never forgot the death of a child. She had never forgotten either of them, her own flesh and blood. Never been allowed to nurture them and watch them grow. Fate was cruel.

The Dublin ferry docked in Liverpool as normal. The grey rain beat down, welcoming the passengers to England in its inimitable fashion. An elderly priest accompanied a younger nun as they went through the formal customs and immigration procedures. Father Patrick Ryan and

Sister Mary were ushered through with the deference their positions were due. Special Branch operatives watching through two-way mirrored windows checked the names on the monitor screens in front of them.

Automatically, they checked the data banks for links with any known terrorist organizations, for the IRA particularly had made use of the clergy in the past. No links showed up, and so they gave the nod to the regular customs officials to let them through unhindered.

Carrying only small overnight bags, the two members of the clergy walked the short distance to the Avis stand, where Father Ryan collected the keys for the car they had booked in his name. Putting the bags in the rear seat, Father Ryan handed the keys to Sister Mary. His long legs were not really suited to driving long distances in such a small car. Still, anything bigger would not have seemed appropriate. He consulted the roadmaps as Sister Mary drove. The motorway system was good, and barring roadworks which were the curse of modern transport, they would be in Teesside by early evening.

By his reckoning, with luck, they would have maybe two days to prepare for Gabriel's arrival. He would not rush in blindly, for he would have learnt by past experience, and Gabriel truly had more "past" experience to call on. Still, Patrick Ryan was no spring chicken himself, and he owed Gabriel for the scars he now carried, which still caused him some discomfort in the damp weather. Idly, he fingered his side, where the scars lay.

Gabriel had tried and almost succeeded in killing him while Lucifer had inadvertently saved his life. How strange the workings of fate. Sister Mary noticed him staring into space. "Are you all right, Father?" she asked, concerned.

Father Ryan nodded, turning to her. "Yes, my dear, I was just thinking for a moment. This 'reunion' is long overdue." He smiled a vulture's smile, the loose skin beneath his jaw tightening for a moment.

"Yes," Sister Mary replied. "It is." Her fingers tightened imperceptibly upon the steering wheel as she drove, the wipers whipping back and forth across the screen, trying to displace the rain. Ryan noticed the mood change that suddenly came over her and smiled wryly.

Chapter Forty

Lucifer was flying again, and this time, he had wings. Someone was flying alongside him. Someone he knew, but the name just wouldn't come. It was a strange dream, full of javelins and stones and rope nets. Strange painted people clubbing and taunting, and then of him and his unknown friend finally being forced down onto a grey stone altar and sharp knives digging into his flesh as his wings were cut away.

Lucifer awoke in a cold sweat. The dream had been so vivid. Had it happened? Was it real? He didn't know anymore. *It couldn't be real, couldn't be*, he reassured himself as his breathing slowed. There were no angels. At least not anymore, and he drifted off back into an uneasy sleep.

Chapter Forty-one

The south of Portugal was beautiful at this time of the year, the weather not yet too hot, and the tourist industry not yet in full flow. The drive south through the countryside was enjoyable. He could have made better time on one of the motorways, but Gabriel preferred to cover his tracks well. A tail could be concealed less easily on these country roads, where there was less traffic.

He arrived at the dock just before dusk, and the harbormaster greeted him, alerted by the call Gabriel had made on his mobile phone earlier that day, instructing him to ensure the boat was fuelled and fully provisioned for a seven-day trip.

Gabriel went to a small inn, which he had frequented in the past, for an evening meal, which he washed down with a half bottle of local wine. Then he took a long, slow walk around the docks. Finally satisfied, he went aboard the small sloop. Digging out his maps, he spread them out on the table, mentally plotting his route along the coast and up the channel. The hazards of the channel were preferable to the more circuitous route up through the Irish Sea and along the Scottish coastline.

The weather front, slowly building out there in the Atlantic, would be here in a few days. If he timed it right, he would be sailing into Hartlepool on the back of the fierce storm. He stowed his few cases carefully. Set an automated alarm system on the hatches and then set his watch alarm for three in the morning, intending to slip away before dawn. He undressed and crawled into the small bunk. Get what rest he could while he could and enjoy the trip in the boat. He knew he wouldn't enjoy what lay ahead. Doubtless, the church would have some surprises in store for him. That was expected. He had a surprise for them too.

Chapter Forty-two

The Vatican City was a sovereign state. Inviolate and ruled by Papal decree. Its innermost workings were more of a secret than China's Forbidden City. The church still kept its secrets, and the most secret of these secrets was kept in an underground world, beneath the very streets of Rome, unbeknownst to the Italian populace. Shortly after the Vatican City was formed, certain of the catacombs in good repair were sealed off from the officially designated tourist areas, and the church set about renovating and modernizing the underground world. It was now a city beneath a city, visited only by the most trusted of the Holy Church's faithful. Scarcely a hundred people in the world knew its secrets.

Within this underground world, a dark ornate chamber was the setting for a meeting. The men who sat around the walnut table gave little thought to the priceless paintings and icons which adorned the walls, for they were long used to such opulence. The world's riches had long since been gathered for their benefit, and money and riches scarcely held any significance to them these days. Their skins were pale, some pale enough to clearly show the veins prominent and pulsing vibrantly with something which was no longer blood. They very rarely went out into the light of day, having become accustomed to their underground world. The sunlight was painful to their eyes. Those outside the innermost circles would know them only as strangers, the faces and identities receded with memory and time. Once, each had sat upon the See of Holy Rome. Today, that honor was reserved for another, one who, in time, would be offered the gift of Blood of Christ, should he be deemed worthy. Now this conclave was referred to as the Council of Vampires by the many underlings who served it.

"What word of Ryan?" The voice was leathery and came from the eldest, most venerated of their gathering. One or two of the others joined him in looking to the head of the table.

"He travelled to England last night to personally oversee the operation. Sister Mary accompanied him."

"Ah yes," chuckled another of them. "The delightful Sister Mary." He laughed as if at a personal joke. "I trust she will be invaluable to the success of the operation?" he asked.

"Indeed, she will."

"I still don't like it," rasped an aged wheezing voice, not from the eldest at the table but from one within whom the blood, the precious blood, was losing its efficacy. "Gabriel is not to be underestimated. We have paid for that mistake in the past. It might be a mistake to use her in this way," he cautioned.

"True … true … I understand the history, yet she has proven herself a reliable operative over the years."

"Very well then. Contingency plans." Alonso Borgia looked around the table at his familiars. "I trust enough of the faithful have seen our little 'miracle'?" He smiled, showing rotting teeth.

"You're not suggesting …?" interjected one of the others.

"It will be no contest and no risk," Borgia assured the others, who were quick on the uptake. "As good as Gabriel is, he is no match for our 'friend,' I assure you," he stated. A few nods around the table agreed with him.

"The conditioning is strong enough?" queried one doubter.

"Oh yes." He chuckled in reply. "The brainwashing is quite complete, reinforced by his known hatred of Gabriel, and even if it isn't, we have other means of persuasion. Modern drugs and technology are so efficient."

"I preferred the methods of the Inquisition myself," complained another.

"You old fool! This is the modern age now. Learn to embrace it as the rest of us have done," another scoffed at the derision.

"How then will we put our pawn in position?" asked one of them.

"Why, he'll fly there, of course!" the aged one chuckled, and after a few moments, the room reverberated to a cacophony of unholy laughter.

Chapter Forty-three

"Sure, and that's the prettiest damn nun I've seen in me life, Sean!" One of the IRA men chuckled to his friend as the both of them watched Sister Mary get out of the car in the car park , her bare legs on display momentarily as she swung them out of the car. Both she and Father Ryan wore normal civilian clothes, having stayed overnight in a local hotel.

"Worth a few Hail Marys, to be sure." Sean rubbed his crotch suggestively as he chuckled with his friend.

"You'd get more than a few for fucking a nun, and that's for sure." Davey laughed. "Damn me if it wouldn't be worth it though," he admitted as he watched the nun walk towards them. He threw his cigarette on the ground and stood on it to put it out.

Davey was the older and taller of the two men. In his midthirties and a good ten years older than the more impressionable Sean. His ginger hair was short whilst Sean grew his black hair a bit longer. Both were dressed casually in jeans. Davey had on an old grey roll-neck sweater whilst Sean wore a simple white T-shirt. They just looked like ordinary friends meeting up in a car park.

The local clergy knew nothing of their visit, and it would be kept that way. Father Ryan wore a dark green alpine weatherproof jacket, hood down despite the fine rain. Sister Mary wore a longer coat, her blonde hair tied back into a long braid. They greeted each other as typical friends meeting by chance after Ryan recognized the two men. An innocent enough place for a meeting, plenty of people about so their presence wouldn't be too noticeable.

They went into the Fairfield pub and took a table near the back of the lounge. Davey went to the bar to order drinks. A street map of the area was unfolded on the table, pencil marks indicating the area of concern. Sean explained the problem.

"Patrick and Con are set up here and here," he said, indicating the entrance from the main road to the cul-de-sac where Lucifer now stayed and the only other possible exit down through the walkway along the open green. "We can't get any closer without being too obvious," he explained. Ryan nodded.

"Gabriel will have the same trouble," he mused. "He won't try it. He'll find a way to get to him away from the house."

"How many cars do you have on standby?" asked Sister Mary.

"Including yours, that makes four," Davey answered. "Pat and Con have one each parked close by. We swap the cars around every six hours during the day. At night, we get in closer, just use the one car parked down the street, though within sight of his house."

"We've got the mobile phones to keep in touch, and we got lucky with a rented house less than a mile away. Anything happens, we can get there in a few minutes," he reassured Ryan.

"I know Gabriel," Ryan warned. "If anything happens, you might not have a few minutes!" They were feeling cocky. Neither of them had gone up against anyone like Gabriel before. He was not going to tell them anything further.

"We've been up against the SAS, Father. We know what it's all about, don't you worry," Sean laughed over the top of his beer.

"Laddie, the man we're waiting for would eat your precious SAS bogeymen for breakfast!" he warned. "You are to take no chances. Confer with me before taking any action," he insisted. "I'll take one of the phones. Myself and Sister Mary are booked into the Swallow Hotel. It's not far," he explained. "If Lucifer moves, you phone me instantly. We can be with you in ten minutes or so. You can direct us by phone if he's mobile."

"Sounds far too complicated to me, Father. Why not just kill him and have done with it?" asked Sean.

"You'll find him a rather hard man to kill," answered Sister Mary.

"Besides, dead, he's no use to us. We have our reasons for keeping him alive. You don't need to know them," answered Ryan. "What have you observed about Lucifer's daily routine?" he asked.

"About nine o'clock, he comes out of the house and walks to the newsagent's on Oxbridge Lane. Then he walks back through the park and then along the walkway. If it's raining, he skips the park and comes straight back, along the main road. He collected a hire car yesterday, so he's obviously thinking of travelling further afield. Only times he's been out of the house since we started watching him," Davey explained.

"Sometimes, the kid from next door goes to see him," Sean added. Father Ryan seemed to be thinking things through in his mind for a moment.

"Ah yes, the boy," Ryan mused. "His curiosity it was that brought us here." He chuckled. "Sister Mary will work on the park angle. A chance meeting next time he goes through there. Mary, you'll have to move into the safe house from tomorrow. Make him think you live locally." Mary nodded. "Very good, that should do for now, but don't anyone get too cocky. Lucifer might not be as dangerous as Gabriel, but that's only because he hasn't had the same practice. Do not underestimate him," Ryan warned. "Lucifer's suffering a bout of amnesia as the result of an old wound. That's our only advantage at the moment. We know where he is, and we know Gabriel is trying to find him. Ideally, this operation will end with both of them in our power. Gabriel will do anything to keep his friend alive, and that may be the key to taking him."

Chapter Forty-four

The next day, Father Ryan's mobile phone went off as he and Sister Mary were enjoying a light luncheon in the hotel restaurant. He answered it, maintaining a calm outward exterior. Sister Mary watched his face for any hint of what was going on.

"He's mobile. The boy is with him." Ryan recognized Sean's voice. "The boy's mother came out with them and gave the boy something like a carrier bag. Full, it was. Then she let her son drive off with him. We're following about two hundred yards behind them. Looks like they're heading for the A19."

Ryan checked the weather outside the restaurant window. He had also checked the weather forecast. It was still sunny today, and if the weather forecast was to be believed, the stormy weather wouldn't be here until tomorrow. He knew how Gabriel worked by now, had studied him, crossed swords with him once, and almost a second time in Marseilles. Other operatives had filed brief reports on him over the years. Those reports all added up, and though far from complete, they served to build up a picture of the man and his methods of operating.

"Maintain a discreet surveillance. I'm not expecting any contact before tomorrow. Check in every half hour. Ryan out." He pocketed the phone and resumed his meal. "How did your 'chance' meeting with Lucifer go this morning?" he enquired.

"I couldn't very well throw myself at him, Father." Sister Mary showed her annoyance, pausing with her own knife and fork. "All I did was say hello. Anything else would have been too forward, might have put him more on his guard instead of at ease."

"Tomorrow, you'll have to step things up," Ryan insisted. "Gabriel will make contact in the next forty-eight hours if he's true to form. He'll spot those two too easily. That's the trouble with England, you need better resources for an operation of this type." He took another mouthful of food, chewed, pondering. "I've had word from Rome." He waited till her eyebrows raised before continuing. "They think we need backup. I don't think we do. You and I, more importantly you, should be able to get the upper hand on Gabriel this time." He smiled a vulture's smile, the loose folds of flesh tightening under his chin.

Gabriel, at that moment, was eyeing the dark weather front approaching from the Atlantic. He was sailing quite comfortably up the coast of Portugal, heading for the English Channel. It would be touch-and-go whether he would make Hartlepool before the worst of it hit. His small yacht wasn't made to ride out a storm of that magnitude on the open sea.

He made an adjustment to the sails, stepping over his safety rope. If the winds increased too much, he would need to rely on that safety rope all the more to prevent himself being blown off his feet on the slippery deck.

Chapter Forty-five

The village was called Osmotherley. Picturesque and not too big, just on the edge of the North Yorkshire Moors. It was a scant half hour's drive from Central Teesside, just off the A19. Luke had volunteered to show Lucifer some of the local sites of interest, and his parents had given their permission. He was being taken first to see something called the Sheep Wash.

Luke directed Lucifer left at the junction, and the road wound up at a steep angle, twisting and turning its way up into the Cleveland Hills, towards the very northernmost edge of the North Yorkshire Moors. Before long, the road overlooked a reservoir down to the right, which filled the valley between the hills and the sharp rise escarpment that delineated the boundary of the moors.

The car labored on the steep road, and Lucifer changed down to second gear before accelerating once more. As the road evened out and wound in and out of a copse of trees, which kept obscuring the view, Luke pointed ahead to where Lucifer could make out a sandy cliff dropping down from the edge of the moors into the valley, where a stream trickled back towards the reservoir.

Lucifer soon discovered why the place had its name, as he had to stop on more than one occasion, as odd sheep just wandered into the road. Cars passed him going back the way he had come. Far ahead, he could make out the colorful rows of cars, which were parked up in the makeshift car park. Not too many people out today, but then that was to be expected with the haphazard weather forerunner of the forecast storm.

Looking up, he noticed the thick summer clouds, heavy with rain, being blown furiously across the sky by the strong gusty winds. He pulled into the car park and easily found a place to park the car. Luke was out almost before he'd switched the engine off, with the enthusiasm of youth, running off towards the stream.

"I love this place. It's great for climbing." He laughed. "Race you to the top!" he cried back over his shoulder challengingly. Lucifer laughed as he got out of the car, watching the boy leaping across the stepping stones like a gazelle. There was a worn semipathway, extremely steep and littered with large boulders and stones, which ran up one side of the sandy cliff face, and the boy was already scampering up it, loose earth falling away beneath his trainers.

The idea of a race appealed to him for some unknown reason, and he began running and jumping the stream with a single bound, tearing up the path after the boy. "Thought you wanted a race?" He laughed as he easily overtook the boy, enjoying the startled look on Luke's face, who tried all the harder to catch him up, but Lucifer reached the top fully thirty seconds before the boy and was stood admiring the view as Luke huffed and puffed his way to the top.

"How did you … catch up … so fast …?" the boy gasped, getting his breath back. Lucifer looked honestly bemused.

"I just ran after you. Must be good at running, eh?" he chuckled. Truly he hadn't thought anything of his running and climbing ability. It must have been more than two hundred feet up that steep pathway.

As the boy caught his breath, Lucifer looked out over the whole of Teesside, a marvelous view. The whole area laid out before him, cut into a vast bowl-shaped valley, the industrial areas, such as ICI over to the east, urban areas to the north, vanishing into the distance, and the farmlands to the west. Behind him, to the south, was wild moorland, the heather all purples and wild yellows. God's Country they called it locally. *What a strange description*, he thought.

The heavy clouds scattered across the skies, and the wind was wilder up here on the edge of the moors. Amusingly, on an impulse, he took the bottom corners of his windbreaker jacket and held them out to the sides, feeling the strong winds filling the material … and then a mad moment of panic as he felt his feet leaving the ground.

"Ahhhhh …" He dropped back to the ground as he let go of his jacket. The wind merely buffeted him now, and as the boy turned around to see what had happened, Lucifer felt strangely embarrassed. "It's nothing … just the wind caught me off balance there for a second," he explained.

"Sure is strong up here," the boy agreed. "Bet a kite would fly for miles," he enthused.

For a brief moment there, the feeling of levitation had caused such joy. Then fear had overtaken him, and he had panicked. He felt at ease with the wind, actually enjoyed the windy weather. His emotions left him strangely exasperated.

"Let's go for a walk, maybe chase some sheep …" Luke laughed, and Lucifer found himself smiling again, setting off after the boy who was already following one of the well-worn paths through the heather. He walked into the wind, enjoying its strangely familiar caress.

Chapter Forty-six

Sister Mary reluctantly moved into the safe house set up by the IRA men on Ryan's orders. She must appear to live nearby if she were to arrange a plausible friendship with Lucifer. She moved her few belongings into the main bedroom. The second bedroom was occupied by two bunk beds, which were used by the Irishmen in shifts. From now on, the men would keep a low profile and, if noticed, would pretend to be her two cousins just over the water for a holiday.

She didn't like the arrangement but understood the necessity. Killers always made her uneasy, and she had noticed the way they looked at her. She had long since become used to such looks, knowing she still looked good, though not in any vain way. She was used to handling men, yet she felt threatened by them in such forced close contact.

Patrick and Con were happy enough to meet her. Patrick was an old-timer in his fifties with thinning grey hair. Con was around thirtyish, short black hair matching a short black goatee beard. He was muscular and barrel-chested, the complete opposite of Patrick, who looked emaciated.

They called her "Sister" with uncalled for levity, though were polite enough most of the time. She noticed more than a few empty whiskey bottles in the house as she did her best to settle in, tidying the place up. On the off chance that Lucifer might visit the house in the next day or so, it mustn't appear the pigsty it was at present. The two men smiled to themselves as they appreciated having a woman around to do the housework. She tried to ignore the cigarette smoke as she felt the old cravings itching away under her skin.

Tomorrow, if all went well, she would break the ice with Lucifer, another chance meeting that would pave the way for her to spend more time with him till eventually Gabriel made contact.

Gabriel. She could still remember how he looked when last she'd seen him, eyes wild and death in his heart. She shivered inwardly. After so many years, just the mere thought of him could still have such an effect on her. He owed her a life, and she was going to take his in repayment. Ryan preached patience but promised that she could have her vengeance when Gabriel's usefulness to the church had ended.

Out in the English Channel, Gabriel swore as the wind started to pick up. The storm wasn't far behind him, its wind filling his sails. He trimmed them back, respecting the wind's awesome power.

He altered course as the huge oil tanker bore down on him, its captain probably trying frantically to raise him by radio, having picked him up on radar directly in the tanker's path. Gabriel was maintaining radio silence, not wanting to risk any unnecessary transmissions being picked up. With luck, he would ride the storm into Hartlepool before the dawn.

Chapter Forty-seven

That night, Patrick and Con took over surveillance, relieving Sean and Davey, who were put in the picture about their houseguest. "Sure and a bit of female company would help us all relax a bit," chuckled Davey.

They let themselves in the front door when they got to the house. They could hear Sister Mary in the bathroom with the shower running. Sean chuckled to his friend, holding a finger to his lips, and they crept up the stairs.

There was no key in the keyhole, and Sean bent down to peer through. "Damn, she's not a very trusting soul is the good sister," he whispered in amused frustration. "Sure and she's hung something up over the keyhole." He stood up and turned away, following the beckoning arm of Davey as he went into the main bedroom.

Davey chuckled as he held up the fresh underwear Sister Mary had laid out on the bed. "Very nice. Not exactly your standard convent issue, is it, Sean?" he whispered as he peered over the top of the obviously expensive slip he held up.

"Bit of a dark horse, this 'Sister' of ours, eh?" mused Sean. "We'd best get downstairs and grab something to eat." He turned to leave the room. Davey took a bit longer, enjoying the feel of the silk between his fingers before he finally rearranged the underwear back on the bed and tiptoed quietly down the stairs.

Once downstairs, Sean opened the front door once more and closed it noisily enough for the woman upstairs to hear, and then he and Davey went into the kitchen to make themselves something to eat from the groceries they'd earlier stocked up with.

Upstairs, in the shower, Sister Mary paused in her ablutions as she heard the door slam shut, realizing who it would be. She continued soaping herself, lowering her head under the hot spray, luxuriating in the warmth and wetness as her long blonde locks matted against her skin.

She had avoided showers for so many years yet had no choice here, for there was no bathtub. The intimacy of the spray and the cubicle brought back memories both pleasant and unpleasant. Her nipples were hard as she soaped them leisurely with the soft sponge, arousing herself almost unthinkingly …

So long … so damn long ago … Her other hand slid automatically down her still sleek belly, fingers delving beneath the golden hair. Moaning, she leaned forward, her head touching the tiles. Her breath came faster, shallower, breathing through the cloying steam as her own excitement quickened.

She gasped, the orgasm coming so quickly … too quickly … and the hot spray of the shower washed away the salty tears that now ran down her cheeks as she sobbed helplessly.

The edge of the storm had hit an hour ago, the sea swells rising to four or five feet as Gabriel struggled to keep control of his sails. Automatic steering took care of course corrections, but he would shortly have to switch back to manual as he approached the Teesside coast. Already in the distance, he could see the dancing mooring lights of the big tankers all lined up, awaiting permission to load or discharge at the Teesport refinery. The lights were relatively still, in seeming contradiction to the waves around him, which tossed his small craft about as if on a whim.

The rain was lashing down, making visibility difficult. Still two hours from dawn as he checked his watch. On time. Gabriel's teeth grated as a trough opened up beneath his yacht, a cross wave catching the bows just as she dipped. Water flooded the deck, sweeping him off his feet, and he was grateful for his lifeline as he regained his footing.

An hour later, Hartlepool's marina lights beckoned, and Gabriel switched to the engines as he trimmed his sails once more. Expecting him, the harbormaster met him at the end of the jetty as he navigated into the calmer waters and directed him to where a berth had been reserved.

He soon negotiated the marina and found the mooring position, where he cut the engines and made fast the ropes fore and aft, leaving just enough slack to account for the rising and falling of the tide. Exhausted, he stripped off his oilskins and then the rest of his clothes. He crawled into the warm bunk bed and was soon asleep, dreaming of warmer climes in times past.

Chapter Forty-eight

In the 'safe' house, 'Sister' Mary slept fitfully. She had retired earlier than normal rather than share a room with the two Irishmen, who proceeded to work their way through a bottle of Kilkenny whiskey with consummate ease. They had ignored her gentle persuasion to keep a sober head in case Ryan or one of the other two men phoned.

Her dreams were dark. Deafening gunfire all around her. Explosions … men dying—correction, being slaughtered by a dark-haired man, whose eyes were filled with an unholy fire.

Her sleep came to an end as the smell of whiskey invaded her nostrils. Her eyes opened to see the soiled bulging underpants of the one called Davey, stood close by her bedside. Trying to maintain her calm, she turned her head slightly on the pillow, looking up past the string vest, which was his only other attire, to see him still swigging from the neck of another bottle.

"Get out," she said as calmly as she could. Davey was over six feet tall and, though slimly built, a good few pounds heavier than she. He was also a lot stronger … a curse of the female sex. Davey just laughed and made to sit down on the bed with her.

She tried to sit up, but a meaty hand grabbed her throat, forcing her head back down onto the pillow. "Ahhhhh … you're hurting …" She tried to flail her legs, but the blankets were too restricting.

"Don't be so unfriendly, 'Sister,'" Davey chuckled. "Have a drink." With his other hand, he brought the bottle to her face, forcing the neck into her mouth and upending it, the warm whiskey filling her mouth as she gasped and spluttered, her hands trying to force the bottle back.

He forced her to swallow or choke, laughing as she coughed the fiery liquid back up, and then relented somewhat, using his forearm to pin her neck back down onto the pillow. "Sure and that's better, 'Sister.' Much more friendly," he said as he swung his legs onto the bed, his free hand moving aside the bedsheets and finding her breast, cupping and squeezing it roughly. "I usually like 'em with bigger tits." He laughed coarsely before his face descended on hers, bruising her lips with his unshaven stubble as he forced a kiss on her.

She struggled anew under him. "Get off me," she cried as his mouth released hers. "You drunken bastard!" The Irishman laughed anew, his hand exploring her body further beneath the sheets as she squirmed, still restricted.

"Sure and that's no language a nun would use," he leered, breath hot in her face. "But then you're no fucking nun, are you, Mary? Nuns don't wear silk knickers!" He laughed, hand clutching her cruelly between her legs.

"Ahhhh …," she cried out. "You're hurting me," she pleaded, desperate. Davey laughed, enjoying his domination of the woman. Sean appeared in the bedroom doorway. He too had been drinking heavily.

"Is the good sister in the mood for some fun 'n' games, Davey?" He chuckled, rubbing the swollen bulge in the front of his trousers. He eyed Mary's seminudity as she lay back on the bed with Davey's hands on her.

"You're just Ryan's fucking hoor, aren't yer?" he leered. "Well you can be my hoor tonight, woman. I'm sure the good Father won't mind if we get a piece of yer ass too." He chuckled, the whiskey splashing out of the bottle soaked her pillow as he began to slide under the sheets with her.

"All right … all right …," she gasped. "Stop choking me, will you?" she pleaded. "I'm no nun, you're right," she admitted. Davey laughed as she confirmed his suspicions. "If you're gentle with me, I'll do what you want. Just don't hurt me, please …," she pleaded.

"Sure and I don't want to hurt you, darlin'," Davey leered, arm coming off her neck as he reached to put the bottle down on her bedside table. "That's not want I want to do to you at all," he leered, stripping the sheets back from her legs and running his hand back up the inside of her bare thigh once more.

"Okay … okay then … Come on … come on …," she urged, spreading her legs. Davey cackled at her sudden eagerness and rapidly began to remove his underpants. Fighting the revulsion she felt, Mary moved one leg further, drawing it back as she urged him on. "Yes … I want it …" Davey chuckled gleefully as he began to kneel between the woman's legs … the one long white leg drawing back as he moved forward, and then his world turned to agony as that same leg shot forward, driving into his exposed genitals with the fury only a woman could inflict.

"Ahhhhgggg … Kkkkkkkkk …" He doubled up on the bed, clutching himself as he shrieked. "Jaysus, ye've killed me …," he sobbed. "Jaaaayysussss …"

Mary spun quickly off the bed as he fell forward, one hand scooping up the whiskey bottle by the neck and smashing it with all her strength against the side of the man's head. Glass, whiskey, and blood splattered on the carpet as Sean looked on through the open doorway.

Still half-drunk himself, he swayed there a second or two, taking in the scene before him. "Christ, woman, you've killed him!" he exclaimed as he saw Davey laying there on the floor, blood pouring from the side of his face where the glass had cut him.

Mary was stood over him, the remaining half of the broken bottle still in her hand, and she was ready to use it. "No, I haven't. But if this animal comes near me again, I will. Get him out of here!" She spat on the unconscious Davey, and Sean tried to get his friend back onto his feet. Failing, he began to drag him out of the room. Mary picked up the discarded underpants with distaste and threw them out on the landing after them.

Trying hard to control her breathing, she slammed the bedroom door shut and stood with her back to it. "I may be no nun, but I'm no one's fucking whore!" she spoke to herself.

Calming down, she pulled the bedside table over against the door so that at least she would get some warning if anyone tried opening the door again. Going over to the dresser table, she put on the small light to examine the bruises on her neck. Red enough, but she knew from experience that marks as slight as that would be gone by morning. Nothing left to need explaining to Lucifer.

Around her neck, the little gold crucifix caught the light, still glistening brightly, almost an antique now. She clutched it momentarily before bringing it up to her lips and kissing it.

Chapter Forty-nine

Lucifer enjoyed his morning walks. He didn't mind whether the sun was shining or not. It most certainly was not at the moment. As he walked, the strong winds buffeted him. The sky was dark with heavy clouds, though it had not started to rain as yet.

Century Radio weather forecast had alerted him to the storm front that was approaching from the Atlantic. He was looking forward to it.

He alternated the papers he bought at the newsagent, sometimes one of the tabloids with the shocking sensationalism, sometimes the broadsheets with the economical and political stories. Depended on the mood he was in and what was happening in the world according to the television reports. Today he bought a computer magazine, having been really fascinated by some of the stuff young Luke had shown him. He wanted to learn more about it.

He had enjoyed yesterday's walk on the moors and so had the boy. Luke had promised to take him to some of the area's other major landmarks later in the week, like Roseberry Topping, the tallest point of the Cleveland Hills, Captain Cook's Monument, Fylingdales, Brimham Rocks. They all sounded fascinating, and he was eager to see them. It was good of the boy's parents to allow him to act as his guide during the school holidays.

He took the short way back along the green, the grass falling away beside the tarmac path towards the small stream which ran through it. Some children were down there at the moment, one on either side of the water, throwing a ball from side to side while their dog kept leaping the stream trying to catch it. He chuckled as he admired the dog's efforts.

Looking back up, he noticed that attractive young blonde woman approaching through the old tunnel under the raised walkway, her high heels echoing on the brick walls. He had seen her first yesterday, said "good morning" to her out of politeness. He had gotten a brief smile and a return greeting from her as they'd passed in opposite directions.

Today it looked like they were both heading towards the small bridge over the stream as she turned down the path some yards ahead of him. He was just about to turn down the same pathway himself, when he heard her give out a sharp cry and turned his head back towards her just in time to see her tumble to the ground.

"Owwww … Owwwww …," she cried as she rubbed her ankle. Lucifer rushed to her side, concerned.

"Are you all right? I saw you stumble." He crouched down beside her. The woman looked up, a pained expression on her face.

"My ankle. I think I've sprained it …," she gasped, still rubbing. Lucifer examined the ankle, not failing to notice the expanse of leg that was now on show as her skirt was in disarray. He concentrated on the ankle, gently putting his hands on it as she gasped again.

"Sorry …," he apologized as he examined it. There was a slight swelling already forming. "Yes, you're going to need that strapping up," he stated. "Do you live near here?" he asked, offering a hand to help her back onto her feet. She winced as she tried to put her weight back onto the ankle.

"Just a few streets away," she said, biting her lip against the pain as Lucifer put his arm around her and tried to help her to walk. She did so with difficulty, whimpering with each step. Lucifer realised within a few steps that it was going to be a difficult walk for her.

"Okay, this is how we'll do it," he said, sweeping her up off her feet and into his arms.

"Ohhhhh," she gasped. Lucifer looked concerned.

"Sorry. Did I hurt you there?" he asked.

"No," she said, allowing herself to melt against Lucifer's chest. "You just took me by surprise there. I wasn't expecting you to be so strong."

"You're light enough. It's no trouble." Lucifer smiled, enjoying the feel of the woman in his arms. "Now if you'll direct me, I'll take you home. It's best if you keep the weight off your ankle for a few days." He walked easily with her in his arms.

Mary directed him left and out towards Oxbridge Lane as they exited the cut. Then, left again up towards Green Lane. "What will the neighbors think?" she half-joked, and Lucifer laughed. He carried her to the door of a house in Windermere Road, and she gasped again as he gently set her down on the step.

"There you are, safe and sound," he pronounced. "Can you manage from here?" He smiled.

Mary fished in her handbag for her keys and opened the door. Seeing she still needed help, Lucifer helped her into the house. "Thank you … thank you so much …," she gasped, still in pain, allowing Lucifer to help her into the front room, where she sat down on the sofa. "There's a medicine cabinet on the wall in the kitchen with some bandages. Could you get them for me?" she asked.

Lucifer went through to the kitchen, noticing a man's jacket hung up in the hall. He returned shortly with the bandages. "You'll have to phone your husband and let him know you've hurt yourself," he suggested as he began unwrapping the bandage.

"What …? Oh this …" She forced a grin, holding up her left hand and displaying her ring. "My husband died. I just wear it out of habit," she explained. "I came over here from Ireland to get away from all the violence. My two brothers are staying with me at the moment, trying to find work over here. They don't want to go back either," she quickly explained, gasping as Lucifer eased her shoe off and raised her leg. "I'm Mary, by the way," she finally introduced herself.

"Call me Lucifer," he said, and she laughed mischievously for a second.

"How devilish. Why not Luke?" she asked.

"One's a derivative of the other, so a new neighbor of mine says. It's an old name. I like the sound of it," he explained, remembering the boy's comments. "Seems to suit me." He chuckled.

Keeping his gaze deliberately on her ankle and avoiding that damned attractive leg, Lucifer began to dress the ankle before the swelling increased, crisscrossing the bandage to give a good support to the damaged ligaments …

"You've done this before. Are you a doctor?" Mary asked.

"No." Lucifer was puzzled for a moment. He didn't think he was. "It just seemed the right way to do it," he answered.

Mary watched him as he dressed her ankle. It would heal itself in an hour or two, and it had taken her ages to find the right spot to commit the injury. The high heels had helped somewhat. She must be careful to keep the bandage on for a few days, so he would not think it odd.

He reminded her a lot of Gabriel, though blond where he was dark. Chiselled, handsome features. She felt a pang of regret for the deception, but it was necessary. She owed Gabriel more than she could forgive, though she had prayed to find forgiveness in her heart over the years.

"There, that should do it. Try it," he suggested, offering her his hand to help her back onto her feet. Gingerly, she put weight on it, wincing only slightly this time.

"Yes, that's much better … I think I can manage." She walked unaided across the room with a slight limp, though Lucifer walked by her side to assist if need be.

"Well, I'd better go then," he said as he started to walk out of the room. Mary followed him, limping slightly and favoring the ankle.

"Thank you so much for helping me. It was very kind of you." She lowered her head slightly, big eyes looking up at him from under her brow. Lucifer turned in the doorway as if to say something, when she leaned forward, putting a hand on his shoulder, and kissed him lightly on the cheek.

Lucifer was taken aback slightly, almost blushed in fact. "I'll … I'll be on my way then …," he spluttered. "Would you mind if I called by to see if there's anything you need? Best to keep off that ankle for a day or so," he suggested.

"Yes, I'd like that. It's very thoughtful of you." She smiled. "There's my number there on the phone," she said, pointing out the handset on the hall table. "You can phone me if you want. I'd like to talk to you again," she admitted with another bat of her eyelashes.

Lucifer could feel himself being drawn in. She was an attractive-enough-looking woman. Yes, he would call her. "Well, good-bye for now." He turned and started off down the path as she waved from the doorstep.

She watched him go and then finally closed the door. Patrick and Connor were watching from the top of the staircase. "He fell for it then, did he?" Connor asked.

"Yes," admitted Mary with an ache in her heart. "He fell for it."

Chapter Fifty

Hartlepool was filling up with shoppers by the time Gabriel surfaced from his warm bed aboard the yacht. He had allowed himself five hours sleep, his watch alarm reaffirming his own internal alarm.

He went into the galley, pausing to switch the immersion heater on in the shower cubicle before cooking himself some breakfast. A simple cooked breakfast of eggs, beans, and bacon, mopped up with a slice or two of bread. Not the healthiest of fares for most people, but then he could eat most things without any lasting harm to his system.

He felt better with something inside him. A hot shower would complete the job of waking him up. Not as powerful as he would have liked, the shower still did its job, and he felt a lot more refreshed as he toweled himself dry.

Some twenty minutes later, hair still damp, he walked along the wooden jetties, admiring the modernization work that had been recently completed along the waterfront. Apartment complexes which must cost a fortune in rent. Yachts of all shapes and sizes were moored here with few empty berths.

He, first of all, found a bank along the high street, where he could change a small amount of escudos, though not enough to be noticeable. The English currency he came out with should suffice him the few days he expected to be here.

Then he went up the street and along York Road where most of the shopping area was, and into a stationery shop when he spied through the window that local maps were on sale.

He browsed through a few and ended up purchasing a detailed street map of the Teesside area, which included Stockton, and also an ordnance survey map, which showed all the topographical features as well as the roads.

Further down the road, he stopped and entered a Burger Bar, though he just ordered a cup of coffee. He sat down in one of the booths at the back and started to peruse the maps he had just bought.

He needed to hire a car and do some driving around. He could see from a quick perusal of the Stockton area that extraction could not be easily done from Lucifer's new home. There was only one way in by car and one way on foot. He would expect that both would be watched.

Once he had decided upon the best chance of success, he would have to get in touch with the boy and arrange a meeting away from the house.

Later that day, he verified the surveillance setup by the church. The man in the car was easy to spot, and the second man loitering in the walkway was conspicuous enough by the dressing on the side of his face.

He was lucky enough to strike up a brief conversation with a couple of kids out walking their dog, a fine-looking boxer dog who he quickly befriended, kneeling to stroke it and let it sniff his hand. Dogs were good judges of character, he had found. Walking with them a ways, to anyone watching, he appeared to be their father.

Ryan visited the house that afternoon after checking up on Sean and Davey himself. Mary greeted him at the door, and he sat down to partake of a cup of tea with Patrick and Connor at the kitchen table.

The two IRA men confirmed that there had been no sightings up to now. "You know his description, but he doesn't know yours. I daresay he'll spot Sean and Davey easily enough. Unfortunately, we are limited in what we can do for surveillance. That works both ways. He'll try to get Lucifer away from the house." Then he turned his attention to Mary.

"I see Davey's not looking too well this morning." He waited for a response. The two Irishmen shifted uncomfortably in their seats. "Walking a bit funny too," he added.

"Look, Father, Davey was drunk …" Patrick tried to excuse his friend's actions.

"It was nothing I couldn't handle, Father." Mary spoke to calm the waters. "Patrick's right. Davey was drunk. He won't repeat his mistake," she reassured him. Ryan turned his attention back to the two men.

"Just so there *is* no mistake … You've probably guessed by now that Mary here isn't a nun. That was just a ruse we used for the Ferry Customs and Special Branch. But she is a very old and dear friend of mine." He paused, looking both men squarely in the eye. "She is to be treated with the utmost respect, and if any harm befalls her, sure and I'll cut your balls off if Mary doesn't do it herself!" he added with a snarl.

Both men had worked with Father Ryan before, on more than a few missions for the IRA. They knew he wasn't joking. "Sure and we'll take the best of care of her, Father," Connor reassured the older man.

"See that you do," he warned. Then, finishing his tea, he got up from the table, and Mary escorted him to the door. "Things went well this morning, I take it?" he asked

"Yes, Father. He was quite concerned for me. I think he'll phone."

"Good … Good … See as much of him as you can over the next few days. We need someone close to him."

"Do we really need to kill him, Father? He seems such a gentle soul." She was starting to feel guilty about the church's plans for Lucifer. Father Ryan smiled wanly, lifting a hand to stroke the side of her face gently in a soothing way.

"Hush, child. Remember now, that was how you viewed that butcher Gabriel when first you met him." Mary hung her head.

"Aye, Father. I did." She stood reproached.

"Remember that, child. Gabriel's war against the church has gone on too long. He must be made to pay for his crimes. Brother Lucifer betrayed our church, siding with his brother out of misguided loyalty, or perhaps his brain was even affected by having his medical treatment so abruptly terminated that day in the catacombs."

"I have heard the tales, Father," Mary acknowledged. "I still remember …," she started to say but then was silent.

"Either way, that's why this special organization exists within the church. The Pope himself authorized its creation, using men like myself, who were once men of violence or soldiers. We are the church's Sword of Solomon, if you like, dispensing final justice at the Pope's behest," he reiterated her indoctrination to her.

"That's why I joined it, Father, I know." She felt tears brimming up in her eyes as unwanted memories came flooding back. "I have my own justice to dispense to Gabriel," she promised. "He killed my child, Father. I thought my first loss was bad enough, but the second was more than I could bear, and though I burn in the fires of hell for what I do, I will see him pay for that!" she vowed, clutching the little gold cross to her bosom.

Chapter Fifty-one

"I still say it's a bloody stupid day to get married on," Luke's father complained as he struggled to fasten his tie. Luke could hear them arguing in their bedroom.

"She's one of my oldest friends, and you've known about it for ages. So stop moaning."

"No true supporter would get married when the Boro are at home. I paid good money for these season tickets." He still struggled with the tie, for he rarely wore one.

"Well, it's only one match, and that nice Mr. Angell has agreed to take Luke since your dad's feeling poorly," his mother went on. "It probably won't be that good a match in this horrible weather, anyway."

"It's not *only* a match, it's the bloody Mackems!"

Next door, Lucifer was looking at the season tickets he had been loaned. Three of them. Him, Luke, and? Should he phone her? He couldn't make his mind up. He knew nothing about football himself. Did they play football in Ireland? He didn't know.

Mary's phone rang just after eleven. "Hello? Stockton 699169?" she spoke.

"Morning, Mary. It's me, Lucifer ...," a nervous voice spoke at the other end of the line. "How's the ankle?" he asked.

Mary nodded to answer the curious glances from Patrick and Connor, who had come down the stairs, their sleep broken by the sound of the phone ringing. "Hello, yourself. My ankle is still a little sore, but I'm managing. It's nice to hear from you," she added.

"Do you like football?" he asked out of the blue. Mary didn't know how to answer such an unexpected question for a second. "It's just that I suddenly find myself going to see a match this afternoon, and I have a spare ticket. I thought a bit of fresh air might be good for you."

"Football?" she looked at the horrified faces on the two men. "I watch it on the telly sometimes, but I've never been to a match before," she added. The two men were gesticulating wildly, though in silence.

"That makes two of us then. I volunteered to take my neighbor's son. Shall I pick you up about half one then?" he asked.

"Yes. Okay. Half one would be fine. See you then." She put the phone down.

"Oh, bugger … We're going to have our work cut out for us for sure. Get Ryan on the phone."

Chapter Fifty-two

Lucifer called to collect Mary on time, helping her to the car as she continued to walk with a slight limp, though her ankle had healed overnight. Introductions were made in the car, and it set off, heading for the A66.

Two cars followed at a distance. Ryan was not with them, preferring to stay back out of the way. He doubted whether Gabriel would arrange a meeting in such a crowded situation, but they couldn't take a chance, and so all four IRA men were to try to keep tabs on them.

All three cars soon got caught up in the usual match-day traffic jams, and then it was just a case of following the car in front as Luke directed Lucifer towards the car park where they had a reserved space. Luke flashed the badge on the way in and got waved through. Sean and Davey were two cars back, and they got stopped.

"Three quid, please …," said the attendant, holding out his hand to collect the money.

"Three quid?" argued Sean. "That's bloody extortion!"

"Well find your own place to park then," said the attendant gruffly.

"Shut up and pay the man, ye tight bastid!" ordered Davey, and the attendant begrudgingly gave them their parking ticket, and they drove through, parking just down the line from Lucifer's car. "Hurry up. They're going out the gate." Davey was worried they'd lose sight of them in the crowd.

Pat and Connor's car was coming through the gate as they were rushing to catch up with their target. Reluctantly, they left their guns in the car, as police were all over the place. Sean rushed ahead, Davey walked slower, still feeling his aching balls, waiting for the other two men to catch up.

Once joined up with Pat and Connor, Davey directed them towards where he had seen Sean disappearing. As they were drawn along with the crowds, Connor suddenly pointed out the simple fact that everyone else there was wearing match colors, scarves, or team shirts.

"We'll stick out like nuns in a brothel," he pointed out.

"Well, let's get something from these street vendors then?" suggested Pat, and they approached a couple of the vendors' stalls, where a diminishing number of items was still on sale, though going rapidly.

"Giz one o' them scarves, pal?" asked Pat.

"Fiver, mate, please." Pat handed over the money. Connor bought the last remaining scarf.

"How much for the striped shirt there, mate?" asked Davey. The vendor looked at him for a moment and then back to the shirt. He looked at him a little strangely and then replied.

"You can have it for eight quid." He smiled. "Hope it brings you luck," he added with a chuckle. "Hope you enjoy the game." He grinned. Davey pulled on the shirt over his sweater and rejoined Pat and Connor who had scarves wrapped round their necks. They hurried towards the impressive-looking Riverside Stadium, where Sean was waving to catch their attention.

The four of them huddled up in the crowd as Sean related what he'd seen. "They went in through Gate 57. It's all-season ticket, and the game's a sellout, anyway," he explained. "We'll just have to spread out outside here. One of us goes back closer to the car park, and the rest of us just try to spot him leaving at the end of the match. Mary will do her best to make sure he doesn't go walkabout."

Inside the stadium, the teams were just coming out onto the pitch as Lucifer, Mary, and the boy were taking their seats. By the way Luke was cheering, it was obvious that the team in the red shirts was Middlesbrough. Today's opponents, Sunderland, were wearing their away strip of pale yellow shirts, though normally they would have worn their famous red-and-white striped shirts.

As the teams kicked a ball about before the start of the match, Lucifer picked out the tall defender with the Latin features. "The big man at the back. I think I know him from somewhere ..." He pointed him out to Luke, who was struggling to open a packet of Maltesers.

"That's Festa. He's from Sicily. You don't want to mess with him. He's dangerous," the boy added with pride. Lucifer was nonplussed for a moment.

"Why? Is he Mafia?" he asked. Luke almost choked on a Malteser as he laughed.

"No, he's a black belt at karate ..." The boy chuckled. "You're weird." Mary laughed along with the boy, though she was now wondering just how much of his past Lucifer was starting to remember.

Outside the ground, Sean, Davey, and Connor were spread out on the east side of the main car park, each of them hovering near one of the fast-food stalls. Pat had gone back closer to the car park to pick them up when they came back to their car.

Davey leaned on a fence, munching away on a hamburger as two policemen approached him. He was aware of their approach, trying to remain calm, though inwardly sweating.

"Wouldn't hang about too long there, mate," one of the coppers advised him in a friendly tone.

"It's a free country, isn't it?" he retorted, trying to play down his accent. He just had an inbuilt hatred of authority and couldn't stop from replying to the policeman in that way.

The officer opened his mouth to say something but then was pulled away by the other policeman. "You have a nice day, pal. Even if you don't have a ticket. You just soak up the match atmosphere." He grinned. The two went away and then suddenly burst out laughing to themselves.

"Bastids!" Davey muttered to himself under his breath. He heard a tremendous roar go up from inside the ground, guessing a goal had just been scored.

Inside the ground, Lucifer and Mary were caught up in the celebrations as the home side went one nil ahead, Craig Hignett crashing in a twenty-five-yard effort off the inside of the post and silencing the away supporters.

The atmosphere inside the magnificent stadium was electric, with thirty thousand supporters cheering on their two teams, flags and banners waving. "Why does everyone boo those three men in black? Surely they don't play for either side?" Lucifer asked the boy.

"We just boo them because they're always crap," Luke explained. "The match officials always cost us a couple of goals a game because of their bad decisions," he added.

"You'll have to explain the rules to me at halftime." Lucifer shook his head in exasperation.

The match ended up a comfortable win for the home side, and people started leaving the ground about ten minutes before the end. Sean, Davey, and Connor were keeping a sharp eye out for the group of three or anyone fitting Gabriel's description.

The exodus increased as full time approached, with more and more people filling the concourse. A red tide began sweeping out of the ground as people made their way back to their buses and cars, all eager to get out and try to beat the traffic jams.

Davey was desperately trying to catch sight of a recognizable face, when a loud cry went up from the approaching crowd. "Get the fucken' Mackem bastard!" was quickly echoed by other voices, and a dozen or more red shirts began running towards him.

Suddenly alarmed, he looked frantically behind him and then looked back as he realized the significance of the striped shirt he was wearing. "Oh, fuck me ...," he cursed as he started to run, the howling mob at his back.

Stuck in traffic some five cars behind Lucifer's, Connor used his mobile phone to advise Ryan of the afternoon's events. "Father, we're on our way back. No contact that we saw, but we have a problem ..."

"What problem might that be then?" The voice sounded weary at the other end of the phone.

"Davey, Father. The last we saw, he was being loaded onto an ambulance. It looks like he's been taken to the hospital. He looked in a bad way, Father," he expressed his concern.

Ryan was silent for a moment. "The boy does seem to be rather accident-prone, wouldn't you say now? I think perhaps I'd better visit him in my official capacity, even if it's only to deliver the last rites," he added after he had broken the connection.

Chapter Fifty-three

Priests were a fairly common sight in hospitals, administering to the dying, comforting the grieved ... so no one thought it odd to find Father Patrick Ryan wandering around North Tees Hospital on the Saturday night, which was normally one of the busiest of the week for the hospital staff.

A few polite enquiries resulted in him being directed up to Ward 5, where the patient from the Riverside attack was in a private room. "Terrible, Father, simply terrible but not unexpected. 'Twas only last month they played up in Sunderland, and the Middlesbrough invalid supporters' bus got bricked, and three of the old and infirm were badly injured. Wouldn't surprise me if the police didn't turn a blind eye to a bit of getting your own back, eh?" the sister suggested.

"Shocking, but with human nature being what it is, it's very understandable, Sister," he agreed, wishing the woman would go now that she'd shown him to Davey's room.

"He's heavily sedated, Father, and we found no identification on him, so we can't contact his family. He might not be able to speak," she warned him as she showed him into the room. Father Ryan waited till she had left the room before going over to the bedside.

Poor Davey was indeed in a bad way. More bandages were added to the dressing already around his head. One leg was in a cast and raised upright. A tent over the other leg revealed damage there too. One arm was heavily bandaged, the other lightly so. A bag of blood hung on a stand by the bed, with a tube attached to a drip in his arm.

An impressive looking piece of equipment was at the far side of the bed, and numerous sensors were attached to Davey's body and feeding back into it. Ryan approached the bed, noting Davey's eyes were closed and heavily bruised. He found it hard not to laugh. One of the IRA's hard men, beaten to a pulp by a bunch of bloody football hooligans.

"Hello, Davey. Can you hear me?" he asked lightly, noting the slight response in the flickering of eyelids. One eye opened slightly, though the other one was too swollen. "Not having a good week, are we, Davey boy?" He smiled grimly. "The police are downstairs, waiting to question you."

Davey's one good eye widened, and one arm trembled slightly. He was too heavily sedated to do more. Ryan hovered closer like a vulture, circling around his dying prey.

"Can't have them running a check on you, now can I, son? Once they link you to the IRA, and they will, the mission will be at risk." The one eye followed Ryan's hand as it approached the transfusion bag, old fingers snaking down along the red tube towards the catheter in his arm. "It all comes down to the blood in the end," he mused as he gently unplugged the plastic tube. Leaning forward, he brought the connector to his mouth, squeezing to open the little nonreturn valve and blew into the tube.

Davey's eye was going bloodshot, head moving oh so slightly as he tried to fight the sedation. His brain still functioned enough to know he had just been killed.

Ryan methodically refastened the tube into the connector, using his handkerchief to carefully mop up the small droplets of blood that had leaked from the tube. Then he turned his attention to where the blood was now resuming its flow towards Davey's arm, pushing the small air bubble ahead of it slowly but surely.

He had maybe five minutes before the monitors went off, recording a heart seizure when the air bubble reached its target. Making the sign of the cross, Ryan left the quivering Irishman to say his silent prayers and made his way back out of the hospital.

Chapter Fifty-four

On board the yacht, Gabriel was making final preparations. He pulled his laptop out from the valise, switched it on, and connected the modem to his mobile phone. He had studied the surrounding areas, visiting likely spots, and decided where his best choice of making the extraction would be.

The storm would hit with its full fury tomorrow, and he intended to take full advantage of it. Opening Outlook, he began to compose an e-mail message to the boy.

Once he sent it, he left the laptop switched on, awaiting a reply. This done, he pulled another small case out and opened it up, spreading its contents out on the bunk bed, checking it minutely to ensure there was no break-in any of the circuits that ran through the memory-plastic and that the battery connections were solid. The batteries had been tested thoroughly and were good for two hours. That should be just enough.

The beep from Luke's machine alerted him to the e-mail that had just arrived. Opening it, he saw it was from Gabriel. He had been expecting some sort of contact. It had been nearly a week since he had last been in touch.

No need to be alarmed, but our mutual friend is being watched. I've seen the watchers, but they haven't seen me. Your phone may also be monitored, so be careful if you use it.

It's too risky to come to the house. Lucifer will have to be moved to a more accessible place. You'll be followed when you leave, but let me worry about that. Here's what I need you to do ...

Luke read the e-mail and rattled off a quick reply, excited by the thought of all this intrigue. It was fun. Like Cops 'n' Robbers. In the back of his mind, part of him wanted to confide in his father, but knowing him, he would probably forbid Luke to do what Gabriel wanted, and he couldn't let the mysterious Gabriel down. He just couldn't ...

Chapter Fifty-five

The next day, Luke shuffled about on the backseat, studying the map of North Yorkshire as the two adults talked in the front of the car. He had been taken aback when Lucifer had suddenly suggested inviting Mary along and could not formulate a believable argument against the idea. It was obvious Lucifer was taken with her, and in truth, Luke liked her too, but Gabriel would only be expecting the two of them, and so he hoped it would cause no complications.

He returned to studying the map as Lucifer drove south on the A19. The route would take them out past Thirsk and Ripon, old market towns of the last century and still popular tourist spots because of that. Almost a two-hour drive from Teesside was the place Gabriel had chosen for the rendezvous. Off the B6265 was a place called Brimham Rocks, which the boy remembered from his youth, when he had climbed all over the place.

Monstrous natural rock formations and giant boulders made up Brimham Rocks, carved by the wind and rain over the centuries, another popular tourist spot, though Luke thought they would be the only people there today in this foul weather. The rain lashed down, making Lucifer drive slowly and carefully, and he could feel the strong winds buffeting the car as the gusts hit it broadside on.

The location and route would make the people following them all the more visible, Gabriel had explained, and would draw them away from Teesside onto a playing field of Gabriel's choosing. Overhead, thunder rumbled ominously, loud and threatening. Lucifer increased the speed of his windscreen wipers.

Mary chatted with Lucifer quite lightheartedly as she tried to visualize the route they were taking with her knowledge of the area. She felt reassured by the loaded automatic and the homing transmitter that she carried in her handbag. Father Ryan and the other three men would be using it to track and follow her to their destination. If today was the long awaited reckoning with Gabriel, Ryan would not be far behind.

Chapter Fifty-six

The storm howled at its height as Gabriel made the climb up the awkward rock face, its surface smoothed by centuries of erosion due to the wind and rain. At last, he got to the top and stood for a moment, buffeted by the winds as he enjoyed the view.

The strangely shaped monoliths scattered the landscape as far as he could see, all varying in shape and height. Some even had whole trees growing out of their very rock. He took off his knapsack, opening out the contents.

He was expecting Lucifer and the boy shortly. Expecting them to be followed too, but he was confident he would be able to foil their plan and then retrace their steps back to Teesside, where hopefully they would not be expected to go, and leave on the yacht.

Taking it out of his rucksack, Gabriel shook the bodysuit out, checking its integrity before stepping into the finely woven plastic fibers interlaced with the fine circuitry. Until the last twenty years, the technology had not existed to create such a suit, and only he had the ability and the physiology to implement it.

At first glance, the suit looked ill-fitting with long loose sleeves hanging down to his feet. His hands fit into the gloves like ancient Roman cestii—neat flat power packs against the back of his hands, controls in the palms of his hands. He took out his knives from the knapsack, strapping them to his thighs, and then he was ready ... He thumbed the switch in the palm of his left hand and felt the magnetic clamps fastening the suit at his wrists and ankles.

He was so akin with the wind. It was his friend and lover in a way no other person except Lucifer could understand. It roared about him with a vengeance, pleading, begging him, until Gabriel could stand it no more.

He thumbed the control in his right palm, sending electrical current along the tiny circuits, which ran throughout the bodysuit, the charge sufficient to cause the memory-plastic to change shape, the long loose sleeves stiffening, the gloved fingers themselves growing with reinforced metal extensions.

The wind embraced him, and with a savage exultant cry, Gabriel flung himself from the top of the rock face, giving himself up to the mercy of the winds.

Gabriel felt himself lifted once more, arms beating violently down as he took to the air, soaring high in seconds, hundreds of feet above the strange rocky monoliths.

So free again, so joyous, he laughed as he used his arms, fingers delicately controlling the artificial wings. He had tried out the suit in the Sierra Madres last year, finding it more cumbersome than his previous real wings and modeled as it was on the wings of the prehistoric pteranodon. It was more of a hang glider if truth be told, but modeled to his unique physiology, it gave him back the skies. His light body weight gave him sufficient lift in strong winds to enjoy the freedom of the heavens.

He climbed and climbed, seeking out the heavens, laughing as the rain fought him, seeking to throw him back, but he would not be denied. Up into the clouds he went, feeling the static charge building, knowing it was dangerous for him to fly through these storm clouds with an electrical power source about his body, yet Gabriel had always enjoyed flirting with danger.

He withdrew as he felt the static charge in his hair, plummeting and dropping like a stone, as behind him the air split with a vengeance, white forked lightning seeking the ground, and the deafening thunder roared in his ears. Gabriel laughed once more and then turned his attention to the ground, seeking out the road and points of reference.

He spotted his car where he had left it, pulled off to the side on one of the minor roads, away from the main tourist entrance, which was closed. The barriers he had removed earlier. He flew northeast, following the road, keeping just below the fringes of the heavy cloud as he looked for the vehicle whose description the boy had given him.

Ten miles along the road, Gabriel spotted the car. Satisfied, he continued on, scanning the sparse traffic on the road for the pursuit vehicles. He could identify one car, he knew. If they had changed cars or used another vehicle, it would be more difficult.

As it was, Ryan was driving with Connor in the vehicle he had driven up from Liverpool. The other two men were driving the vehicle Gabriel had spotted earlier when checking out the surveillance on his friend. They kept a good five miles behind Lucifer's car. The homing transmitter in Mary's purse was good for a fifteen-mile radius, and Connor was good at reading the handheld scanner to direct Ryan as he drove.

Ryan thumbed the send button on his two-way radio as he relayed a message to the men in the following car. "Only a few miles now. Stay alert, and wait for my orders," he warned them. Then he changed frequencies and spoke again. "How far away are you?" he asked.

The voice that replied was weary and almost lost in the wind. "Not sure. Visibility is poor."

"Look for a place with many large rocks. When you find it, stay out of sight and await instructions. Do you understand?" he asked.

"I will do as instructed," answered the monotone voice, half carried away on the howling gale.

Ryan put the radio back on the dashboard. "Still on course for Brimham Rocks?" he asked Connor.

"No variation, Father," answered the IRA man.

"Good. Then we'll take the fork ahead and come in around the other side of the place using the back road. That way we'll cover both exits," he explained. "Slow down, and watch your speed around that corner," he warned. "The road surface is wet and dangerous."

Aloft, Gabriel flew steadily northeasterly, his strong arms were needed more for control than impetus. He let the wind do most of the work, reading its nuances like a well-read book. Finally, he saw a vehicle he recognized, swooping down for a cursory examination, though not low enough to be seen amid the fury of the elements.

Two men in the car. Two men whose outlines looked familiar. If they turned off towards the Rocks, it would be them. No one else would be visiting the place in a storm of this magnitude. He reached for the heavens once more, biding his time.

Pulling up at the car park in Brimham Rocks, Lucifer was not surprised to see no attendant in this foul weather. Most people stayed indoors during storms such as this. He felt quite at home somehow in extreme weather, relishing its attempts to express itself on his puny insignificant "human" body. Nature was a fierce and unrelenting adversary and strangely familiar to Lucifer.

Young Luke was first out of the car, slamming the door behind him. "Let's find a nice high spot and watch the lightning," he yelled before running off in the direction of a huge flat rock, which projected out over the large valley, affording a wonderful view of the countryside.

"Excitable, isn't he?" Lucifer smiled at Mary. She nodded, remembering her own childhood briefly. A loud crack of thunder overhead made Mary jump, and Lucifer was quick to console her, reassuring her they would be all right.

"It's all right. I quite like storms. There's something about the wildness of nature." She allowed him to put his arm around her as they followed the boy. Mary's eyes scanned the surroundings as she walked, watching, waiting. It would be here, she knew. She could feel it somehow. Her time of vengeance was almost at hand, and finally Gabriel would be made to pay for his sins.

Lucifer himself meant nothing to her other than a means to an end. She did not want to kill him, but Father Ryan, her mentor, had assured her that he was just as evil as Gabriel himself, having joined him in committing many acts of terrorism against the church.

Ryan had shown her the film footage and, in years later, the video evidence of the raid on a facility in Madrid. Two old men murdered in cold blood. Terrorists, both of them. Gabriel more so, as he had killed her unborn child. An eye for an eye was called for, yet Ryan wanted him alive, his blood too valuable to the church. She still didn't know if she would use the gun or not.

Her religious beliefs had always taught of mercy, and she had firmly believed in such teachings. Yet her heart had been broken twice over by the man, this demon from hell, if such he was. Today, old ghosts would finally be laid to rest.

Chapter Fifty-seven

Sure now that it was the correct car, as it turned off the main road and began driving up the approach to the Rocks, Gabriel waited till the car approached the rise and the sharp bend thereafter, and then he suddenly plummeted like a hawk, straight for the car, approaching from almost directly ahead.

Sean saw only a massive shape falling towards the car, cursing as he turned the wheel, screaming as the car slid over into the ditch, where the mud cushioned the crash.

Gabriel's wings beat, flaring, as he sought the safety of the skies once more, satisfied the car was now immobile. It would not get out of the ditch unaided. No one dead so far. Perhaps if the fates were kind, the escape would go unhindered. He climbed high, heading back for the Rocks, where he knew Lucifer and the boy would be waiting.

The two Irishmen looked rather sheepish as Ryan's car pulled up, and they started attaching the towrope to help pull their car out of the ditch. "You'd better hope Mary manages to delay him," warned Ryan. "The bend doesn't look too bad. You must have been driving too fast for the conditions," he reflected. The two men said nothing, neither of them really sure what they had seen in the storm that had caused them to run off the road.

Chapter Fifty-eight

From a height, he saw them standing on the huge flat rock. Lucifer, the boy, and a woman. Puzzled, he soared higher, almost into the clouds, as he pondered the import of the third figure. He could only assume it was the boy's mother, having no other information on which to base his decision, and he decided to make his presence known.

He swooped down, some distance away from the rock, letting himself be seen. Startled, the figures on the rock crowded together. "Look at the big bird!" cried the boy, pointing. Gabriel circled above them as they watched.

Slowly, he swooped lower, approaching the flat rock from the valley side, flaring his wings as they stepped back from the edge, allowing him plenty of room to land.

Their mouths gaped at the sight of this angel come to earth, eyes staring wide with wonder. Lucifer's with the first glimmer of distant recognition as he had hoped. The woman! Something about the woman. She looked so familiar. Traces of blonde hair escaped the headscarf she wore against the elements.

Then the alarm bells went off inside his head, gasping as though an invisible hand had reached into his chest and solidified around his heart. It couldn't be! It just couldn't be!

Now it was Gabriel's turn to gape in sudden recognition, sudden realization, frozen with shock as the woman regained her senses, clawing open her handbag and fumbling for the gun, a gun she quickly pressed to Lucifer's temple as she grabbed him from behind, taking him by surprise.

"Mary ... what ... what are you doing?" he exclaimed in sudden shock. His mind whirled, fog lifting in slow swirls. Gabriel, his friend Gabriel ... Mary ... with a gun ...

"Stay still. Still, I say, or I'll shoot you now," Mary ordered. Her lip trembled as she tried to remain in control of herself and the situation, though if truth be told, she was unraveling at the seams. All the planning, all for this moment. She had to stay calm, but her knuckle was white on the trigger, which Gabriel noticed only too well. Luke backed away, horrified at what was happening.

Slowly, Gabriel was mentally piecing together the unknown events of the last fifty-eight years. There was only one explanation, one that inwardly sickened him. For one brief second, his heart had soared higher than his makeshift wings could carry him, and then the crushing revelation had brought with it only blackness and despair.

"I take it this is no chance reunion?" Gabriel said sullenly, baleful eyes glowering out from beneath his dark rain-soaked brow. Mary looked wildly at him, her eyes barely focused as her mind flashed back oh so many painful years.

Back to the day she had recovered from the anesthetic and Father Ryan telling her that her second child had been delivered stillborn, dead because of the mental stress she had been under at the time, caused by Gabriel and his murderous assault in the catacombs.

"Take off that ridiculous suit," she ordered. "Father Ryan will be here soon, and he will see you delivered to the church, to pay for your crimes." She spoke hurriedly, the gun wavering back and forth from Gabriel to Lucifer.

"So he lives too?" Gabriel shook his head. "I wonder how?" he asked rhetorically.

"Mary ... Mary, put the gun down ... please ... I think he's a friend of mine," said Lucifer, memory beginning to flood back in bright sudden flashes, which made his knees weak, and he wavered on his legs unsteadily ...

Gabriel locked eyes with the woman, burning coals glowered out from under the dark wet fringe which clung, dripping to his forehead. "Her name's not Mary, Lucifer," he said simply, and then to her he spoke again. "I always said I would introduce you, didn't I?" he choked on the words. Overhead, a tremendous thunderclap exploded , and sheet lightning lit the face-off in an eerie sheen. "Lucifer, meet Laura Donovan."

Chapter Fifty-nine

The rain was intensifying, driving hard as the four people confronted each other. Gabriel touched the palm switches that deactivated and released the straps on his suit and carefully stepped out of it under Laura's watchful stare.

Mentally, he was weighing up his options. If Ryan was coming, there must have been another car, one he had failed to spot. Perhaps coming in on the back road where he had hoped to make his escape. How much time did he have?

He stood there, seemingly obedient, as Laura continued to threaten Lucifer with the gun. At his side, his hands were level with the knives strapped to his thighs, a fact she had seemingly overlooked, though he was loath to use violence against her. Instead, his fingers began to move, trembling as though with nerves.

Lucifer's eyes caught the movement, and Gabriel locked eyes with him for a second. His mind was clearing enough to remember, recognizing the hand signals for what they were. His own fingers began to twitch in response.

"Laura," he began the overdue conversation with difficulty. "Believe me when I tell you I thought you had died beneath that cave-in."

Her eyes glared with hatred as she rounded on him. "No.

I remember it all so well!" she accused. "All you wanted to do was kill Father Ryan. I watched you, and the roof came down, and I cried out for you." Her words were filled with pain, and Gabriel could hear the anguish in her voice. "You chose to save your brother and left me there as the German troops arrived. You left me to die!" she accused, her eyes now as wild as the storm that raged above.

"That's not true," he pleaded. "You were drugged, frightened, and in shock at the time. That's not what you really saw, Laura, believe me."

"How can I believe you?" she sobbed. "I've seen the films and the video footage of your attacks on the church over the years. You're just a terrorist as Father Ryan has so often told me. Not once did you try to find out what happened to me. My injuries healed, but the mental scars I still carry. You abandoned us, Gabriel. Father Ryan sent word to you because I begged him to, but you never came, never even sent word." She was crying now, her tears washing away in the downpour, but she would never be able to cry away the hurt she felt inside at his betrayal.

"I received no word from Ryan," he stated plainly. "Until a few minutes ago, as with yourself, I didn't know he had survived. I'm telling you the truth, Laura. I've never lied to you, never wanted to hurt you in any way."

"You're still lying. I've known Father Ryan ever since I first came to Rome. I trust him implicitly," she defended her father figure.

"What other lies has he told you then?" Gabriel insisted. 'That I and Lucifer are terrorists? What did he tell you it was that you were drinking, Laura?" he asked accusingly.

"What? What do you mean?" she looked momentarily puzzled.

"You said your injuries were bad, yet here you are in the full bloom of health, looking no older than the last time I saw you some fifty-eight years ago. The miraculous elixir he gave you to drink," he accused. "What did he say it was?"

"The derivative of your blood, you mean?"

"No derivative, Laura. That's another lie. It can't be recreated. What you drank was this," he said, reaching up to his cheek and using a sharp fingernail to scratch open a deep cut on his cheek so that blood ran freely as the rain washed it down his cheek. "Look at the wound, Laura. See, it's already closing," he demonstrated. "That's why I and my kind are so eagerly pursued by your church. What they can't recreate, they wish to preserve. They hunt us for our blood!"

"You're talking in riddles. You're trying to confuse me," she stammered, using her gun hand to brush back a lock of matted hair out of her eyes.

"When ingested by humans, our blood increases your regenerative system, in effect, increasing your lifespan," he explained. "But its effects are limited, lasting only fifty to sixty years and then more must be ingested. The effectiveness deteriorates with every ingestion."

"What do you mean, 'humans'?" she asked, puzzled.

"Haven't you guessed yet, Laura? Lucifer and I aren't human. We're the last of a dying breed, hunted almost to the edge of extinction by your beloved church. Our lifespan is infinite as far as I'm aware—mine, anyway. Lucifer I don't know about since the church conducted their experiments upon him in those catacombs. His body no longer works as effectively as my own."

"You're mad!" she accused. "Stark, raving mad."

"Not mad. Forgetful maybe, but so would you be if you'd lived as long as I have. The mind is a wonderful thing, but like a computer, it can only hold so much data," he admitted. "My most distant memories recall a migration of my people. There were dozens of us then, before the rise of Rome. We fled north and west, trying to escape the spread of human civilization. Then we were captured by your ancestors, and me and Lucifer had our wings taken from us. Real flesh and feathers, Laura, not like this artificial thing I've been wearing," he explained.

"It's true, Laura, if that's your name …," Lucifer butted in. "I'm starting to remember. We are virtually immortal. We can be killed, yes, but unless the wound is of itself fatal, our bodies can recover."

"Lies, all lies." Laura refused to believe. "You're just trying to confuse me. Father Ryan will be here soon."

"Lucifer and I are all that's left, Laura," Gabriel explained. "Your church and others have hunted us over the centuries. They would either kill us or keep us as their lab rats. Why do you think they want us so badly?"

"They said they need to utilize the rare compound in your blood for the serum. It can be of immense benefit to mankind."

"Our blood and that of others of our kind has been horded by your beloved council for centuries. My people have been butchered and dissected, their blood drained, just so that you humans can extend your life spans. Have they made any moves to publicize that? Your present Pope knows nothing of what goes on in the underworld of the catacombs. Perhaps as yet he isn't trusted by the present incumbents? I know Alonso Borgia of old." He could sense her confusion.

Laura shivered as she stood there, holding her ground against the driving rain and wind. Gabriel's words sounded so sincere, and yet her memory reminded her they always had during their brief affair in Rome. Yet Father Ryan had looked after her like a second father after she had learnt of her own father's death. He had recruited her into this secret papal organization. He had not abandoned her like Gabriel had.

"You still abandoned us!" she screamed in accusation, her mind whirling, the gun shaking in her hand.

Suddenly, her choice of words was noticed by Gabriel. "What do you mean, Laura? What 'us' are you talking about?" He was suddenly fearful of the answer.

"Our baby, Gabriel! Our baby!" she sobbed. "You simply abandoned us, and I couldn't bear it. It was stillborn *again*. You tore my heart out, you bastard!" She gesticulated wildly with the gun now, and her finger tightened on the trigger. "I should kill you now, and to hell with Ryan, the church, everybody. I've dreamed so often of killing you!" Lightning exploded overhead once more, the thunder deafening and rolling away over the immense alien landscape of the huge rocks. Gabriel's face was white against the fury of the storm.

Gabriel's own emotions were running high now. She had been pregnant with his child, the realization slowly sinking in. No wonder she hated him now with such ferocity after such a tragedy. Offspring from the unions of angels and humans were rare, but the children were usually gifted with unusual physiology by their fathers.

It was a sick joke that the foundation of the current Holy Church had been Michael's own son, crucified by the Romans against the Christian Church's beliefs, and while the aerie had been powerless to prevent his execution.

A horrid thought suddenly overtook Gabriel. "When did you ingest the blood, Laura? It's important." He started to move toward her and then stopped as she leveled the gun on him once more. She looked like she knew how to use it.

"Father Ryan gave it to me a few weeks after they dug me out of the rubble," she explained. "Why is the date so important to you?"

"Because the offspring of angel and human are notoriously healthy, Laura. Even without you ingesting the blood, the child would not have been stillborn. Did they show you the baby's body?" he asked.

Laura looked stunned, taking a small step back away from him. "No. No, you're lying again." Laura shook her head from side to side. Lightning reflected in her wide eyes. "You *have* to be lying. Father Ryan would never do that to me. Never …" She started to tremble now, her eyes widening further as she tried to deal with the horrific revelation. Mentally, she flashed back to that awful time—the drugs, the medication, the labor, and finally the horrible news.

"Think about it, Laura," Gabriel pleaded. "They had you carrying *my* child. After pursuing me and my kind throughout the centuries, you really think they'd pass up an opportunity like that?"

"Oh my God! My God, no … Nooooo …" Laura screamed as the brutal truth finally began to reveal itself, and Gabriel seized the opportunity to make one sudden movement with his hand. Lucifer whirled with a speed Laura wouldn't have believed possible and simply plucked the gun from her hand before she could react, his thumb holding the hammer back, and preventing it from falling as gently as he could.

She stood there, shivering … almost catatonic as Gabriel rushed to take her into his arms once more, and she fell sobbing into his embrace. "Laura, I …" He didn't have the words to express himself and simply held her, letting her cry her tears as Lucifer consulted with the frightened boy.

"Can you start a car?" he asked.

"Yes, I can start one, but my feet can't reach the pedals too well," Luke explained.

"Just go back to the car, start the engine, and keep it running. We're going to have to leave here very soon and very quickly." He gave the boy the ignition keys, and Luke ran off to do what Lucifer had asked.

"So long …," Laura sobbed. "I've hated you for so long. Only my hatred of you kept me going," she cried into Gabriel's shoulder. "Ryan promised me that one day we would catch up with you."

"It's okay. I'm here now. I thought I'd lost you, and now you're here with me again. That must count for something." He held her tightly, not wanting to let go of her after so long apart.

"It's all so fantastic. I can't take it all in." She brushed the wet blonde hair out of her eyes. "Is our child really still alive then?" She hoped against hope. Time was so cruel. Gabriel comforted her.

"Alive and maybe not much older than you, probably." He kissed her forehead. "I can't believe the church would have allowed any harm to happen to it." He held her at arm's length now. "Rest assured, I'll be asking Ryan about it just before I kill him!" he said vehemently. "This time I'm going to make sure the bastard stays dead!"

"Gabriel, headlights coming up the road. Two sets." Lucifer warned, pointing away in the distance from their vantage point. "We don't have much time."

"The transmitter in my handbag. It's leading them right here," Laura cautioned, sniffing back her tears and rubbing her eyes as she fumbled inside the bag for the transmitter.

"Give it here," said Gabriel. "Take your car, go back up the secondary road, and head for Hartlepool. The yacht is moored in the marina."

"The sloop?" Lucifer asked.

"Yes. Wait for me there. I'll lead Father Ryan a merry chase before I have my little talk with him. Give you plenty of time to clear the area," he promised, starting to put on the flying suit once more. "How well are they armed, Laura?" he asked.

"They've got handguns. There are four of them including Ryan. Some of them also have special paintball guns." Lucifer laughed derisively.

"They won't do much good against even me." He laughed in self-mockery. Laura quickly disillusioned him.

"These guns will," she explained. "Inside the balls are a special anesthetic compound, not paint. Skin-absorbed in seconds. They've tested them on wild animals. Unconsciousness sets in within a few minutes," she warned. "The real handguns are a last resort and meant for use against any unseen interference from the police or other outsiders."

Gabriel finished fitting the suit. Thumbing the palm control switches, he felt the suit come alive once more, stiffening and moving as he flexed his fingers. The wind seemed to seek him out, rushing about him once more, filling the special memory-plastic woven mesh. "We'll see how good their aim is then," he said defiantly. "I'll give you plenty of time to get clear. Go now, and don't look back," he warned.

"Gabriel," Laura pleaded. "Let Ryan go. Don't try to take them all on by yourself. They're killers. I don't want to lose you a second time." She ran to him, embracing him as closely as the strange flying suit would allow. He kissed her gently on the forehead.

"Sorry, Laura, but today is the day Father Ryan finds out if there really is a heaven or a hell!" he promised. "The others I'll avoid if I can, but Ryan and I are overdue a final reckoning. He has our child, and I want to know where."

Lucifer held her comfortingly as Gabriel stepped up to the edge of the overhanging rock and let the wind fill his wings as he threw himself at its mercy.

Laura gasped as his body dropped over the edge and then marveled at the sight of this human bird of prey as it rose on an updraft into the raging sky above, as if daring the lightning bolts to strike him down.

Gabriel rose high and fast. In seconds, he was lost from view amongst the low dark clouds. Sheet lightning momentarily revealed a winged figure high above, and then they saw no more, and Lucifer ushered her towards the car to make good their escape.

Luke was gunning the accelerator with a vengeance as he warmed the engine up. He climbed over into the passenger seat as Lucifer slid in through the driver's door. Laura got into the rear of the car.

Lucifer buckled up with one hand as he pulled away and hurriedly made the turn away from the main entrance, speeding off quickly down the back road, the wheels momentarily losing traction on the wet gravel before he compensated, slowing his speed accordingly to suit the conditions,

As Ryan hurriedly approached the huge rocks he could see in the distance, he thumbed the control on his two-way radio once more. "Are you there yet?" he asked impatiently.

"Yes, I'm ready," answered a windswept voice. "I can see Lucifer, the woman, and the boy driving away in their car. Gabriel is nowhere in sight."

Ryan looked at the IRA man, carefully studying the scanner for the position of the homing beacon. "I'm still getting a signal," he replied.

"Okay," said Ryan grimly, "if Gabriel wants to play games, we'll play by my rules. Stop that car, and bring Lucifer here to me," he ordered into the two-way radio.

"Very well" came the weary reply.

Lucifer swore as the wipers could hardly handle the amount of rain obscuring his windscreen. He fought to keep the car on the road and maintain a decent speed to outdistance any pursuit. Headlights didn't reach far, and only brief but bright lightning flashes added to the visibility momentarily.

Through one such flash of lightning, Laura pointed up ahead on the road. "Stop, it's Gabriel!" she cried, pointing out the winged figure silhouetted on the rain-swept road ahead of them. Lucifer slowed the car instantly as the distance between them closed, the headlights starting to pick out the figure now as he stared, his blood slowly froze in his veins

"No, that's not Gabriel," he spluttered, seeing the mighty wings flex and beat, propelling the huge form towards them, the mighty spear raising, pointing straight at the car. He shuddered as realization of their attacker's identity sunk in. "It's Michael!" he blurted out in awe.

"Look out!" Luke cried, and Laura screamed as the mighty spear came crashing straight through the windscreen of the car mere seconds later.

Chapter Sixty

The cold rain on her face through the shattered window and the boy's crying woke Laura, who had passed out as the car had ran off the road. Her face felt sticky with blood, and she wiped the back of her hand across her cut forehead, wincing at the torn flesh which was slowly trying to knit itself back together. Things healed that much slower these days.

The driver's door was no longer there, for she could see it lying on its side quite some distance from the car. Lucifer was no longer there either.

She climbed into the front of the car to check on the boy, who was holding his arm and trying not to cry. She forced herself into action, reassuring the boy first of all. He winced as she examined the arm, gently manipulating it. "It's likely just bruised, Luke," she reassured the boy, who began to stifle his tears, which stemmed more from the shock of what had just happened to them. "Did you see what happened?" she asked.

"The … the big man with wings … he … t-tore the door off with his bare hands …," Luke blurted out. "He just pulled him out of the car, and then all I saw was feathers … and they disappeared." He still rubbed his arm but had stopped his tears as Laura soothed him.

She got out of the car to examine its position in the ditch. Quickly, she realized the front axle was shot, and the car would be going nowhere. "Come on, Luke. We have to go back to Gabriel's car. We have to warn Gabriel they have Lucifer. We have to warn him, warn him about Michael." Laura was feeling the effect of shock herself but knew the cold shudder that was now going through her was all too real, not imaginary.

It was all true. All of it. As fantastic as Gabriel's story had been. She had wanted to believe him, yes, but now she had seen the evidence for herself. Angels … real angels … Michael was a living winged angel and obviously controlled somehow by the church. She knew how Ryan worked after all these years. He was cold and calculating. He left nothing to chance.

Gabriel had to be warned. "Hurry," she rushed the boy as he climbed out of the wrecked car.

Ryan and the three Irishmen parked up in the main car park as pleased as Gabriel had been that in this awful weather, the place was deserted. The readings they were getting from the tracer were erratic; Gabriel was trying to be clever, always on the move yet keeping to the side of the monoliths away from the back road, trying to leave an exit clear for Lucifer to escape. Ryan had to admire his resolve. He knew Lucifer wasn't the real prize here, not with his polluted blood, yet he was still prepared to put his own freedom at risk to save his friend.

Still, science moves on, and today's minds wouldn't make the same mistakes once they had Gabriel to experiment on. They had better equipment, better facilities. Ryan believed they could synthesize the blood successfully with modern science.

All four of them looked up in awe as Michael swooped down out of the low clouds, bringing the unconscious Lucifer to be used as bait once more. The three IRA men crossed themselves even though they'd been briefed on what to expect.

"He's real, so he is. Jaysus …," exclaimed Patrick.

"I've never seen anything like it," added Connor. The two Irishmen were dumbstruck at the sight of a real flesh and blood angel.

"Nor will you again, boys. Michael is the last of his kind. The last with wings, anyway." He stepped forward to greet the weary angel as Michael alighted with his unconscious friend in his arms. "You have done well, Michael," Ryan congratulated him. "Now give him into the keeping of our friends." He indicated the Irishmen.

"I like this not," boomed Michael's deep thunderous voice. "Lucifer is my friend. He and I were lovers once. So long ago …" His voice saddened. "I would not have harm come to him," he warned, and Ryan tightened his grip on the control box he kept in his pocket, ready to press the button, which would cause the implant in Michael's skull to activate, causing untold agonies.

"We need Lucifer only to draw out Gabriel, my friend. You know this," Ryan reiterated. "We only want Gabriel. Once we have him, your Lucifer may walk free. You have my word."

"Your word ...," he scoffed. "I have had similar promises through the years, all to no avail. Still you keep me like a pet."

"Michael, Michael ... Look around you. How many other winged men do you see?" Ryan tried to placate him. "In this modern world, you are a freak, a rarity. You would be hunted down for sheer novelty value. Our church keeps you safe, provides you a haven of sorts. Are you not comfortable? Do we not cater to your almost every whim, except where it concerns your freedom?" Michael glowered at the priest, used to his rhetoric. "We want only your safety, my friend."

"Is that why you put this device in my head?" Michael glowered, tapping his temple and stepping forward menacingly, causing Ryan to back up and Patrick to draw his gun.

"It's okay, Patrick. Michael knows that was thought a necessity at the time and nothing to do with me." At a signal from Ryan, Sean and Patrick came forward to take Lucifer's unconscious body. "Now we can force Gabriel out of hiding, and once we have him, Lucifer can go free. We will not bother him again, I promise you."

"Gabriel." Michael's face darkened at the mention of the name.

"Ah yes ... There's no love lost between the two of you, is there?" Ryan taunted, though carefully.

"It was Gabriel who caused Lucifer to be captured by the Druids. His fine wings shorn from his back, and he could no longer fly with us. I was forced to leave him behind and take the aerie north," he reminisced sorrowfully. "Gabriel and his damn games!"

"Well now, help us, Michael. Fly high and wait for my signal. We may take Gabriel without your help, but if I signal, then come at once. I daresay Gabriel will be pleased to see you again." Ryan smiled grimly.

"Not half as pleased as I will be to see him," Michael warned.

Chapter Sixty-one

In the clouds, Gabriel circled and soared, using the strong gusts bouncing off the huge rocks to fly in a roughly elliptical pattern. Another ten minutes should suffice, and then he would seek out the priest.

He was startled momentarily by three loud successive gunshots, which echoed above the roar of the storm. A voice followed behind on the wind, a voice he still recognized …

"*Gabriel …*," it called. "*Your plan didn't work. We still have Lucifer*," it taunted. A lie? Trying to get him to show himself too soon? Gabriel turned against the wind, arms working the plastic wings, heading towards the sound of the priest's voice. "*Gabriel …*," it cried once more as Gabriel homed in on the cries, keeping just within the constantly shifting clouds. He played with fire as he had done most of his long life, for he could feel the charges building up in the clouds he passed through. The metal filaments in his wings chanced fate this close to the source of the lightning.

At last he saw them, stood off to one side, in the lee of one of the huge monoliths. Ryan and four men, one of them on his knees, slumped as one of them tried to hold his face up. No bluff then. Ryan and his friends had somehow recovered Lucifer. What had happened to Laura and the boy?

Fearful of their fate and tired of these constant threats, a bloodlust descended upon Gabriel. Today was a day for vengeance. He swept down into view, and one of the men cried out, pointing. All of them looked up, his appearance not causing as much consternation as he had hoped. Perhaps Lucifer had ... but no, his friend would not betray him.

All of a sudden, the four standing suddenly galvanized into action. "It's him. Christ, he's flying too!" Gabriel heard the words but didn't understand them.

Ryan put the Luger against Lucifer's head slowly. "Come down, Gabriel," he called. "We've played this game before. You'll lose now as well." He smiled grimly.

"Let him go, Ryan," Gabriel answered in reply from his relatively safe position above them. "It's me you want. Let him go, and I promise you, you'll get me. You want me, and I want you, priest!" he spat the word out like a curse. "This is your day of reckoning, Ryan!" he promised.

Ryan and the three Irishmen looked at each other. "Shoot him down," he ordered, and the three men drew their paintball guns and started blasting away. Accurate though they were, the paintballs themselves were bulky, and the wind and rain slowed them down. He dodged them with ease.

"Let him go, and I'll come down," Gabriel promised.

Furious, Ryan lifted the transmitter to his mouth. "Take him," he said simply.

As Gabriel floated on the winds, safe enough from their guns and paintballs, no matter how much nerve toxin they carried, he saw two of the men point upwards again, not at him this time, at something else.

His head turned; a flicker of movement, a shadow in the clouds had caught his eye. What was it? His nerves were on fire. That unknown sixth sense of his that had kept him alive for so many centuries was screaming at him. What was it?

All of a sudden, a dark patch appeared through the cloud, growing bigger and more distinct every second. Gabriel's eyes widened in sheer disbelief. It couldn't be!

"Time to die, Gabriel!" thundered Michael as he swept down out of the thundercloud, his mighty spear aimed for Gabriel's heart.

Chapter Sixty-two

Laura and Luke hurried back along the road towards where they remembered Gabriel had left his own car parked. The rain was heavier than ever, and both of them were now completely soaked through.

Luke was moving his arm easier now, forgetting the pain for the moment. Laura's forehead wound had stopped bleeding, the flesh still sore. They had heard the gunshots and had started to run.

The car was where they had remembered it, and they found it unlocked. Laura saw no keys in the ignition and searched in and around the driver's seat till she found the keys on the sun visor. Seating herself, she fired up the engine. Luke slid into the passenger seat alongside her. She gunned the accelerator, slewing the tires as she skidded and turned the car around.

"Alive! Alive I said!" Ryan screamed into the transmitter as it seemed Michael would skewer Gabriel on the end of his mighty spear, for Gabriel was totally transfixed by the appearance of Michael, having thought him long since dead. At the last second, screaming in frustration and fury, Michael reversed the spear, slamming the butt of it into Gabriel's side. Even they on the ground heard his anger.

Shocked, it took the blow to make Gabriel react. React … react … don't think … just react … His mind had been dealt an even greater blow than his body. Winded, he fell from the sky, trying to force his arms to manipulate his plastic wings as he fought to seek out the updraughts, lungs working agonizingly to take a breath of the ozone-laden air.

Michael was alive! He and Lucifer weren't the last after all! Could there be more? Today was a day for shocks. Yet Michael was obviously working with Ryan. Why? How? He heard his former friend behind him, swooping down on him once more. He had no doubts as to who would win this uneven contest. His pale imitation plastic wings against the glory of Michael's flesh and feathers.

Yet, Michael could have, should have, killed him with that first blow, when he was frozen with shock. Michael had just cause to hate him, blaming him for Lucifer's torture at the hands of the Druids.

There remained a chance, albeit a slim one. If Michael was working to orders, then Gabriel had an edge, and Gabriel had walked similar knifelike edges all his life. Michael was strong and fast, fearless even. Yet he wasn't the brightest or the most skilful of their breed.

Gabriel didn't bother turning as Michael closed the distance between them but simply waited till the other's shadow approximated the same size as his own and then folded a wing, diving to one side even as he felt the brush of greater wings sweeping past him and Michael's roar of anger and frustration.

Gabriel clawed for the heavens, arms working furiously to put as much distance as possible between himself and Michael. Already, the angry angel had pulled out of his own dive and was looking around for Gabriel.

Michael's wings beat powerfully, driving himself upwards in pursuit of Gabriel as he sought the safety of the obscuring clouds. He closed the distance in seconds, Gabriel veering away at the last moment. "Is this what it's come to, Michael? Angel fighting angel? What lies have they told you?" He dove again as Michael's spear caught him another glancing blow, to the head this time, and his senses swam.

Michael followed him down. "No lies from them and none from you," he bellowed. "Lucifer goes free, and you get a slow death at the hands of the church. I can live with that!" he snarled. "It's the least you deserve for what you did to him, to *us* ..."

Gabriel flew awkwardly, seeming to fly right into the top of one of the huge rocks. But then at the very last moment, his wings found some lift, beating the air as his feet touched the tip of the rock. Bending his legs on contact and then snapping straight once more, Gabriel executed a backwards somersault as he tucked his wings in close to his body. Michael's wings beat as he hovered in surprise at the maneuver, and Gabriel slammed into him, hands reaching to grapple the other's spear.

"You were never the cleverest among us, Michael." Gabriel taunted him deliberately, and as the huge angel fought to break his grip, Gabriel slammed his forehead into Michael's face, feeling cartilage snap and the hot flow of blood as Michael cried out in pain, momentarily blinded.

Gabriel let go his hold, dropping like a stone then seeking the updraughts again, climbing once more, using the rocks for momentary cover. He soared high, the Irishmen pointing him out to Michael, who ignored his still-streaming nose and flew up after him. But he wasn't quick enough this time, for Gabriel found the clouds, the heavy dark clouds. He could feel the static charges building, the hair on his head felt itchy.

The dangerous game of cat and mouse through the clouds began, and this was where Michael's own wings worked against him. For as Gabriel's manmade memory-plastic wings were so lightweight, and he, in fact, glided more than flew, he was that much quieter than Michael, whose heavy wings' beat Gabriel could hear even though obscured by the clouds.

Michael was getting more and more frustrated at his inability to catch the wingless angel. Twice now he came at Gabriel using the deadly tip of his spear despite the cautioning he received from Ryan by the implanted radio. From the ground, Ryan could see very little of the deadly duel in the skies.

Gabriel led him on, seeking ever more heavily laden clouds. It would have to be soon. Michael was that much stronger and faster. He was getting closer all the time.

The blackest cloud of all, so laden with electricity, he could see its outline shimmering. He headed straight for it. Michael cried out, closing the gap between them as Gabriel broke free from the clouds for a moment.

Gabriel's nerves were screaming. The charge was building, building ... Now, it had to be now! He thumbed the control of his flying suit, the memory-plastic relaxing as he folded his arms and legs, allowing himself to fall like a stone, as behind him, the sky erupted with a savage, primordial fury. The electrical charge finally exploded in the form of a tremendous bolt of lightning, seeking the path of least resistance to earth, and Michael was in the way, his mighty iron-tipped spear a perfect conductor.

A scream, unlike anything heard on this earth for centuries, echoed even above the crack of the lightning, so reminiscent of Gabriel's own screams so many years ago as his wings were cut from his back.

Gabriel thumbed his suit controls once more, the material stiffening just in time for him to spread his arms and halt his fall to earth. Turning, he saw, with no great satisfaction, Michael falling to earth, those mighty feathered wings aflame.

Full of compassion for his former friend, Gabriel swooped to earth to try to offer some aid, beat out the flames if need be. But as he did so, he lost track of the position of Ryan and his men.

A cry from a wakened Lucifer alerted him, but it was too late, as they came out from behind a large outcrop of rock, only yards from him, and he cried out, feeling the explosion of one of the paintballs against his arm. Another hit to the body and another to his leg. Gasping, he felt the nerve toxin paralyzing his body. His arm was numb in seconds, and he felt his legs weakening.

Ryan and his men shouted with triumph as Gabriel slumped, trying to stay on his feet, and then their cries turned to horror as a still-burning Michael rose up behind Gabriel, wings aflame, spear raised on high, like an apparition out of hell.

"No. He dies! He dies!" he roared, hurling the spear with all his waning might at Gabriel's chest.

Frozen into immobility as much as Gabriel himself, the Irishmen could only watch, and it was only the recovered Lucifer who was galvanized into action. "Michael, no … Nahhhhhhhh …" He flung himself in front of Gabriel in a split second, trying to force his friend out of the way of the deadly spear. Too slow by far, the force of the blow taking the spear almost a foot out the other side of his body.

He took what seemed like a long time to fall to the ground, lifeless, and the Irishmen looked on, shocked, but not as shocked as Michael himself, who had wanted so badly to kill Gabriel and who had now killed instead his former lover. Indeed, even through the centuries, he had never stopped loving Lucifer, never stopped cursing Gabriel for his role in their parting.

He looked on for three, four seconds, ignoring the pain of his still-smoldering wings, his mind finally snapping, and he roared in anguish and frustration, rounding on the Irishmen."Your fault. Your fault, yours, not mine, yours ...," he accused, starting towards them painfully then ignoring his pain and running at them, bellowing his hate.

Connor and Patrick began blasting away at him with their handguns, terrified, as most of the shots missed. Some didn't, but for all the blood and flesh they blew away from his body, Michael kept on coming, his mighty arms sending Connor smashing into the nearby rock face and leaving a messy trail of blood on the rock as his body slid to the ground.

As mighty hands reached for him, in desperation, Ryan triggered the transmitter in his pocket, and the explosive charge implanted in the angel's brain did its work; Michael's skull exploded, showering them all with blood and brains.

On the ground, Gabriel could do nothing except sob helplessly. Lucifer was dead. Michael was dead, and they had him at last!

Chapter Sixty-three

Too late. They were too late! Laura felt like screaming as she heard the gunshots. Don't let him die. Please God, don't let him die! She spoke a mental prayer, and then, minutes later, the boy pointed.

"Look, up in the sky."

The winged figure fell in flames, his screams heard above the thunder and the lightning, like Icarus denied the heavens. Gritting her teeth, she floored the accelerator, the car bouncing uncertainly across the rough inner roads between the monoliths, in the direction of the angel's fall to earth. Who was it? Gabriel or Michael? Over such a distance and through such awful wind and rain, she couldn't tell.

Sparks flew off the front wing as the car scraped against the side on one such monolith, and she fought the steering wheel to keep the car going forward. "Can you drive?" she asked Luke through gritted teeth.

"I'm not allowed to. I'm underage …" Luke explained.

"That's not what I asked. Can you drive or not?" she asked, her mind working frantically.

"I think so. I've watched my dad do it. It doesn't look so hard. My feet can reach the pedals these days," he said proudly. Laura at once began to slow down.

"Slide over onto my lap. Come on, do it now," she urged, and Luke reluctantly began to do as she bid him, hands gripping the wheel as he slid across in front of her. Laura held onto the wheel as she in turn slid out from under the boy, allowing him to sit fully in the driver's seat.

The car slewed momentarily till the boy got the hang of it. He started to grin wildly as he realized he was really driving the thing, his feet working the pedals, albeit roughly.

Laura reached around him to fasten his seatbelt around him. "Not too fast. Just keep it on the road," she warned and reached for her handbag, unfastening it and taking out the automatic, cocking it grimly.

"Are you going to use that?" the boy asked, looking worriedly across at her.

"Oh, yes. I'm going to use it." Laura promised herself. She would use it to free the man she loved, and if Gabriel was dead for all Ryan's lies, she was still going to use the gun.

Chapter Sixty-four

"Tie him up. The drugs won't last forever, and he's a hardy one is our Gabriel, aren't you, son?" Ryan chuckled, pleased at the successful outcome of his mission. He watched as the IRA men stripped the flying suit off Gabriel and used plastic ties to fasten his wrists behind his back and then fasten his ankles together. "Make sure you take his knives. He's rather good with them, I believe."

Gabriel lay there, conserving his strength, waiting for his body to fight off the paralyzing effects of the drug that still raced through his system. He glared up at Ryan, ignoring the other two men.

"He goes in the backseat of the car," Ryan ordered. "Connor's body will have to go in the boot and Lucifer's as well."

"What do we do about the big fella, Father? Sure and we've no room for him, wings and all," Patrick asked. Ryan pondered a moment.

"You still have that can of petrol in the boot of the car?" he asked. Patrick nodded. "Then use it all. Burn his body till there's nothing recognizable left," he ordered. "I was hoping to leave no trace behind, but we've ended up with a few bodies too many," he reflected.

As Patrick began to fetch the petrol can, Ryan helped Sean move Gabriel into the rear of one of the cars. Then they started to move the other two bodies, messily removing the huge spear from Lucifer's body. Sean threw it down alongside the dead angel. "Better make sure that gets burned too, Pat," he said.

"Sean and I will drive on ahead with Gabriel." Ryan explained as Patrick began dousing the angel's body and wings with petrol. "I have arrangements to make to move him to one of our facilities. You bring the other car with the two bodies and follow on when you're through here. Then we'll dispose of the car and the bodies over one of the cliffs somewhere on the coast. We'll need more petrol, so stop and fill the can up at a petrol station somewhere on the way. I want a nice big explosion when the car goes over to avoid any evidence on the bodies." Ryan was as thorough as they come. He had done this sort of cover-up many times before, even before his association with the Holy Catholic Church.

They left Patrick to his grisly chores, and Ryan and Sean got into the car. As Sean started the engine, Ryan turned in his seat to keep an eye on Gabriel, who still remained slumped lying down on the backseat. Gabriel tried to remain motionless, giving the impression that the nerve toxin was still paralyzing his body, though in truth, his body's regenerative system was already fighting it. He already had limited movement in his arms and legs.

"Head back towards Teesside," Ryan instructed Sean. "We've a man to see about the use of a tanker. We need him transporting to the south coast, where we have a special facility waiting for him. They'd like him back in Rome, but I've assured the council the English scientists are amongst the best in the world. The facility is easily on a par with anything in Italy. Besides which, my superiors don't have to arrange the transportation overseas. It gets more awkward these days." He gave a wry smile.

Sean set off, taking the same road he came in on, heading back out towards the main road. Above them, the storm was finally moving on, the sky lightening somewhat, though it was still raining.

Behind them, Sean suddenly noticed headlights. "Christ, he must have been quick," he exclaimed, assuming the car to be driven by Patrick. Ryan looked out through the rear window of the car.

"That's not Patrick!" he cursed. "It's Mary," he said grimly. Gabriel's heartbeat quickened as he willed his body to move, to fight off the drug in his system. His fingers clenched and unclenched behind his back, out of Ryan's view. "I never thought the bastard would turn her after all this time. All her conditioning." He shook his head. "Such a pity," he said and took out his Luger.

Winding down the window, he reached out and fired a shot at the pursuing car. Gabriel heard wheels squealing on the wet surface as the car behind swerved to get out of Ryan's line of fire.

The rear screen shattered seconds before Gabriel heard an answering shot in reply, and Sean cursed as the bullet whizzed through the body of the car, leaving a starred hole through the front windscreen. "Fuck! Where did she learn to shoot like that?" he cursed, gunning the accelerator and weaving now himself.

"Mea Culpa, I'm afraid." Ryan grinned wildly, reaching out to fire a second shot at the pursuing car. "She was an excellent student." He laughed wildly. Gabriel began to move his legs slowly, agonizingly slow, drawing them back.

He forced his body into action, slowly hooking his bound wrists over his ankles while Ryan was distracted. He was sweating with the effort, his system on fire as it fought off the toxin. At last, he had his hands in front of him again.

"Shit!" cursed Ryan, suddenly alerted by the movement on the rear seat, but before he could get the gun back inside the car, Gabriel's hands came over the top of Sean's head, wrenching back immediately. The effect was instantaneous.

Sean screamed, his hands flying up off the steering wheel to grapple with the constriction around his throat as Gabriel tried to throttle him. Ryan grabbed for the wheel instinctively as the car headed for the ditch, hauling back on it at the last minute but only forcing the car to skid across to the other side of the road.

"Damn you," he cursed as Sean's struggles prevented him from recovering control of the still-accelerating vehicle, the front wheel catching the edge of the ditch.

Behind, in the pursuing car, Laura quickly understood what was happening in the car in front, seeing the struggle through the shattered rear window, and told Luke to slow down.

She watched as the car dipped into the ditch by the side of the road, it's momentum carrying it up again, bouncing off a fencepost and then smashed through the fence completely, bouncing high once more before coming down again to rest on its side.

Hardly had the car come to a stop when she noticed two figures grappling as they fell from one of the opened doors. "Stop the car. Stop the car," she cried as the boy clumsily braked, forgetting for a moment to dip the clutch.

Luke managed to bring the vehicle to a stop about thirty yards behind the crashed car, and Laura hurried to open the door. A shot rang out, and she looked around to see Gabriel falling away from the partly overturned car, scrambling to his feet as Ryan climbed out onto the bodywork of the car, leveling the gun as Gabriel tried to get quickly clear, but his drugged body wouldn't move fast enough. "Not this time, Gabriel," Ryan shouted a warning, and as Gabriel continued to stagger away from the car, the Luger cracked once more, and Gabriel cried out as the bullet tore through his thigh, and he fell to the ground.

Laura screamed at the sight of him falling, and as Ryan turned, the Luger aiming in her direction, she fired, once, twice, in quick succession. Ryan's shot went high as he fell back off the car, crying out in pain as one of the bullets from her gun hit him in the shoulder.

Adrenaline pumping furiously, Laura acted on instinct alone, closing the distance to the car rapidly, angling her run towards Gabriel while keeping a watchful eye on the car. Ryan was out of her sight but no less dangerous. She knew the man had more lives than a cat.

Laura risked a look back at her own car and waved the boy back inside as he started to get out. Then she continued on to where Gabriel lay clutching at his thigh, trying to stop the bleeding.

"It's okay. I'm all right," he grimaced as he tightened his handkerchief into a crude tourniquet. "Once this damn drug wears off, I should be fine," he said, annoyed with himself. "Good shot, by the way." He managed a pained smile. "Ryan ran off through the cornfield using the car as cover. He's wounded, but he's still got the gun." He could see the look in her eyes. "Let him go, he's still dangerous."

"So am I!" she said resolutely. "You have no idea just *how* dangerous!" Her eyes flared wide, and she turned quickly away from him, keeping low as she ran over to the overturned car. She checked inside to see Sean slumped over the wheel. His neck was obviously broken.

"Laura!" he called out to her. "Laura!" But she didn't hear him. Her mind was set, and nothing would change it. Looking quickly around, she saw where Ryan had entered the cornfield, and she quickly followed his tracks, feet squelching into the mud. "Fuck it!" Gabriel swore as he forced himself to his feet.

The flow of blood was easing. As long as he could stop the bleeding, his wound would heal all the faster. Yet he had no time. Laura was chasing that mad priest across the countryside. He gathered Laura had been given training whilst under Ryan's care, but what sort of training, and how good was she?

He limped over to the overturned car to find a weapon. As he did so, Luke finally got out of the car, having looked in his rearview mirror to see headlights approaching through the rain.

He stepped out into the middle of the road to wave the driver down to get help. The car slowed as the headlights picked out the boy. Patrick smiled as he recognized the boy. He was already drawing his revolver as the boy rushed up to the car, unsuspecting.

Chapter Sixty-five

Laura ran after Ryan as fast as she could, feet slipping in the mud till she kicked off her shoes and went barefoot. It proved to be quieter, anyway. There was no way she was letting him get away after all he'd done.

As she approached the copse, she heard him cry out and looked up to see bushes moving over to her right. Crouching now, she slowed her pace. Ryan was wounded but still mobile. He had taught her a lot over the years, taught her too much.

Controlling her breathing, she kept low, traversing the edge of the woods, looking for movement and dark patches that shouldn't be there. Growing up on a farm, she was well versed in woodcraft. She had been born in the countryside and knew all about hunting game, stalking prey. The rain both helped and hindered her. Ryan's tracks were easy to follow, but moving was noisy unless she took it slow, and Ryan was moving, trying to put as much distance as he could between them.

She heard him cry out once more, heard the sound of breaking twigs, and she rushed forward using the sounds to mask her own movements. Ryan had slipped and slid down a muddy bank. She saw him across from her, trying to climb up the other side, which was just as muddy, just as slippery.

His right arm hung limply at his side, the sleeve of his jacket dark red with the blood he'd lost. His collar bone was damaged, she guessed, from the way he was holding himself. In a lot of pain. Good.

Ryan used his left hand to put the Luger in his pocket, needing leverage to help himself up the slippery slope. Laura rose up behind him as he did so. "End of the road, Father," she said coldly as Ryan froze at the sound of her voice.

He turned around slowly, face contorted in a half-smile against the pain. "Laura, me child. So you've come on your own then?" he asked, scanning the woods behind her for sight of Gabriel.

"I think this little talk is best kept between just the two of us, Father. Don't you agree?" she asked, face set like a mask.

"Maybe so. Gabriel knows very little about the last fifty odd years, does he?" Ryan asked. "I understand there are certain things you'd rather he remained ignorant about." His breathing was still labored as he tried to catch his breath from his exertions. "You always were good with that gun, weren't you, Laura?" He smiled again.

Laura felt in control of the situation now, and she hefted the gun comfortably in her hand. "Fifty-eight years ago, Father, I was pregnant with Gabriel's child. You told me it was stillborn. You lying *bastard*!" she accused.

"Ahhh, so that's what all this is about?" He managed a chuckle. "I wondered how he managed to turn you against me so quickly."

"You knew I'd already lost one child." Her voice was pained, the memories still haunting her. "How could you put me through that agony again?"

"It seemed the most plausible excuse at the time," he started to explain then looked up quickly over Laura's shoulder. "I thought you said you came alone?" he queried.

Laura automatically half-turned and instantly cursed her own stupidity as she heard Ryan's gasp as he fumbled the Luger out of his pocket with his left hand.

Dropping onto one knee, Laura whirled, her gun hand reaching out, pointing and firing all in one smooth movement. Ryan screamed as the bullet shattered his forearm just below the elbow, falling backwards into the mud. The Luger dropped from nerveless fingers.

Carefully, as Ryan gasped at the fresh pain and lay there panting, she made her way down the slippery bank. "Now we'll have our little talk, Father." Laura aimed the gun at Ryan's left kneecap. "Forgive me, Father, for I am about to sin." And then she pulled the trigger.

Chapter Sixty-six

Patrick had the boy in an armlock before Gabriel could do anything. The gun was at his head and Gabriel at his mercy. For he hadn't yet had time to retrieve any weapons out of the wrecked car. He could see his knives, but no way could he reach them before Patrick could use his own gun, either on the boy or on himself.

"Where's Ryan?" he asked gruffly. Gabriel answered quickly before the boy could blurt anything out.

"He shot me and then went after Laura as she ran off into the woods. They tried to rescue me," he lied, looking despondent.

"No more than the traitorous bitch deserves. No loose ends, that's our Father Ryan for you." Patrick smiled. Just then, they heard the first shot from the woods, and Patrick laughed as he saw Gabriel wince. "Just you sit yersel down there, nice and easy like. The good Father will be with us shortly," He smiled, bidding Gabriel to sit next to the wrecked car.

He kept the boy within reach, leaning back on the bonnet of his own car while they waited. Minutes later, they heard a second gunshot, which puzzled them. Then came a third and, finally, some minutes later, a fourth and final shot.

Long minutes passed with none of them knowing what was happening in the woods. Patrick was getting cagey. Ryan was usually more thorough than to need four shots to finish anyone, four shots separated by minutes. What was he doing?

Suddenly, as the rain began to ease off, he saw Laura's blonde head approaching from the far side of the cornfield, and his blood froze.

Gabriel saw him tense, and he edged closer to the open car door, where his knives lay.

Patrick turned, catching the movement. "Still now and not one fucken' word, or I'll blow the kid's head off," he warned. Luke tried not to let his fears show, but the events of the day were catching up with him.

Gabriel guessed Laura was returning and not Ryan. That in itself was good and bad. She'd survived Ryan, yet now Patrick was waiting for her. If he tried to warn her, the boy was as good as dead.

Not enough time. Gabriel cursed as Laura came out from the field, her face looked sad, her eyes stared blankly ahead. She was in shock. Patrick stepped out from behind the car, leveling the gun at her. "Where is he, bitch? Where's Ryan?" he demanded.

Laura focused once more, recognizing the Irishman, taking in the scene, Gabriel frantically using hand and eye movements to try to communicate something to her, but she wasn't Lucifer, and she didn't understand the frantic movements of his fingers.

"Where he belongs. In hell," she answered in monotone. The big man looked shocked. For a moment, he didn't really believe her. Then seeing her eyes and her shell-shocked state, he suddenly knew she was telling him the truth.

"Then you're dead with him," he said flatly, raising the gun.

"*Noooo* ...," cried Gabriel, lunging for the car door and his knives, trying to draw his fire. Patrick fired once, his shot going high as the young boy suddenly elbowed him in the balls, and he cursed as he let the child go.

Laura brought her own automatic up to bear on the Irishman, finger tightening as her arm straightened, the hammer falling uselessly on an empty chamber as she froze. Lost count. Stupid woman. She'd lost count. Eight shots and out. Her gun was empty.

Patrick's gun wasn't empty, and his second shot was on target. Laura screamed as the shot took her in the chest, whirling her around and throwing her down onto the road.

With a snarl of satisfaction, the big Irishman whirled around to turn his attention back to Gabriel, surprised not to find him still sitting there, and then a sudden flurry of black launched itself from the top of the car, bowling into him and knocking him backwards off his feet.

Only Gabriel got up, leaving Patrick laying there, the handle of the knife still sticking up out of his chest. He went quickly over to where Laura lay. His eyes saw the wound, and he heard the bubbling in her throat. He knew the wound had caused serious internal damage. A nearby hospital and they might have a chance, but there was none such for miles.

The bullet seemed to have perforated a lung and severed one of the main arteries coming from her heart. She was losing too much blood, coughing it up as well as leaking it from the bullet wound itself. Helplessly, he knelt down beside her.

Still conscious, though barely, Laura looked up at him. "Hold me, Gabriel." She tried to raise a hand. "Hold me one last time. I always felt so safe in your arms." She coughed up more blood as Gabriel lifted her.

"Laura … I …" Her fingertips brushed against his lips.

"A daughter. We have a daughter …" She managed to smile, and even though the blood covered her chin, Gabriel thought he had never seen her look so beautiful, so happy. He felt like crying but couldn't spoil her mood. To have found her again and then lose her again so soon. It was almost more than he could bear. "Mirabelle … they named her Mirabelle …" She coughed again, the blood more dark, more crimson now, if that was possible. "Cold … so cold …" She shivered in his arms. "Find her … find her for me …" Her eyes closed, and Gabriel could no longer hold back his tears, shaking her violently.

"Don't you *dare* die on me again …," he cried. "Listen to me … Laura, listen." Her eyes opened finally, though she was weakening rapidly. "There's a chance. My blood is old …" he explained hurriedly. "Old and more potent by far than anything they may have given you to drink back in Rome. That's why they want me so badly," he went on as he pulled the handkerchief tourniquet off his leg, letting the rich blood flow freely again out of the wound, which was now slightly smaller than before. "If we can stop your bleeding, the blood will keep you alive long enough for me to get you to a hospital. You have to drink," he said, moving her head down to his thigh.

"No … don't want to … Enough trouble …," she apologized, feeling weaker. She swooned once more, her head dropping back till Gabriel shook her once more.

"Laura, you must. If not for me, for yourself, for Mirabelle. She needs a mother. Somewhere, wherever she is, she needs you," he pleaded with her. Laura smiled weakly up at him as he cradled her head in his lap.

"Will … will I live forever? Like you?" she asked.

"Forever is a long time … but I'd like to share it with you." He smiled, pressing her face down to his bleeding wound. "Drink deep," he pleaded and was rewarded with her mouth's suction on his wound, her throat working as she swallowed the hot vital blood.

Finally, raising a hand to wipe away his tears, he was reminded of the boy's condition. Luke was still suffering from shock and visibly trembling. He had seen sights this day that no boy his age ought to have seen. "Luke, it's okay. Trust me," he implored. "I need something to help plug this wound and stop the bleeding. See what you can find in the car." The boy sniffled but turned to do Gabriel's bidding while he continued to cradle Laura's head in his lap.

Luke searched through first one and then all three cars. There were no medical kits or anything in any of them. Just then, he remembered his sandwiches, which were still stuffed in his jacket pocket. They had been wrapped in cling film by his mother, and he had seen a program once on television. Hurriedly, the boy took the sandwiches out of his pocket, and he began unwrapping them and discarding them as he tried to smooth and clean the cling film. He hurried over to Gabriel, holding up the cling film to let the rain wash it.

"You need to press this over the wound. I saw it on a medical program once," Luke explained, and Gabriel quickly understood the boy's suggestion. As Laura had by now ingested enough of his blood, he laid her gently back down on the ground. Quickly, he pulled open her raincoat and then her blouse. Strong nimble fingers ripped her bra in two, revealing her blood-soaked breasts, and a bit embarrassed, Luke turned away.

Quickly, Gabriel pressed the cling film over the wound, fingers smoothing it, feeling it "cling" to the skin, the sticky blood helping the adhesion. Then he fastened her blouse back up and just tied her belt loosely around her to hold her coat together.

Effortlessly, he picked her gently up off the floor and carried her quickly to the car, laying her on the backseat as Luke opened the door for him. Then he quickly retied the handkerchief around his thigh although the flow of blood was noticeably decreasing.

They set off eagerly, Gabriel wasting no time. He asked Luke to hand him his cellular phone out of the glove compartment as he drove and used it one-handed to call a number.

Luke heard him talking hurriedly in Italian. The conversation continued for a few miles down the road; Gabriel hurriedly took a side road. Luke saw the sign whizz past too quickly to know in which direction they were headed, but back towards Ripon still, he supposed.

The boy looked worriedly into the rear of the car to check on Laura. Her eyes were closed but he thought he could detect a slight rising and falling of her chest, so she was still alive, he hoped.

Chapter Sixty-seven

After a frantic drive through the driving rain, Gabriel finally took another side road, this time leading up to an old country house, set back and isolated from the road. A middle-aged balding man was stood outside waiting to receive them, and Gabriel halted the car a scant feet away from him.

"Bring her inside, quickly …" The man wasted no time nor did Gabriel, who scooped Laura out of the car and rushed to follow the man inside the house. Luke tagged along behind as they led the way to a surgery of sorts.

Gabriel set Laura down on a black vinyl padded table, surrounded by bottles of anesthetic gas and trays of surgical implements. The balding man was already prepping a syringe as Gabriel began removing Laura's coat.

Luke decided to wait outside the room. The stranger nodded to him. "My wife is waiting in the kitchen. Go to her, and she'll get you dried out in front of the fire." He smiled. Luke did so, nodding in return.

Gabriel took off the blood-soaked blouse and bra, leaving the cling film in place as the seemingly older man gave her the injection. Then he began to swab her down. "What blood group is she? She'll need a transfusion, and I don't keep much here. I'm retired, officially anyway," he explained.

"You have plasma?" Gabriel asked.

"Not a lot, as I said," explained the man.

"You can give her more of my blood if she needs it." The old man's eyes widened, not quite understanding Gabriel. Then he noticed the bloody trousers.

"You're wounded yourself," he pointed out.

"I'm a fast healer," he explained, tearing open the trouser leg even more to reveal what was left of the closing wound. The blood had stopped flowing altogether now. Just a reddish livid section of skin was all that remained of the wound.

"Help me with this equipment. Just do as I instruct. My wife would normally help me, but I daresay the boy needs a bit of company right now, if what I've heard from our 'friends' is correct," he queried. Gabriel just nodded and wheeled the large bottles of gas around to Laura's head.

In the kitchen, Luke was soon seated in front of a roaring fire, his jacket hung up over an old-fashioned fireguard, steam rising up off it as the flames began to dry it. The woman fussed over him, giving him a bowl of fresh homemade soup to drink. Ordinarily, Luke wouldn't have touched homemade soup with a bargepole, but it was hot and he was cold and soaked to the skin. He compromised when the old woman made him some bread and butter to eat it with.

Outside, the bad-weather warning was fortunately still in effect, and no one else was expected out on these exposed roads. Two pizza delivery vans pulled up at the scene of the accident. The men were soon at work, rearranging the scene of the accident. Two of them went off in the direction of the woods.

Hours later, after he had joined the boy in the kitchen for something to eat, Gabriel placed a call from his mobile to the boy's parents, introducing himself as Lucifer's brother, explaining he would be bringing the boy home late, and then he let Luke speak to his parents himself, cautioning him to be careful what he said.

After a lengthy surgery assisted by Gabriel, the operation to remove the bullet was a success, and the doctor had managed to reinflate the perforated lung. Laura rested now under sedation. Gabriel felt safe in leaving her in the doctor's care for a few hours. At eight o'clock, he drove the boy back home to Teesside.

Chapter Sixty-eight

Gabriel stopped the car at the end of the road. "I can't come any further, Luke. They'll ask me too many questions. You too, probably." He grinned wryly. "Just tell them half the truth, that I found my long-lost brother, and I'm taking him back to South America with me," he suggested.

"Will I ever see you again?" the boy asked. Gabriel gave a short laugh and shook his head sadly.

"I don't think that's a good idea. I don't keep my friends, Luke. They all have a habit of dying on me eventually. They call me the Angel of Death for a reason. I don't want to frighten you, but have you ever given any thought to it? Can you imagine what it would feel like if many years from now when you're old and grey, you suddenly look across a restaurant or bar and see me there, looking back at you, looking exactly as I am today? Could you handle that? Some people who've had near-death experiences say it's exactly like that when they feel their time is up. Death is constant, unchanging. You might even say death and I are old friends, so similar in many ways. I've known the death of friends and loved ones, have even courted and desired death myself on occasion. It's not easy seeing the world changing around you while you just remain simply unchanged by it all," he reflected sadly. "Being immortal is not as pleasant as you might think. Oh, it gives you time, if nothing else. You can use that time to plan, invest, make yourself rich and comfortable as I have done. But time is a never-ending one-way street, down which I must walk forever. I have no idea where that street will take me, Luke. Death is the only way out, and I have seriously considered it more than once in my dark times. Try not to have too many dark times yourself, Luke. They're not pleasant," he emphasised with a wry smile, slightly forced. "But this world is getting ever smaller, Luke. Who knows? It's possible we might bump into each other again. But do drop me an e-mail from time to time, won't you?" he asked. On impulse, the boy reached across and hugged Gabriel, who returned the hug with the same affection. "You'd better go before your parents get too worried." He reached across to open the car door, and the boy got out.

Luke waved good-bye as he started to walk and then ran down the road towards his house. Gabriel blinked his headlights once in reply and then reversed out onto Oulston Road and drove off towards the T-junction.

Chapter Sixty-nine

It was after midnight when he got back to the doctor's house. He found a black enameled coffin waiting for him in one of the large rooms at the back of the house. "Your friends brought him while you were gone. You can leave him here for a day or two until you can make arrangements. I can get you the necessary death certificate and organize the shipment of the body for you," the doctor offered.

"Thank you," he answered sincerely and then went over to the coffin and placed a single hand on its surface. "Lucifer, my old friend. Your long years of torment are over," he said so softly that the doctor could hardly hear him.

Then the doctor's wife came into the room. "If you'd like to see her, she's just woken up from the anesthetic," she said. "She's still very weak, you understand? But she's got a bit of color back in her cheeks. I think she'll be fine." She smiled.

Gabriel entered the makeshift surgery by himself, the doctor and his wife holding back out of courtesy. Laura's long blonde hair had been cleaned, no longer matted with blood. Her eyes opened at the sound of the door opening and closing.

He drew up a chair and sat down next to her, reaching out for her hand, and was pleased when he felt her fingers gripping his own. "Will I live then?" She smiled up at him from the pillow, still feeling a bit weak, and talking was a strain.

"Yes, my darling. You'll live for a long, long time." He smiled back. "Welcome to forever."

Outside, the night sky was black, and the rains still came down. The storm had moved on, but in the heavens above, the rumble of thunder could still be heard.

The End

Preview

Belladonna
(The Second Book of Gabriel)

Chapter One
Revelations

The morning sun shone down, reflecting brightly off the disturbed waters of the private swimming pool in the walled estate. As yet, the water was still cool but would warm up throughout the day, heated by the sun's rays. The whitewashed walls of the villa were hard to look at on sunny days like this, for the sun and heat reflected off them, the shimmering curtain of heat forming a modicum of privacy from a distance.

It was a fine, if typical, morning just outside Buenos Aires. The sweet smell of flowers was on the light breeze, and the noisy cicadas were heard across the lawn separating the pool from the lush garden and trees.

Laura Donovan swam gracefully and energetically, cutting through the water like a fish as she completed her twentieth length of the pool. The water was still cool in the hot Argentine sun, and she paused at the end of the pool, turning and hooking her elbows onto the paved edge, her naked breasts glistening wetly and invitingly as Gabriel paused from reading his newspaper and turned to look at her.

She smiled wistfully, enjoying his appreciative stare. The scars of her recent bullet wound were barely noticeable and would disappear entirely, Gabriel assured her. She found it hard to credit the speed of her recovery. As a recipient of the Blood of Christ many years ago, she had experienced an accelerated metabolism but nothing like what she had experienced after drinking Gabriel's unadulterated life's blood.

Gabriel stood up from his late breakfast, and untying his robe, he draped it on his chair. Naked, he dove into the pool to join her, surfacing alongside her as her arms reached out for him, thrilling in the sensation of his naked body pressing up against her.

Skinny-dipping was a pastime she was getting used to, secreted away here in Gabriel's villa. His manservant Manuel discreetly stayed away from the pool area when either Gabriel or she was using it. A simple buzzer by the table sufficed to call upon him when needed.

Gabriel kissed her, softly, tenderly. Her lips opened to take his tongue. Laura loved him with all her heart, and she knew the feelings were reciprocated. She could feel him hardening down there, despite the coolness of the water. Chuckling, she reached her hand down to grasp him, Gabriel gasping.

Her head dipped down below the water, and Gabriel gasped once more at the sudden heat he felt but for a moment, and then she surfaced, laughing, as she swept her long blonde hair out of her eyes. "Mine, all mine ..." She chuckled. Then shrieking with laughter, she pulled away and began swimming away from him. Gabriel surged after her, eager for the chase, his powerful strokes overtaking her halfway down the pool, and caught her leg, pulling her back into his arms, and she surrendered willingly this time.

Up in the computer room, Manuel was dutifully checking feedback from the search program instituted by his master and downloading e-mail responses from many of Gabriel's varied associates across the world. He had enlisted worldwide aid in tracking down a woman known only as Mirabelle. Contacts old and new were requested to find out anything they could about a woman Gabriel could only give the vaguest details about.

Certain questions had to be phrased so as not to reveal anything about her longevity; therefore, old contacts were only asked about possible sightings of such a woman in the distant past and not seemingly possible sightings of her in present-day circumstance, though some of these contacts, the ones Gabriel maintained more frequent contact with, had their obvious suspicions about his continued youthful appearance.

There was still a chance that Mirabelle was no longer among the living. Only seemingly immortal and very hard to kill, it could still be done; indeed it had been done in the past. Gabriel thought himself the last survivor of his species. Or had, until learning about his daughter.

Gabriel had no description of her, only a name. Not much for his friends around the world to go on, and he focused most of his hopes on his maintained Mafia contacts in Rome. Even after Grimaldi's death, his family had continued their support in whatever activities he required. It had been a sad and private funeral in a small cemetery in the foothills overlooking the sprawling city.

It was always risky to venture into Italy, even via Sicily, where the Mafia was so strong. The Holy Catholic Church was always there in the background, hovering like a vulture and awaiting the opportunity to strike. Still, he had wanted to go. A senseless death. One of many in the Mafia's internal feuds over the years. The Grimaldi clan remained his staunchest allies amongst the Mafia even unto present day, and it was there he hoped to have most success in the possibly fruitless search.

Manuel gathered up today's printed matter, sifting through it, preparing for Gabriel to peruse later in the day. Sightings of women—some blonde, some dark, some modern, some dim remembrances of years past. Gabriel looked for similarities of either description or personalities ...

If she had been brought up within the church, then obviously as a child she would have been fostered somewhere, and as an adult, she would have maintained close relations with the church, possibly as a nun? There were so many possibilities.

Manuel had been diligently sifting this information for the last few weeks, descriptions came and went, but a name kept cropping up from time to time, both from past and recent remembrances, possibly a codename. Belladonna.

Was the name coincidental? Was it indeed the same woman? Manuel took it upon himself to initiate further searches using various points of reference unearthed by Gabriel's large network of contacts thus possibly saving his master time in his research.

Belladonna was indeed a codename it seemed and used within the Sword of Solomon organisation. The codename had been in use for the last forty years, but no further information was available to him. Perhaps Gabriel himself knew of a way of hacking into the Vatican's private computer systems?

Later that afternoon, after lunching with Laura, Gabriel was presented with the latest search updates by his manservant, and he sat down in his study to go through them, occasionally initiating further internet searches via his computer link at his desk.

His own hacking skills were formidable, better even than that young English boy Luke. Still, the Vatican's system was locked out from external interference, as there was no physical link between external phone lines and its own private internal communications setup. What firewalls existed were extremely sophisticated. If he could find a way to access them, it would be no problem to find out everything he wanted to know, but there was presently no way in, not even a mobile phone allowed in the place.

Was the codename handed down from one operative to another? Or was it indeed used exclusively by one person? Was that one person his daughter? He needed a description, and descriptions seemed to vary judging by the few people who had actually caught sight of her. This Belladonna seemed to be a very shrewd operator. Not many people ever got a good look at her and lived to tell the tale. As deadly as her nom de plume, to be sure.

It was time to ask Laura of her time spent with the organisation. Perhaps her memories might give them a clue. Laura was out in the gardens, enjoying herself with a pair of pruning shears among the shrubbery, when he called to her and joined her there in the shade of an overhanging tree. She turned to greet him, kissing him lightly as he embraced her. Gardening was a long-forgotten pleasure in which she now indulged herself in this home of Gabriel's and in which she was beginning to feel at home herself.

"We need to talk," he spoke softly, using a finger to lightly brush her pouted lips. "Let's go into my study, and I'll show you what I've found out to date." Arm in arm, he walked her back inside the house.

Scattered across his desk were reports and printouts, and he scooped up a few of them as he sat down with Laura on the soft upholstered sofa. "Cast your mind back to the time you spent with Ryan in Italy … All the reports I'm getting back are pointing to a female operative within the Vatican's organisation, who uses the name Belladonna. Does the name ring any bells?" he asked.

Momentarily, a shadow fell across Laura's eyes as she sought to drift back in time, searching her memories. "I seem to recall hearing the name, but I don't think I've ever come across her," she replied. "The Sword of Solomon was a *big* organisation, and the people that worked for it, the actual 'operatives' very rarely came into contact with each other," she explained. "Only the cardinals dealt frequently with their network of agents."

"Then we need a better description of whom it is we're looking for, if indeed this Belladonna is our errant daughter." Gabriel smiled ruefully. "I think you'd better get changed. We're going to take a little ride up into the mountains," he explained.

An hour later, as Gabriel's four-by-four negotiated the well-worn mountain track, Laura's curiosity could stand it no more. "Just where is it you're taking me?" she asked. Gabriel turned around from the wheel and smiled mysteriously as he peered over the top of his mirrored sunglasses.

"I recall your surprise when you realised the truth about me and my origins. Well, let's just say you still have a lot to learn about this world in which you live, Laura." He smiled wistfully. "In my many years, I have seen countless strange and unexplained things. Things which you and most of the modern world write off as fiction and fairy tales to frighten children and adults alike. Some of them aren't," he added warningly. "Some of these '*myths*' still walk this earth."

Laura looked puzzled by Gabriel's words, and he relented and continued. "We're going to see an old woman, who lives up in the mountains. Her name is Juliana," he said simply. "She is a witch."

A further two hours went by, the roads were getting narrower and progressively worse till it seemed they were nonexistent. Laura was starting to think Gabriel had lost his way, when she noticed a wisp of smoke rising above the tree line in the distance.

Within a small clearing, a tiny log cabin nestled against the rising slope of the mountain. A small stream ran past, mere yards from the old-looking structure. Gabriel finally halted the vehicle about fifty yards from the place, raising a small cloud of dust. He switched off the engine and beckoned to Laura to alight.

Together, they began to approach the cabin, which showed no outward signs of life other than the plume of smoke from the chimney. "Perhaps she's not home?" suggested Laura.

Gabriel gave her an amused glance as he took off his sunglasses and put them in his top pocket. Then he reached for the door to turn the handle, opening it to reveal a dark and gloomy interior. The strange smell hit Laura as he beckoned for her to precede him into the cabin. "Hello? Anyone home?" she called out softly, slightly wary.

"Do you think I'd leave the door unlocked if I wasn't home, child?" an amused aged voice replied from the murky interior. "In these troubled times?" Laura stepped back, momentarily startled, backing into Gabriel as he followed her inside.

"It's okay, she won't bite. Lost her teeth years ago, didn't you, Juliana?" Gabriel joked and then quickly ducked as the old woman's stick swung through the air, his lightning-fast reflexes enabling him to grab hold of the offending weapon. "No way to treat your guests, Juliana," he scolded her, wagging a finger admonishingly.

"Arrogant as ever. Come here, and give an old woman a hug." She smiled. Gabriel let go of the stick and moved forward, arms widening to embrace the wizened old figure, when the stick swung back and caught him high on the forearm before he could block the blow a second time.

"Owwwww ...," he cursed. "Juliana, that wasn't funny," he warned. Laura stifled a chuckle as she sensed the intimate rapport between the two of them.

"You're late," the old woman snapped. "I was expecting you an hour ago. The soup's almost ruined," she announced, turning away into the interior of the cabin, which Laura noticed, as her eyes grew more accustomed to the dim light, went deep into the actual mountainside.

The strange smell, she recognised now for what it was—a pot of soup boiling away on an old cast-iron wood-burning range. "I had it brought up here years ago," Gabriel explained. "Her only condescension to these modern times."

Gabriel and Laura took their seats on plain wooden chairs around a small kitchen table. There were only three seats, though plainly enough room for four around the table. Seeing Laura's look of slight puzzlement, the old woman offered an explanation.

"The missing chair broke. It went into the stove." Juliana chuckled as she ladled the thick aromatic soap into bowls. She handed out the bowls and then offered a basket of fresh home-baked bread around.

The three of them settled down to enjoy their soup as Gabriel explained to Laura his relationship with the old woman. "I came to

Argentina in 1964 ...," he began. Laura's eyes flashed a warning, interrupting his narrative momentarily. "It's okay. She knows about me," he reassured her and then continued. "Lucifer and I had been stalked halfway across Europe by former friends of yours, and we needed to put a lot of distance between ourselves and the Vatican at the time." He paused, dipping the fresh bread into the soup, and then wolfed it down hungrily. "The military junta was causing havoc with the populace back then, so it took a lot of money to ingratiate ourselves and buy the villa. Friends of friends put me in touch with Juliana's husband, who was a member of the opposition party at the time. He helped open a few doors for me back then. Then came the dawn raids as the junta clamped down, and Juliana and her husband were arrested." The old woman concentrated on her soup as Gabriel recited his memories of unpleasant times. "Marco was put before a firing squad within hours of his arrest. Fortunately, we managed to get to Juliana and remove her from the prison before she was due to be executed as well."

"You went into the prison to get her out? I've passed that place. It's a fortress," Laura exclaimed in surprise.

"Not me, personally. Lucifer was the one who went inside. I just took care of a few 'distractions' to take their minds off things."

"He only blew up half of Buenos Aires," the old woman cackled. "Never heard fireworks as good before or since." She managed a pained smile.

"Since then, Juliana has lived up here in the wilds. Her choice, even though things have improved with the military over the years."

"Is peaceful here. Where else should I live?" Juliana shrugged her shoulders, breaking off more bread for her soup.

"You could live anywhere now Maldano's dead," Gabriel complained mildly.

"Who's Maldano?" asked Laura.

"Generalissimo Maldano was the bastard who trumped up the charges to have members of our party arrested," the old woman explained. "He survived the fireworks, but he did not survive me." She smiled cruelly, an expression which did not seem to fit on her face.

"You killed him?" Laura asked in disbelief, for the slight figure of the woman in front of her, even as she must have looked thirty years ago, did not seem capable of such an act.

"Not personally." The old woman chuckled as Laura looked puzzled. "A little of this, a little of that ..." She shrugged her shoulders, obviously not prepared to go into details.

"I told you," Gabriel butted in, "she's a witch." Juliana started to laugh and then coughed and spluttered as some soup caught in her throat, and it was Gabriel's turn to laugh. Laura, too, as the old woman turned to hit him with the spoon.

"That night, I crossed a line over which there can be no return," Juliana reminisced. "I had power then, but I had never used it for my own benefit and never in such a manner. His death was not easy." She returned to her soup, her explanations over for now.

The three of them continued with their meal, only small talk interrupting. Laura felt the old woman's eyes on her throughout the meal, and she caught the glance Juliana shared with Gabriel, who nodded quickly in affirmation of whatever it was that passed between them.

Gabriel had told her about the instinctive, almost telepathic, bond that he had shared with Lucifer before the chemical torture he had undergone beneath the catacombs of Rome. Apparently, it was quite common among Gabriel's kind, another benefit of the strange blood which now also flowed through her own veins. She had noticed a similar "bonding" between the two of them lately, more instinct than true telepathy, but hadn't had chance to raise the subject with Gabriel yet. As if sensing her interest, Juliana looked across the table towards her and nodded slightly herself, her dark eyes catching Laura's own.

After the meal was concluded, Gabriel explained the reason for their visit, which again, the old woman claimed to already know, and Laura wondered if indeed Juliana was joking at her expense. She watched as the old woman washed out the large black pot, which had contained the soup, and then went out of the shack to refill it with water from the tiny mountain stream. She came back in momentarily and began adding to the pot a mixture of herbs and strange-looking things she kept in jars of preservative on a shelf in a dark alcove in the corner of the kitchen. She then placed the pot back on the range to boil.

"A strange story," Juliana commented as they waited for the pot to boil. "A daughter neither of you knew existed and now seek to find." She shook her head, long greying hair hiding her face for a moment till she swept it back. "Mirabelle is a nice name. If she still lives, I can help you. My magic, helped by yours ...," she added pointedly, "will reveal her to you."

As the small pot gradually bubbled and boiled, Laura enjoyed listening to the interplay between Gabriel and Juliana. It was obvious she knew of Lucifer's death, and Laura assumed that Gabriel must have visited her at some time since his return to Buenos Aires, for he was always flitting here and there, leaving her to convalesce on his estate.

Eventually, the steam rose from the boiling pot, and Juliana used a rag to lift it off the range and brought it onto the table around which they all sat. "Roll up your sleeves," the old woman instructed. Gabriel nodded at Laura to do the same as he rolled his sleeve up, baring his forearm.

Juliana went away into the darkened alcove once more and came back brandishing a small wickedly curved knife, the edge of which looked strangely black with age. Gabriel knew what was expected and held out his arm over the still bubbling pot.

The old woman turned his arm, exposing the vein, which she sliced through quite deftly, and red blood flowed, dripping into the boiling liquid. Laura was taken aback momentarily and then, seeing it was expected, offered her own arm, wincing as she felt the hot slice of the knife and her own blood mixed with Gabriel's in the boiling concoction as the old woman began her strange mutterings—half-whispered, strange monosyllabic sounds, guttural, and basic, like no tongue she had ever heard before.

The wounds on their wrists began to noticeably close, healing themselves as the blood flow diminished and then stopped altogether. Still, Juliana kept up her chanting. As Laura looked on, the swirling steam coming up out of the pot seemed to contain shapes, as if containing something "else" within.

A face, for it was surely a face, was taking shape within the steam. Gabriel and Laura looked on avidly as the face took shape before their eyes, solidifying, growing clearer by the second. A young woman's face, looking in her early twenties. Black hair, skin that strange golden sheen of Gabriel's. Laura's own eyes stared back out of the steam at her. A beautiful face which suddenly made Laura gasp involuntarily and also caused a cold shudder to run down Gabriel's back.

"Your daughter," announced Juliana.